MW00884751

JENNY
OF THE
WOODS

Joseph Stamp

FOR TED

". . . We know what we are, but not what we may be."
—Ophelia, Hamlet. 4.5.42–43

Part One

CHAPTER ONE

Jenny Woods clutched her book. It was the only semblance of comfort she had on the school bus of rowdy teenagers. They had just left the Bronx and were headed towards the destination of their class field trip: the Balsam Lake Mountain Wild Forest preserve. In other words, her personal hell.

These excursions were theoretically supposed to build character strengths, such as resilience and independence by exposing students to the outdoors and new challenges. Somehow a day trip to the wilderness was going to "create community". Jenny cringed at the lame sell-it-to-parents talking point because it was just an excuse to charge more tuition. Rather than creating any kind of community, most of her classmates goofed off and splintered into their various pre-established social circles to talk about gossip, celebrities, or the latest social media drama. She always ended up by herself.

Being half Puerto Rican did open some social doors for her with the fellow classmates who looked like her. There were a handful of people she would sit with at lunch, but she didn't feel the need for company. All of the fulfillment others found in companionship and social activities, she found in preparing for college. Once she left high school and made it to Columbia University, she could restart her social life surrounded by people even smarter than she was. Then she would finally be herself. But it was only September. The twenty-fourth, to be exact. Senior year had just started, and though she was more than ready for college, she still had to graduate from high school. The only thing standing between her and Columbia University was 259 days. She planned to walk across that graduation stage, grab her diploma, and keep it moving because she was

1

over this school.

There were many debates on where the best seat on the bus was, but the consensus was the very back. It wasn't just that it was the farthest seat away from the teacher, who always sat at the front of the bus talking with the driver about who knows what. Whenever the bus hit a bump, the entire back bounced up and down. Probably because of an old axle that needed repair, or just because the suspension was failing. So, at the exact moment the bus hit a bump, you could jump out of the seat and the momentum would send you up high in the air. For some reason everyone thought this was funny, and not a glaring safety issue.

In Jenny's opinion, the often-overlooked seat in the middle of the bus right over the wheel well was the best. It offered a footrest, and with this glorious support she could put her feet up, sink down into her warm hoodie, and read. When she'd claimed it today, she put in her AirPods, started her Spotify reading playlist, and pulled out the book *Starfish* by Peter Watts. Unsurprisingly, no one sat next to her. She'd thought that focusing on the pages in front of her and staying out of everyone's way would act as social camouflage.

"I can't believe Jenny brought a book. What a loser."

Crap. Didn't work. Eric Wilson sat right behind her. She could pick out his arrogant privileged patois without her eyes leaving the page. His black hair and cold blue eyes exuded an overabundance of confidence. His mother was some big-shot defense contractor and let him have parties at their mansion on the weekends. Well, she used to let him have parties, but last summer a viral video upended his life. As it goes, at a random party, someone caught Eric doing drugs on video. No one knows who filmed it, or why they released it online, but if it weren't for his mom Eric would have been expelled.

"I mean seriously, who brings a book to a hike?"

Jenny felt heat rise in her cheeks. But she pushed her emotions away and pretended she didn't hear him. She pulled at her long ponytail and tried to read the words on the page. If she reacted to anything he said, it would just fuel their incessant make-fun-of-the-smart-kid game. By now, she had reread the same sentence in her book six times. Screw it, she thought, time to say something.

"Maybe you should try reading a book, Eric." She yelled at him from her seat," Then your mom wouldn't have to pay for you to get into Harvard."

"I'll have you know, J.Lo, I got in because I passed the SAT."

"Ahh nice, call the Latina from the Bronx Jennifer Lopez. That's not racist at all."

"I'm not racist! I have tons of Black friends."

"Wow. Yeah. You really proved me wrong there. Idiot."

Jenny whipped around and sat back in her seat, letting her last comment hang in the air. She took a few focused breaths namaste style, turned up her music, and forced the world away so she wouldn't have to listen to whatever lame retort Eric could muster. Just as she fell back into the book, hands roughly grabbed at her ears and suddenly her AirPods were gone. Her cheeks bloomed hot with anger. She wanted to scream, but she knew from experience this would only make it worse. Instead, she sighed, stood up, and slowly turned. Eric pretended to be oblivious, with a wolfish grin on his face that made her want to punch him in his dumb overbleached teeth.

"Please give me back my AirPods," Jenny said.

"I don't know what you're talking about," Eric said, skittishly looking around at his friends for approval.

"Come on. I know you took them."

"Seriously, J.Lo. I don't know what you mean."

She could feel everyone's eyes on her. She had hoped for just one pair to show a hint of empathy. Her eyes met Logan Camillo of all people, but after a moment he looked away. After Eric got in huge trouble for that video going viral, he interrogated each of his friends and, without a shred of evidence, settled on his best friend Logan as the videographer who leaked it. The exile he faced was brutal: No eye contact at school, no texting, no communication. Everyone started treating Logan like an outcast. He lost tons of followers on social media, and Eric created a Logan hate group online and told everyone to invite their friends to join. The worst part was that they all thought it was just a joke.

Logan couldn't risk being ostracized even further, so no sympathy there. Her anger boiled over. She stepped into the aisle and stood next to Eric's seat. She knew he had her AirPods in his hand. He didn't even try to hide them.

"Eric, give them back."

"Oh, these cheap Chinese knock offs? They're garbage."

With one swift motion, Eric threw the AirPods out the window. She watched them sail behind the bus and disappear. Jenny stood motionless, seething with anger, unsure about what to do.

"Please stop harassing me," Eric said and pushed Jenny away. Then he stuck his foot out and kicked her black-and-red Jordans, which made her stumble and fall onto the dirty bus floor. The back of the bus exploded with laughter, which drew the attention of their teacher at the front of the bus, Mr. Blumfit.

Blumfit, brother of the principal, had no formal training but somehow managed to get some kind of certificate to be a substitute teacher. When the previous history teacher retired, they put him in charge of the school's history courses as a "long-term auxiliary." No one know what that meant, or when they might get a real teacher. His complete knowledge of American history centered around Cubs baseball statistics from the 1980s.

"What's going on back there?" Blumfit yelled from the front of the bus.

"Jenny is out of her seat and harassing me, sir!" Eric said.

"Jenny, just um . . . sit in your seat. Or else it's detention for you!"

"But Mr. Blumfit," Jenny argued. "Eric—"

"I don't want to hear it!" he replied and turned his back to continue his conversation with the bus driver.

"Sit down, loser," Eric whispered in Jenny's ear.

Jenny dragged herself back into her seat. The fresh memory of Eric nonchalantly tossing her AirPods out the window looped over and over in her head like a GIF. He'd also scuffed up her Jordans on purpose. Sure, they weren't her best pair of shoes, because it'd be wild to wear a good pair of Jordans hiking. Looking at them, she saw that they were pretty beat up, but they were her favorite and no one scuffs her Jordans except her. She calmly grabbed her green canvas backpack from the floor and placed *Starfish* inside. Internally, she was fuming. She had to get even. There would be no way for her to calm down until he felt what she felt. Jenny slowly turned around to face Eric.

"What are you looking at, J.Lo?" Eric said.

Jenny smiled and cleared her throat.

"I want you to know something."

"What's that?"

"I'm the one that filmed you at that party. It was me."

Eric lunged at her.

CHAPTER TWO

One of the worst clichés Jenny loathed to read in books was the whole slow-mo action sequence trope. Like suddenly the main character gets into a fight, adrenaline starts pumping, and then the character sees everything in slow motion. Until now, she'd never had the chance to test the theory of whether time actually slows down during a fight.

Turns out, time doesn't slow down. It goes by at normal speed, same as the rest of life. The only good thing about this fight was finally getting the answer to that question. Everything else sucked.

Eric threw himself over the seat at Jenny, who flinched and tried to dodge, which was less like an action-film dodge and more like just falling into the aisle. She was half successful, but Eric's hands caught her hoodie as she fell. His momentum and their mutual weight sent them both down to the floor. Jenny spilled backward and Eric fell headfirst into the seat, colliding with the wheel well. Hard. When he pulled himself up his eyes snapped from dazed to enraged in an instant.

"What's wrong with you?" Jenny tried to yell, but her voice cracked and sounded weak in the heat of the moment. She hated herself for it.

"My face! You did this!" Eric screamed.

"Fight! Fight! Fight!" the kids yelled from the back.

Jenny tried to pull herself up, but Eric threw himself at her again and they fell into the seat across the aisle. Jenny covered her face as Eric hit her. Everything was a blur of pain and noise. Bright white lights flashed across her vision with every blow to the head. Blow after blow, Jenny squirmed and tried to protect her head, but she couldn't see where the next hit was coming from. After what felt like an eternity, Mr. Blumfit lifted Eric off Jenny and threw him back into his seat like he weighed nothing. Jenny looked around at all of the stunned eyes. No one thought Mr. Blumfit had the strength or will to intervene, let alone toss Eric around like a ragdoll.

"Everyone shut up!" Blumfit yelled to an already silent bus, spittle flying from his mouth.

Blumfit's face was flushed red. "What the hell is wrong with you all? I turn my back for one second and next the thing I know you're at each other's throats. And everyone else, yelling and screaming like a bunch of idiots. You are all one year away from going to college and becoming adults. And Eric, just . . . What's wrong with you?"

"Blumfit, I can't believe you did that to me," Eric said. Then his mouth turned up into a shit-eating grin. "I'm going to call my parents and they'll get you fired."

"Mr. Blumfit," Jenny said. "He scuffed my shoes, and threw my AirPods."

"I don't want to hear another word from either of you. Eric, just . . . there's no need to call your parents. Okay? Jenny, move away from him. Don't go near him for the rest of the trip."

"Mr. Blumfit, he—"

"If I hear another word from you, I'll recommend two weeks of suspension. Do I make myself clear?"

That threat was met with silence.

"Jenny, come sit up here in the front. Eric, just stay in your seat. The rest of this bus ride will be silent. I'd better not hear any talking. From anyone."

Jenny grabbed her bag and moved to an empty seat near the front. Eric went back to his own seat. Blumfit handed her some Burger King napkins to wipe herself off. She glanced over her shoulder at Eric, who looked furious. Someone had given him a wet wipe to wipe the bus floor grime off his face. Jenny sat down and touched her temple, wincing at the sharp pain. A small lump was swelling and felt like it would bruise. She dreaded returning home. How would she explain the bruises on her face to her father? Worse, how would he react once he found out who did it?

Blumfit settled back into his seat. His empty threats to the other students only kept them quiet for a few moments. As soon as he turned his back, everyone whispered to each other about what had just happened. Jenny stared at the floor, trying to process all of it when a ball of paper hit the back of her head. Jenny unraveled it and read the two words scratched onto the page:

You're dead.

Jenny tensed up. It had to be Eric. The lie about the video echoed in her mind. She knew it would make him angry. It didn't matter whether or not it was true. It wouldn't hurt her social status. And she had been at the party, so it could have been true. But it didn't matter now because all she felt was fear. The anger had evaporated and left her terrified of what might happen next. Looking around, Jenny realized she had no allies here. If something went down, who would defend her? For the rest of the trip, she would steer clear of Eric. She reached into her backpack and pulled out a package of tissues, using the last one to blow her nose.

Things awkwardly drifted back to normal for the rest of the drive. When they finally arrived at their destination, the fight felt like a weird distant memory. She hoped it would stay that way.

"All right, everyone, grab your backpacks and gather outside," said Mr. Blumfit.

The sun and crisp mid-September air did wonders to improve Jenny's spirits. It wasn't too cold out, even if it was technically fall, but she felt glad she had decided on her thick hoodie. The soft brown fleece inside was just warm enough to not overheat. She joined the rest of the kids gathering at the start of the hiking trail.

"Okay kids," Blumfit said. "We are going to hike along the Mill Brook Ridge Trail. Form a line and stick with your assigned hiking buddy, okay?"

"Mr. Bum-fit?" said one of the popular kids, causing all the others to chuckle at the mispronunciation.

"What is it, Jax?" Blumfit said with a frown.

"You never assigned us partners," Jax said. The parliament of teenagers all nodded in unison.

"Well, then everyone partner up. You need a hiking buddy so we all can keep track of each other."

A wave of dread and anxiety overwhelmed Jenny. Partnering up for classes was her least favorite thing in the world. Jenny stood waiting to see which poor soul would be sentenced to join her on the island of misfit toys.

Logan appeared out of nowhere with a weird smile on his face. Jenny tensed when their eyes met.

"Hi Jenny. I'm Logan." He smiled at her and extended his hand toward her.

Jenny reached out and shook Logan's hand. "Nice to meet you, Logan."

"No one wanted to be my partner, so I thought I'd go with you. I hope that's okay."

7

"Um, yeah. That's okay." Jenny was caught off guard by how cordial he was acting.

"I wanted to tell you how good it felt to watch you mess with Eric," Logan said with a laugh. "Are you ok?"

Jenny caught Eric looking at them, but he quickly turned back to his circle of friends..

"Yeah, I'm ok. My head is a little sore, but I'll manage."

One by one, the groups started off onto the trail, led by Blumfit, with Jenny and Logan decidedly in the back of the line He was super friendly during the walk, telling funny stories and asking questions. Alarm bells were going off in Jenny's head. Is Logan being nice to trick her, or something? Jenny had read Stephen King's *Carrie*. She knew what happened when people suddenly started acting nice to the nerdy awkward girl. On the flip side, if this wasn't a trap and Logan was being genuine, she didn't want to alienate her one ally on this hike.

"You didn't actually film that video, did you?"

Ahh, was this what he was aiming towards, being friendly to try and get the truth out of her? If she did film it and post it online, she essentially caused his social exile. How mad would he be if it were true?

"No, I didn't, I just said that to piss Eric off."

"Well, that certainly worked."

"You didn't film it either did you?"

"Nope. Not that anyone believes me."

"Why did Eric pin it on you? Weren't you like his best friend?"

The group came to a narrow bend in the hiking trail at the top of a steep hill. The walking slowed as Blumfit took them through the bend with caution.

"When his mom somehow found the video, she threatened to ship him off to military school. Eric refused to take responsibility and went on a vicious mission to out the person who filmed him, which only made kids talk about it more."

"The Streisand effect"

"The what?"

"Never mind. Even if he found the person who filmed it, that doesn't change what he was caught doing."

"It did though. He blamed me because his mom doesn't like me. Maybe because I'm Italian? I honestly don't know, but he convinced her that I faked the video, that he would never do cocaine, which he does, and that I set him up. She bought it, and he avoided military school."

"Wow. And then he exiled his best friend."

"Yup. I tried to tell people I didn't do it, but no one believed me."

"The court of public opinion is swift and fierce."

Up ahead, Blumfit slipped and fell, and everyone laughed. Jenny looked over the edge of the hill they were on and tried to see down to the bottom, but the trees and foliage were too dense to see where it ended.

They stayed at the back of the line, away from Eric and his entourage. She learned that Logan played cello and wanted to attend Julliard someday. He was the oldest in his family and had four younger siblings. He liked to read too, but he had to hide it from Eric when they were friends, who evidently had something against books. Now that he was an outcast, he was reading again.

"Can I ask you something?" Jenny said.

"Sure thing."

"Why did you let Eric control your life?"

This question seemed to catch him off guard. He looked down at the ground and his face blushed red.

"I . . . don't really know," he said. "I wasn't really actively doing it. I guess I just went with the crowd. But after I was exiled, I didn't know what to do with myself. Ended up having a panic attack after like three weeks of no one talking to me. Had to go to therapy, and that's helping I guess."

"That's cool."

"Yeah. I never told that to anyone."

A cool breeze rushed past them, swaying the leaves in the trees. Logan looked like he wanted to say more, but before he could, someone shouted from the front of the line. Jenny stood up on her toes to see what was happening, but the narrow trail made it impossible to see around the crowd.

"What do you think is going on up there?" Jenny asked.

"Oh, it's probably Eric," Logan said.

"What do you mean?"

"Well, he said he had a good idea for a prank."

Jenny went into high alert. Her anxiety spiked and her heart pounded. Is this the moment, after opening herself up to Logan, he would reveal that it was a joke all along?

"A prank for who?"

"Blumfit. I think. Eric wouldn't say."

So that was it. Logan had no clue. Jenny guessed that Eric had kept him in the dark because he was too nice of a guy to willingly go along with it. Right on cue, Eric emerged from the line of hikers and stopped in front of them.

"How's it been, Logan? Has the wolf taken a bite out of you yet?" Eric asked, pointing at Jenny.

"What's happening up front man?" Before her eyes, Logan's body language transformed. His shoulders folded in, making him look smaller and weaker, and his voice went up an octave. Jenny felt sorry for him.

"Oh, Blumfit is helping out Jax. He 'fell down'," Eric said, enunciating with air quotes.

"So, that's the prank on Blumfit you were talking about?" Logan said.

"No, stupid, that was just a diversion," Eric said.

Out of nowhere he pushed Jenny hard, sending her backward off the narrow trail. Jenny heard Logan shout. After a moment of weightlessness as she fell over the edge, her back slammed into the ground. Her world became a violent, blurry tornado as she tumbled down the side of the hill. Only one thought passed through her mind: *I'm falling.*

Her stomach climbed into her throat. Dozens of blows hit her from every direction as she collided with rocks and trees. Every second felt like an hour. Her speed picked up and she fell faster. She tried to grab on to something, anything, to stop the world from spinning. Then her body bounced off something, and there was another moment of weightlessness. Her stomach went into her throat. Everything spun, it was all too fast to focus. Finally, she hit the ground hard and her momentum sent her flying. Her head smacked into a tree and she blacked out.

CHAPTER THREE

At first there was nothing. Blissful nothingness. Pain slowly brought her back to consciousness. Before she opened her eyes, she became aware of a dull throbbing at her temple. The sore spot from the fight with Eric had renewed itself. As she opened her eyes, she became aware of other, new pains. Her arms and back were sore all over, and every breath took effort. Her face stung from a few cuts. She felt like she had been hit by a car and then thrown off a cliff.

Through the fog of pain, the memories slowly crept into her mind bit by bit like a slideshow. The bus ride, the fight with Eric, pairing up with Logan, climbing to the top of a hill along a narrow pathway . . . and then a push. Eric really tried to murder her and Logan had watched it happen. Jenny wanted to scream. She imagined herself hurting Eric in a hundred different ways. Why did people look up to this self-centered privileged kid? Why did he have to pick on her? And now he tried to murder her. The next time she saw him, she vowed to stab him in his eyes. Not kill him, just blind him for life. Seemed like a fitting punishment.

Next to her was a large rotting tree log that appeared to have fallen years ago, sitting undisturbed until she had smashed into it. She used it to help pull herself up and propped herself against it. She took a few deep breaths and rubbed her eyes, trying to push away the pain and focus on surveying her new surroundings.

The steep hill that had delivered her to the forest floor loomed in front of her, jagged and unwelcoming. The slope met the ground beneath her feet at a harsh angle—she could climb up, but it would be difficult even with a clear trail. Jutting out from the incline were rocks and mangled trees. The black dirt looked wet and muddy. All of that combined with the harsh angel of the hill. Climbing up would be a real challenge. She craned her neck back, hoping to glimpse the hiking trail at the top. But the thick foliage made it impossible to see.

The small clearing she found herself in had a carpet of dead leaves mixed with little green plants. Without the knowledge of what these plants were, she decided to avoid touching them at all costs in case there was poison ivy. Thin beams of light penetrated the heavy canopy above, speckling the forest with yellow light. The worst part of it all was the silence. It unsettled her gut in a way she had never felt before. It was so quiet that her breath sounded like sandpaper. She could hear her heartbeat. The forest felt like a different planet compared to the loud and bustling sounds of the Bronx. Here, her ears strained to hear but was only met with deafening silence. A slight breeze ruffled the leaves and branches above her.

Jenny slowly stood up, carefully testing each joint to see how much damage her body had taken on the way down. She prayed nothing was broken. She shifted her weight from foot to foot, testing out her ankle joints. No sharp pain. Just aches and soreness.

"Nothing broken, but everything hurts," she said to herself. Her voice was loud in the surrounding silence.

She stretched her back and paused. Her backpack was gone. Her hands went to her pockets. Phone was gone too. Panic sank in and her heart pounded. Even if she had no way to contact anyone, surely Blumfit and the class would be searching for her. There had to be protocol for when someone went missing on a field trip. It wasn't reassuring to know that her fate rested in Blumfit's hands.

The blood drained from her face. What if Blumfit didn't realize she was missing? What if Eric made Logan swear not to tell anyone? Jenny strained to remember if anyone else had seen her fall, but most of it was a blurry fog. Eric had power over Logan, but would he force him to be complicit in attempted murder? She felt she had bonded with Logan and their shared feeling of being outcasts. He had opened up and seemed like a genuine person. Was it all an act? Maybe he'd made a deal with Eric to restore his reputation and end the social ostracization.

Jenny shook her head, dispelling these thoughts. There was no point in focusing on them now. They made her angry, and anger didn't solve her current problem, which was quickly turning into a bad situation. She was lost and needed to get home, which—according to the Google Maps route she'd studied before they'd left for the trip—was about one hundred and forty-five hundred miles due south-east. To get home, she needed to find her backpack and her phone. It was easier to focus on small goals for the time being. Things she could solve right now, rather than let the toxic thoughts creep into her head and kill her motivation. She would deal with all of that later. Hopefully.

Jenny stepped up to the base of the steep hill. It was a miracle that she hadn't broken something. Twisted trees, sharp rocks, and scraggly bushes jutted out in every direction, leading upward into the tree canopy. She didn't know a word in the English dictionary that could describe the looming mass in front of her. "Hill" seemed too small a word, and it certainly wasn't a mountain in the traditional sense. Something in between. Regardless, from where she stood, falling down this beast appeared impossible to survive. Yet here she stood, and in one piece.

She did the only thing that made sense: try to climb it. After all, her class might still be at the top. But even if they weren't, the trail leading back to civilization would be. She could find it, follow it back to the road, and walk home if she needed to.

Once she began to climb, it became clear rather quickly that her black-and-red Jordans did nothing to help her find footing. They were clearly not meant for hiking. Thankfully she had five other pairs back home, but these were trashed. Seeing them all wet and muddy was heartbreaking. They slipped and struggled to find grip against the muddy hill, and she dropped to the ground. Then she tried to crawl up on her hands and knees, coating them with the cold, wet mud. Off and on, she had to stop when her hands grew numb so she could blow hot breath into them to warm them up. She struggled to make any progress up the steep incline. Throwing cleanliness to the wind, she found that she could dig her hands into the ground like a shovel and use it as leverage to pull herself up, inch by inch.

"I must look like an idiot trying to climb up this hill," she said out loud.

I probably sound like an idiot talking to myself, she thought.

Progress was slow. Her hands and feet ached. After it felt like she had been climbing for hours, she stopped and dug her hands deep into the earth so she could rest and survey the progress. She turned back and saw that she had climbed about twenty feet up. Then she looked up to try to see the top, but it just kept going. To her left was a thin tree that looked strong enough to lean against. She slowly sidled her way toward it until she reached the little sapling, and then swung her legs around so that she sat straddling it between her legs. She laid back against the cold ground and rested, stretching her aching fingers.

As she lay there staring up at the sky, she wondered what time it was. She racked her brain trying to come up with any clues that could help her figure out how long she had spent passed out on the forest floor. She came up with two clues: The sun was still out, and they had started hiking sometime around 10:30 a.m.

"I couldn't have been out for more than an hour, right?" she said.

"Well, how could you know that?" she replied to herself.

"I mean, I don't."

She looked above her, trying to gauge the position of the sun. But the dense canopy of leaves made the sun hard to find. She twisted and strained her neck, looking for gaps in foliage above, and up the hill to the left she spotted a splotch of green. Her backpack. It hung from a thin branch jutting out from a tree stump. Her heart jumped at the sight of it.

It looked to be another twenty feet up the hill. Her hands already hurt like hell from the climb, and the rest of her body felt sore and in need of rest, but she had to push herself. She needed that bag and everything inside it. She twisted her body around to get a better look. Her backpack hung by its strap off a thin little branch jutting out of the old tree stump. There were no tears in the canvas of her bag, so everything inside appeared to be intact, if not a bit jostled. The tree stump was a stubby little thing, warped and twisted by weather and age. It sat by itself on the side of the hill, surrounded by dark, slippery-looking mud.

"Nothing is going to be easy today," Jenny said aloud.

Her eyes scanned the hill for a pathway, something she could use without needing to dig her hands into the cold ground. There was nothing that she might be able to use as handholds, and the few small trees leading up to the stump looked thin. A couple rocks stuck out from the side of the hill, but they were covered in sleek mud, so they couldn't be relied on either. No clear path emerged. Jenny sighed and flipped back onto her stomach. Her left foot dug deep into the ground to create a firm base. Then she did the same with her right, and pushed herself up a few inches. When she pushed upward, she dug her hands into the cold, wet ground to keep from sliding down.

"Slow and steady wins the race," she said.

She continued to climb this way, flat on her stomach like a soldier crawling under barbed wire. It reminded her of World War One stories she'd read about in a book called *The Guns of August*. Soldiers in that war spent most of their time in cold, wet trenches. They would climb out of the trenches to push toward those of the enemy's, crawling around barbed wire while under gunfire. This horrible area between trenches was known as No Man's Land. Compared to that, this hill should be easy.

The history teacher before Blumfit, Mrs. Cooper, had given the book to her. She'd let Jenny call her Mrs. C. She was a tall, gray-haired woman who could make even the most mundane topics in history seem interesting. She didn't use flashy PowerPoint presentations, or cop-out with movies like other teachers, but rather taught by telling stories focused on individual people. She always made it a point to talk from the common perspective because, as she put it, too much of history is about the rich and powerful. She took a different perspective and focused on regular people like farmers, soldiers, and parents. She only touched on the rich and powerful when it was important. She said it was imperative that we remembered the people who had nothing, gave everything, and received none of the glory.

Mrs. C did what few other teachers in Jenny's experience had ever done: treated her students like adults. She didn't pander or hide the harsh truths about history. Her classes were in high demand, and always full. Like most great teachers, the bureaucracy of the education system simply beat her down. For her, it became less about teaching and more about paperwork. So, she abruptly retired and moved with her wife into a small cottage near Woodstock. On her last day, Mrs. C pulled Jenny aside and put a book in her hands.

"Jenny, you're the only person here who will cherish this book, and I want you to have it."

"Wow . . ." Jenny said, examining the beautiful leather-bound cover. It looked expensive. "I don't know what to say."

"This book is why I became a history teacher. Promise me you'll read it someday."

"Yes. Absolutely," Jenny said.

As Jenny continued to climb up the hill, she remembered the first time she'd tried to read the book. The language was denser and more collegiate than the Young Adult novels she was used to. After rereading one paragraph over and over, she just couldn't figure out what it was saying. It was the first book she had given up on, and it made her feel ashamed because she promised Mrs. C. that she would read it. She vowed that it would be the first book she would read when she got back to the real world.

Jenny stopped climbing briefly to warm up her aching hands. The ground below looked far away, and the log she had hit her head against seemed small. Her breath caught in her throat. She had lost track of how high she had climbed, and the height felt a bit scary. Looking beyond the log, the forest floor seemed to go on for miles in all directions. It was hard to see through all of the trees and foliage, but there had to be thousands of trees in this area alone. If the situation wasn't so terrible, she might have enjoyed the view.

15

Enough waiting. It was time to end this. Her hands pushed into the dirt as she climbed upward. The dark mud held firm and supported her weight with each push toward the backpack. When the tree stump was almost within reach, she lifted her right foot and pushed it into the mud a bit higher. The texture of the mud changed and her foot went into the ground without much resistance. When she lifted her left foot out, preparing for the same motion, all of her weight shifted to her right foot and the soft mud gave way under the pressure.

Jenny flailed as she started to fall, and she grabbed at a willowy green plant nearby, but it slipped through her hands. Her body started to slide down the hill. Her speed picked up and before she knew it, she was falling. Again. Instinctively, her arms shot out, and she flattened her body against the ground to stop from spinning out of control. Over her shoulder, she saw that she was sliding right into a small tree that would split her in half if she didn't move. Her hands pushed off the ground with all the effort she could muster, and she rolled onto her back, just barely avoiding the tree. But she couldn't stop the momentum and suddenly her world was spinning again before her back made impact with the ground and the air rushed out of her lungs.

CHAPTER FOUR

For the second time today, Jenny had fallen down this godforsaken hill. She coughed and gasped, struggling to catch her breath. The very real thought that she might die here washed over her mind as the hill, scarred with jagged rocks and twisted trees, loomed in front of her. Guarding against her only way home like a castle wall. How could Eric be so cruel? What had Jenny done to deserve this? Did no one care about her? For the first time in her life, she regretted being solitary. The lone-wolf role came naturally to her, and she even liked it, but this overwhelming sense of abandonment began to make her question her choices.

Jenny shook the thoughts away and sat up. There was no choice but to figure this out on her own. She pushed away the cloud of negative feelings and stood up, wondering how dirty her face looked right now.

"Dad, I really miss you. I hope you're ok," she said. Her dad had struggled with depression for a long time after Mom left, how would he handle this? On the few occasions that Jenny visited her, he always found some excuse not to go with. It took Jenny a few years to understand it was because he still loved her, so seeing her would just tear open the old wound.

The stress of being a single parent weighed him down. He had a full-time job that paid well but kept him busy. Often, he struggled to spend time with Jenny, he had to fight to carve out time on the weekends for her. Last summer she tried to get a job at Macy's, not because she needed the money but for something to do. He refused to let her get the job, saying that studying for college mattered more. She suspected the real reason was because it would mean he would see her less at home on the weekends. Jenny had a hard time really knowing if he was happy. He was good at hiding things. Sometimes too good. These days they felt less like father and daughter and more like roommates.

"It's time to make a plan," she said. "All right. How can I get my backpack?" She surveyed the area.

"I could try climbing again," Jenny suggested. Talking to herself felt weird. "But I don't know how many times I can tolerate falling down that hill."

No ideas came to mind. Nothing around her seemed useful. Plants, sticks, and dirt. Not much one can do with these meager materials at her disposal. The little brainstorming session petered out rather quickly.

"I suppose I could create a rope out of plants and twigs," she wondered. "I feel like that could work . . . but I have no idea how to tie it together, and it probably wouldn't support my weight."

She closed her eyes and conjured the mental image of her backpack. Her green bag hanging off that thin little branch on the stumpy tree. It looked so close to snapping. Her heart skipped a beat. The branch sagged under the weight of her backpack. With a little pressure, the branch would snap and her backpack would fall to the ground. Simple solution. But the problem was getting that pressure.

Jenny opened her eyes and looked up the hill. Her hope wavered. She couldn't see her backpack from here. It was too far up the hill, obscured by thick foliage. Even if she managed to find something strong enough to break the branch, she couldn't throw it and hope to hit it from here. She would have to climb the hill. This problem felt so solvable, but somehow the solution escaped her. It was too steep for her to walk or climb up. She sat down, crossed her legs, took a deep breath, and racked her brain for a solution.

She ran through all of the stories she had ever read, all the movies she had ever watched, searching for any hint that could help her here. Some similar situation that could help her climb the hill. The primary problem was that the ground was not only steep, but wet and slippery. What she really wanted right at this moment was boots with good traction. Could she go barefoot? Even if that helped, her feet would freeze before she even reached halfway to the branch.

Staring at the ground, she spotted ants marching in front of her in a single-file line. Heading someplace important, it seemed. Perhaps a mission to recover food for the colony, or a battle with a rival colony. Her mind went to an old French book she'd read a few years back called *Empire of the Ants*. It was a strange science-fiction novel set in an ant colony outside of Paris. The soldier ants would turn sticks and leaves into tools to accomplish the mission the queen gave them. It hit her not like a bolt of lightning, but like the idea had been there all along. She just needed to stop and think it through. It felt so obvious, she started to laugh. Covering the forest floor were tree branches that had either dropped from the canopy above or were remains from trees that had long since fallen. The line of ants continued to flow below her, and Jenny said a small *thank you* for the inspiration. Then she stood up and set her plan into motion.

She scanned the branches on the forest floor around her. *They had to be thick and strong*, she thought. She couldn't risk them breaking. They also had to be about four or five feet tall to do what she wanted them to do. She spotted a long and thick tree branch to her left. She grabbed it and put it under her arm. She walked in a slow circle around her log, gathering up tree branches as she went. Eight branches managed to fit the specifications. Considering the height of the hill, and how far she could reach, she estimated needing about twenty in total. Dropping the eight she had gathered so far near the bottom of the hill, she made another sweep around the area, widening her circle away from her log. She didn't want to walk out of eyesight for even a moment. Knowing herself, she would get lost and not be able to find her way back. It took some time. There were quite a few branches that were close, but these had to be perfect. When she had twenty in total, she took a moment to rest at the base of the hill.

She pushed one of the branches into the steep hill as far up the side as she could reach. Her hands strained and ached as she twisted the branch and forced it deep down into the mud. She managed to push it into the ground until it was about three feet deep. It looked firm, so she gave it a pull to test its strength. The branch held. Her plan might work. Looking up toward her backpack, she plotted the rest her path—her little ant trail.

With another branch under her arm, Jenny pulled herself up toward the first branch, giving it a real test with her full bodyweight. It still held. So, she put her feet against the base of the branch and stretched up as far as she could reach with the second branch. The weird angle made it harder to find a solid spot for the branch. She couldn't reach too far ahead, and when she found a spot it was difficult to use her full strength because she had little leverage. Her forearm muscles burned with pain as she pushed it into the ground. The effort was exhausting and her arms felt weak. When it was at the right depth, she gave it a tug to test it. The branch felt strong. Two down, eighteen more to go, and her arms were begging for a break.

The work was slow. Branch by branch, she made her way up the hill.

It felt good to have something simple and physical to focus on. For a moment she didn't have to think about the seriousness of her situation. The first ten or so branches, she placed one at a time carefully making sure each one was deep enough and had little to no risk of slipping out. She climbed back and forth, up and down the hill at a slow pace, making sure not to slip or fall.

Once she reached the halfway point of ten branches in the ground, she let herself rest for a few moments. All of her body's alert systems were blaring. Head pounding from the fight, back aching from the fall, arms sore from this plan, and stomach protesting the lack of food and water. From here on out, each branch meant going halfway up the hill each trip. The longer the trip, the more time this would take, and the quicker she would run out of energy. So, she pushed herself on this next trip to carry two branches up the hill. If she could take two at once, she might save some time and energy, and it would hopefully speed up the process. There was still a small sliver of hope that she would be back home in the Bronx tonight, but also the forest had grown a touch darker, and that meant the sun had started to set. She really didn't want to spend the night here.

"Five branches, this plan is actually kind of working. Maybe I do know what I'm doing?"

She took a moment while she held on to the sixteenth branch and looked down to the ground. The four remaining branches looked so far away. Then she looked up to her green backpack. She was so close, less than eight feet away. Another two trips would take a lot of time, and her arms had started to grow numb like her legs always did after a long bike ride. She couldn't be sure how long her strength would last before it all just gave out. But as she stared at the backpack, she grew more and more confident that she could just climb the rest of the way without using her branches. If she could just get within reach and snap the thin little branch holding her backpack, this saga would be over.

She let go of the handhold and dug her hands into the mud. She climbed upward and was about two feet away from the stump when the texture of the mud changed. It felt like fresh playdough, offering no resistance to any pressure. She gave a hard push upward with her feet, trying to almost jump and slide up toward her bag. She stretched her arm out and reached for it. Her fingers grazed the strap, but she couldn't quite grip it before the ground gave way beneath her. She felt herself slide backward down the hill on her stomach. As she gained speed, she reached for the nearest branch in the mud, but her weight combined with her momentum pulled it out of the ground with a wet popping sound.

She flailed as she slid farther down the hill. Her heart was pounding fast as her arms felt for something else to grab. Another branch handhold was approaching, and she grabbed it with both hands, digging her feet into the mud to slow her momentum. Her heart pounded in her chest. The branch held firm. She let herself sit in the moment.

Frustrated with her mistake, she yelled out her favorite curse. It felt rather cathartic to scream out, *fuck*. What a great, stress-relieving word. Her voice and that word echoed throughout the otherwise silent forest around her before gently fading away into silence. It sounded kind of neat and brought a smile to her face. But the levity didn't last long before she realized she would have to make at least two full trips, down and up, to plant the four remaining branches. She wasn't willing to risk a shortcut again. The forest was growing darker by the minute, the brilliant orange light of the sunset softening to a dark blue. Escape now seemed more like an idea than an actuality. She carefully descended the rest of the way down the hill, grabbing two branches quickly to start the ascent again.

Her leg muscles ached and begged for rest. Just two branches left. Each step took effort. Her entire being weighed down with exhaustion. After planting the penultimate branch, she, at last, came to the final branch. She twisted it into the ground with all of her strength. Then she pulled on the branch, testing its security. It felt firm enough, so she used it to pull herself up, her feet slipping along the muddy ground. Her bag was so close but she remained patient. She pushed herself the rest of the way up to the tree stump, reached for the rough old bark with her mud-caked hands, and pulled herself up and over the tree stump. She was coated in mud from the top of her hoodie all the way down to the bottom of her jeans, but it didn't matter because she made it.

She slid her backpack off the thin little branch and pulled it to her chest. She was overwhelmed with a mixture of emotions ranging from elation to anger. She let herself be in that moment for a while.

Once the emotions subsided and her breathing returned to normal, she looked down the hill at her thin line of branches trailing up the side. Pride swelled within her. Her plan had worked. She mentally thanked the ants for inspiring her. She promised never to step on one again.

Jenny looked up, gauging from her new vantage point how much farther she would need to climb to reach the top of the hill. But the sight extinguished any hope that remained within her. About forty feet up, the hill met with a steep cliff face that stretched high up for another twenty feet. It had been impossible to see it from the forest floor below, obscured by foliage and tree branches. How could she have possibly survived the fall? Fate seemed content in taunting her today.

The slick, rocky cliff loomed over her, an ominous presence. She could struggle up the rest of the hill with her sticks, but there was no way she could climb the face of that cliff. Panic set in, and suddenly she couldn't catch her breath.

"*Help!*" she screamed. Her voice echoed throughout the forest, and she hated how weak and desperate she sounded.

"*Help!*" she screamed over and over until her throat was raw.

Jenny took a few deep breaths, forcing herself to calm down. Blumfit might not notice her missing, but some classmate would have noticed by now, right? The crushing reminder that her fate rested in the hands of Eric and Logan brought on a new wave of sadness and anger. Why did this happen to her? Was she going to die here? These thoughts bounced around her mind uncontrollably. That feeling of sheer panic overwhelmed her, but she pushed it away with every ounce of strength she had. The image of Logan, face struck with horror, and the smug smile on Eric's face, the last two people Jenny saw before she fell. The faces of her other classmates tormented her. They were all laughing at her, at her defeat. At the top was privileged Eric who always got what he wanted. The one time that Jenny stood up to him, the one and only time, was a death sentence. All because she wanted to listen to music and read a book on the bus. Now she would starve to death in a stupid forest.

A strong, cold breeze brushed her face. She took a deep breath and tried to focus. The forest had grown darker and her mouth had grown dry. She became deeply aware of how thirsty and hungry she felt. She might be spending the night here after all. She thought of Eric, who was probably enjoying a warm bus ride home right now. A familiar wave of anger washed over her but she pushed it away.

"No," she said. "No, I won't let him hurt me anymore." The sadness and self-pity weren't helping the situation. Right now, Jenny had to live. She had to survive, to get out of here and finally put Eric in his place. She promised herself three things:

She would survive.

She would get home.

She would get revenge.

Jenny slipped on her backpack and, using her self-made handholds as guides, worked her way back down to her "base camp." Since there was still a bit of light, she thought it would be a good idea to take inventory of everything she had with her. She sat facing her log. It was the only anchor she had right now. A focal point— somewhere she could come back to. One by one, she pulled out all of the stuff in her backpack and lined it up against the log.

Starfish by Peter Watts was one of the most important items she had in her inventory. She hoped it wouldn't come to burning the pages for fire. But if it had to, she was prepared. When it came to survival, it had its use.

Next up: A lunch consisting of a peanut butter and jelly sandwich—cut into triangles, of course—inside a Ziploc bag. The rest of her lunch consisted of a fun-sized bag of Cheez Doodles, a Granny Smith apple, and a bottle of Poland Spring Water. Her stomach begged her to eat it all right now, but the reality was that she would have to ration this out for God knows how long.

Next in her inventory were three pens, a wallet, a pad, and a small black stainless-steel pocketknife. She picked up the knife, flicked the blade open, and examined it. Two inches long. Her father had sharpened it the night before so she could take it with her on the hike.

"You sure I should bring this, Dad?" Jenny remembered asking.

"Of course. You never know when you might need it. Always good to have a tool with you," he said.

"Okay. Just feels weird bringing a weapon to a school outing."

"It's hardly a weapon. Think of it more as a tool. Plus, its good luck, you know. My grandfather had it with him in Korea and said it always brought him good fortune. So, now his luck will be passed on to you."

"Grandpa served in the Korean War?"

"Yup. So, take it with you for luck. It was destined for you." He smiled.

"Like Excalibur?" she said.

"Exactly. Except you don't have to pull it from a stone."

Her dad's favorite book was *The Once and Future King*. He had read it to Jenny when she was younger. They must have read it together over a dozen times. He had chosen her name, Jennifer, because it had supposedly descended from the Old-English name Guinevere. She totally understood why her father liked it so much: The Round Table, magical adventures, knights battling for honor and rescuing princesses. She looked down at her Excalibur and wondered if maybe it wasn't so lucky after all. So far today, she'd only had bad luck.

She surveyed all of the items from her backpack and confirmed her worst fear: her phone was missing. A part of her had hoped that she might find it in her bag but knew it had been in her pants pocket. She thought of the tall black cliff she had fallen from, the sensation of falling. Her phone must have flown out at some point and disappeared.

She finished taking inventory by running through everything she had on her person: two beat-up black-and-red Jordans with white shoestrings, a pair of thick socks, jeans, a black leather belt, a T-shirt, underwear, and her warm hoodie. She pulled at her ponytail, it had two hair ties holding it up. She mentally added the hair ties to her list. Though, her hair texture was rough on ties, it would be hard to say how long they would last.

It wasn't a survival kit by any stretch of the imagination, but with everything laid out in front of her, she figured there had to be a way to survive out here. God forbid she would be out here more than one night. She would need to ration her food and try not to drink too much of the water.

A strong, cool breeze blew through the forest and cut through her clothes and deep into her skin. She shivered, gathered up her things, and put them all into her backpack. As unbelievable as it seemed, the possibility that she would spend tonight here felt real. She didn't have a sleeping bag or any way to keep warm. Solve one problem and a new one pops up like the head of a hydra. She would need to figure out how to stay warm, or freeze to death. The exhaustion from the day weighed down on her body but there wasn't time to rest yet. Fire was needed and she had no clue how to make it.

CHAPTER FIVE

The reality that Jenny found herself in could be summed up in a single word: Survival. The sun had set and the warm air cooled to an evening breeze. The darkness encompassed everything, save for a few small moon beams that managed to find a path to the forest floor. At this point in time, she had to assume some group was looking for her. After all, even if Eric had tricked Mr. Blumfit, by the time he took roll call on the bus he would have realized that Jenny was missing. Or if that didn't happen, her father would eventually realize she never came home. Once that happened, it was only a matter of time before a search party would be put together to scour the woods. Jenny figured if she stayed put, her odds of surviving were better than if she tried to wander. She sat with her back up against the log, searching her mind for any memory of how to start a fire.

She remembered the story of Gary Paulsen's *Hatchet* about a young man name Brian who was stranded in the Yukon wilderness after a plane crash. She wished she had that book with her instead of *Starfish*. Brian started fires, hunted, and even managed to catch fish. The book would basically be a survival guide. Jenny sat shivering beneath her hoodie, and then it clicked. Brian had figured out how to start a fire by rolling a stick between his hands fast enough to create heat through friction. That heat, when applied to something flammable like dried grass, created fire.

Jenny went in search of tools. She found a slightly bent stick, a big strip bark, and some long blades of dried-out grass. Returning to her place by the log, she placed the bark on the ground to serve as a flat surface and placed the dried grass on top of it. Then she took the stick between her hands placing one end on the dried grass.

"Thanks for the idea, Brian," Jenny said aloud. "Now it's my turn to make some fire."

Jenny spun the stick in her hands. The challenge was to keep it moving but also keep it in place on the dried grass. She worked her hands back and forth for a long time. Her hands started to ache. After a while, with nothing to show for it, she stopped and let out a sigh. Starting fire always seems so easy in books and movies. The palms of her hands burned, and it seemed she was no closer to having fire.

"It's not like I prepared for a situation where I needed to start a fire," she said to herself. After another session of stick spinning, Jenny gave up and threw the stick at the hill in frustration. She kicked the piece of bark away and the dried grass went flying. The palms of her hands were now red and tender. She slowly balled her hands into fists and endured this pain on top of all of the other pains her body felt at the moment: Throat dry with thirst, a day's worth of hunger, the ache at her temple where Eric had hit her, a dull soreness along her back from two falls down the hill.

"I guess I'm in pretty rough shape." Saying it out loud somehow made it more real. Fear creeped into her mind. Fear of dying, fear of never seeing her father again, and fear of loneliness. It all washed over her in waves. The challenges she would face over the next few days would determine future headlines: *Girl on Class Field Trip Found Dead*, or *Girl Survives Getting Lost in the Woods After Classmate Tried to Murder Her*. The latter headline would need some finesse, but that's what editors were for.

Her stomach let out a low bellow. She should eat a little bit. She took out her sandwich and looked at it longingly. She wanted to wolf down the entire thing in two bites but had to restrain herself. She needed the food to last. She took out one of the triangles and bit off one small bite. She returned the sandwich to the Ziploc bag and tucked it away in her backpack. Then she took out her water bottle and allowed herself a long gulp of water. After all, she thought, you die from thirst quicker than hunger. Her body, while still sore, felt slightly better with the sustenance.

From somewhere behind her, a stick cracked. Her senses went on high alert. Ever so slowly, she turned around looking into the darkness where the sound came from and fought the paralysis of fear. There was nothing. Then she heard a terrifying, deep moan. The noise caused the hairs on her neck to stand on end. What if it was a wolf? A wolf would be able to smell her, and then it would attack and kill her. Fear overwhelmed her. Something was out there.

Another stick snapped, sending her off the deep end. Her heart beat in her chest and adrenaline pumped through her veins. There was no way she would risk drawing attention by running. She pulled up the hood of her hoodie around her head, slowly lay down flat on the ground, and closed her eyes, shutting everything out. She lay there as still as she could for what seemed like an eternity, listening to every sound. Trying to hear the soft pad of wolf paws approaching. More time passed. She strained her ears, trying to listen, but eventually exhaustion took over and she drifted off into a shallow, dreamless sleep.

When she woke some time later, her body had curled up in a ball.

"Everything still hurts. Plus it's cold. Screw Eric for all of this," Jenny said.

The sun was out and the dark, brooding forest had given way to one much brighter, more welcoming this morning. Jenny stood up and stretched her arms and legs, feeling every aching muscle strain against her efforts. She did some jumping jacks to warm herself up and get her blood pumping.

"One night down," she said, now aware of how dry her mouth was. She allowed herself another sip from the water bottle. Her stomach groaned for food, so she grabbed the Granny Smith apple and took a bite. This apple would be her food for the day, she decided, since it was bound to go bad soon. She took another bite and placed it back into her backpack.

The paralyzing fear from the previous evening had subsided, and a new feeling of curiosity bloomed inside her mind. What had made that sound last night, she wondered, and where did it go? Sure, it could be a wolf, or it could be something else. Maybe it was walking along some kind of trail. Every horror story she'd ever read told her not to investigate the trail of a wild animal. However, if she found something like a trail that could lead her out of here, she had to try and look. Jenny debated for a long time whether to take her backpack with her. On the one hand, she had worked hard to get it and didn't want to risk losing it again. On the other hand, if a rescuer tracked her here and saw it, they would know she was close by. She decided to leave her backpack by the log, but not stray too far away from it. She grabbed her pocketknife and placed it in her pants pocket. Not that it would do much against a wolf.

Jenny turned away from the hill and set off, slowly stepped deeper into the woods. As she walked, she scanned the area, taking in her surroundings. The ground leading away from the landing log sloped downward and was littered with dead leaves and tree branches that had fallen from the canopy above. Young, lean plants seemed to thrive on the ground despite the little sunlight that made it down here. Jenny desperately wished she knew what poison ivy looked like. She remembered hearing that it had some spiky leaves, but everything green looked the same to her right now, so she just did her best to avoid brushing up against any plant.

Jenny crossed what she thought looked like a small trail and stopped to examine it. Nothing grew along this thin line in the woods, and she could see the ground. One-half of it extended far to her right, the other far to her left. She knelt on the ground and looked for tracks but couldn't find any. Neither animal nor human. She figured that if this was a trail, it hadn't been used recently. So, probably low odds of a human stumbling past. But she was confident that it was a trail of some sort. She stood up and continued exploring.

Crossing the thin pathway, she continued deeper into the woods. As she walked, she took in all of the smells: deep, rich wood mixed with fresh flora and fauna. It created an intoxicatingly fresh smell of nature. She arrived at a dense tangle of trees, some alive, others dead and rotting. It was impossible to navigate through. Jenny took it as a sign that it was time to head back to her log.

When she crossed the small trail again, she noticed something she hadn't seen before. It was obvious to her now, but only from this viewpoint coming back: Blood. The leaves facing this side of the trail were splotched with dark red blood. Whatever had come through here was injured. She knelt by the plants to examine closer. It was a lot of blood, running up and down the trail, so the creature must have been wounded badly. Now that she knew what she was looking for, she searched the ground and found more blood. She froze at the sight of an animal print in the mud. It was huge, bigger than her hand. Only one animal in the forest had a paw print this big: A bear.

CHAPTER SIX

Mind racing, Jenny hurried back to her log. A bear had been just a few feet away from her last night. It was injured, but what if it had found her? She pushed that aside and focused on the more troubling question: what animal attacks a bear? She couldn't think of anything in the forest big enough to attack one successfully. Bears weighed more than humans and had sharp claws to boot. She arrived and sat with her back up against the log, trying to calm down and ponder her next move. If she stayed here, the bear might wander back through. What if it found her? Even worse, what if the thing that had attacked the bear did? On the other hand, leaving the log would make it harder for the search team to find her. If they were looking.

She ate the rest of her apple. She was about to toss it over her shoulder but stopped. It may be all she would eat today. She nibbled at it to get every possible bite. She contemplated eating the seeds and stem. After all, food is food. "What the hell," she said. "Why not?" She ate every possible bit of the apple until there was nothing left. She felt a drop of water hit her forehead. She looked up toward the sky. A soft pitter-patter of small raindrops fell all around her. The sound of rain drops bouncing off of all the trees and foliage sounded like the applause of a massive crowd. She hoped it was just a quick rain shower that would pass by.

Eric's face flashed in her mind, causing a familiar mix of sadness and anger to well up inside her. Eric had taken things too far. Jenny imagined all of the evil ways to get revenge on Eric and found that her anger subsided a bit at the thought of acts of violence. A pang of guilt hit her for how much she enjoyed imagining acts of cruelty. Her father's face flashed into her mind, and she could almost hear his voice lecturing her.

"Now, Jenny. Violence is not the answer."

"But Dad . . ."

"No. Sorry, kiddo. I can't condone it. Violence only causes more violence."

Jenny wondered if her father's beliefs would hold true when he finds out that Eric had tried to murder his daughter. She felt rage bubble up inside her. She wanted to scream at her father and his annoying "love everyone" lecture. She closed her eyes and took a few deep breaths to calm down. It was more important to focus on the actual problems at hand.

As she stared up at the canopy of trees above her, the drops of rain became louder and steadier. The applause now sounded more like a stampede. This rainstorm seemed intent on sticking around. She pulled up the hood of her hoodie around her head.

When it came down to it, her gut told her it was time to leave. It had been a while since she had fallen here, and there wasn't a sign of a search party. She could sit and hope that someone would find her. Or she could find the trail herself and walk back to civilization. It made sense to wait through the first day, but it was now the second day and waiting made less and less sense for every hour that passed. If someone was coming to rescue her, they would have found her by now. Plus, she needed to find more water, which seemed easy; and more food, which seemed much harder.

"Well, I'm not going to just sit here and feel sorry for myself," she said. She stood up, threw on her backpack, took one last look at her landing log, and left.

When she reached the trail she had discovered earlier, the rain had washed away the bear blood. But the paw prints were still visible in the mud, leading from her left to her right. She decided going left would be the smarter choice, away from the injured bear. Jenny felt pretty good about herself, using logic and clues to make the decision. She thought that maybe this survival thing wouldn't be so hard after all.

The rain had steadily picked up and was falling much harder. Big drops fell all around her, and the ground quickly turned into a muddy mess. As she walked along the trail, she hoped to find a makeshift shelter to stay out of the rain, like a fallen log or a rock outcropping. It amazed her how loud the sound of rain could be. Thousands of gallons of falling water crashing down against plants and trees, drowning everything else out. It was beautiful in a terrifying way. Nothing she had ever read could convey a downpour like this. As she followed the trail, she struggled to take step after step as the muddy ground tried to swallow up her feet.

Her old Jordans were no match for the sticky mud. The warm, welcoming forest of yesterday had given way to a wet and unwelcoming mess of plants and mud.

The forest bloomed with a bright white light followed by a deafening boom, stopping Jenny in her tracks. Thunder echoed through the woods and vibrated in her bones. Terror welled up inside her and she ran, heart pounding against her rib cage in fear. Fear of the rain, fear of thunder, fear of Mother Nature. There was another flash followed by another loud boom that shook the forest. She had never been so terrified.

Jenny's foot caught against a branch on the ground, making her fall face-first into a large puddle of mud and cold water. She pulled herself up to her knees and sobbed, her full body convulsing. Terror overwhelmed her unlike anything she had ever experienced before because she was completely, totally alone. Her clothes were soaked through with cold water, making her shiver uncontrollably. If this continued, she might get hypothermia. It was like everything was trying to kill her.

Picking herself up from the ground, Jenny scanned her surroundings, searching for shelter. The downpour made it impossible to see more than a few feet in any direction. She searched the ground for the trail but couldn't find it. Then it hit her like a ton of bricks. She had been so frantic to escape the storm that she had run off the trail. She scrambled and frantically searched for any sign of the trial but to no avail. It took every ounce of effort to keep herself from sinking back down into the wet earth and just let the hypothermia take over. Not only was Jenny wet, cold, hungry, and thirsty, but now she was also truly, utterly lost.

"Wait a sec, fresh water is literally falling from the sky right now."

Without a second thought, she took off her backpack and grabbed the plastic water bottle. She opened it up and drained the bottle down her parched throat, a wave of fresh energy surging through her. Then she held the empty water bottle up toward the sky and let the rain fall into it. Progress was slow. So she plucked a big green leaf from a small tree—it couldn't have been poison ivy—and folded it to make a funnel at the mouth of the water bottle. Then she watched the bottle gradually fill with rain water, faster than before.

She screwed the lid back on and slipped the water bottle in her backpack. With fresh determination, she trekked forward. Without a trail, she just chose a direction, trying not to worry at the thought of being lost. Lost from civilization, from her log, and from the trail. That meant no direction was a wrong direction. She took little comfort in the thought. With the rain pounding down on her, she wondered how the rest of the contents of her backpack were fairing. The backpack itself was supposedly water-resistant, so she hoped she got what was advertised. But there didn't seem much she could do about it at this point.

Jenny wandered into a small clearing where the rain didn't seem to fall as heavily. In fact, the ground wasn't muddy and it seemed almost dry. She looked up at the thick canopy of trees crisscrossing each other with overlapping leaves. *That's why.*

A high-pitched whimper made her freeze. It was an alien sound, one she had never heard before. It repeated, and this time she discovered the source: A small ball of fur huddled up against the trunk of a tree across the clearing. She couldn't see what kind of animal it was, but it was clearly in distress. Its fur was matted with dry blood. She wanted to step closer to see better and maybe to help, but her gut told her to back off. For all she knew, the animal could be rabid.

A crunching sound to her left made her whip her head around. On other end of the clearing, she could barely make out two small eyes, reflecting light as they slowly swayed from side to side. She stared at them intently, fear welling up inside her. A shadowy silhouette appeared running right at her.

Every ounce of her being screamed *run*, but she was frozen in place, paralyzed by fear. Then the shadow lunged straight for her and she fell to the ground, just barely dodging it. It ran past her and circled back. Jenny got to her feet and turned to face it. An immense coyote stared back at her, teeth bared and eyes burning with rage. Its dark brown-and-gray fur matted with mud, its muzzle speckled crimson with blood.

Realization struck her. Connecting the paw print and blood she found on the trail, the small animal curled up by the tree was a bear cub, and this coyote clearly intended to make it a meal. But one thing didn't click. The bear tracks she'd found earlier were huge, too big for this bear cub to make.

The coyote bowed to the ground, baring its teeth at her. Wide eyed and speechless, Jenny didn't move a muscle. They stared at each other for what seemed like hours. Thunder rumbled in the distance. Jenny broke eye contact for a split second, but when she looked back at the coyote, it charged at her.

CHAPTER SEVEN

Rain pounded down around the clearing as Jenny's survival instincts kicked into high gear. The huge coyote charged, her heart pounding like a drum pumping adrenaline through her system. As a reflex, she dashed to the left but slipped over the wet ground, and the momentum sent her downward. The coyote slid and collided with her, sending them both rolling in a mess of hoodie and wet fur.

Jenny could feel the raw strength of the wild animal as he writhed and bucked, trying to untangle himself from her. She saw a flash of teeth as his powerful jaws lurched forward to bite her, barely missing her face. Jenny pushed against the ground hard and managed to roll out of the way. She seized a thick branch from the ground and got to her knees, but he was already charging at her. She closed her eyes and swung. She felt the solid wood connect with a wet mound of fur, breaking the stick as the nimble coyote bounced back, shrugging off the blow. He stopped, as if stunned that Jenny had fought back.

Frozen on her knees, Jenny stared at him, an ugly creature baring sharp teeth. Her mind raced to find a way to beat this beast. But before she could process her next thought, he charged her again. She tried to dodge to the side, but he clamped onto her arm with his powerful jaw.

Jenny screamed as the coyote violently shook her arm from side to side, and she put up no resistance against his wild strength. A tearing sound made her hope it was from her hoodie and not the tendons in her arm.

He thrashed and tossed Jenny to the side. She hit the ground and immediately felt around for something, anything, to defend herself with. Her hand brushed against a stone the size of a baseball. She threw it as hard as she could. It sailed through the air and hit him on the side of his head.

Without wasting a moment, Jenny scrambled to her feet and slipped her father's knife out of her pocket, flipped open the blade, and flashed it to the animal.

"You see this? Back off or I will kill you."

He stared at her with indifference. Jenny steadied her gaze. "Go away!" she yelled, wincing at how weak her voice sounded. He didn't move an inch. She stomped her foot for emphasis and tried again. "Go away!"

The coyote twisted his head to the side and bared his teeth in a deadly smile before he attacked. Exhausted, malnourished, and in pain, Jenny felt cold surrender wash over her. Giving up felt so easy. She closed her eyes and surrendered to her fate. There was a loud crash and then a thud, but Jenny didn't feel anything. Her eyes shot open. Before her, the bear cub and the coyote were wrestling on the ground in a mess of blood and fur. The coyote, pinned by the cub, struggled to regain its balance. The cub swiped its sharp claws at him, but he reared his head and clamped down on the cub's paw. The cub let out a loud cry and tried to pull its paw away, but it couldn't escape.

Jenny rushed the coyote. She thrust the knife into his face and felt it cut deep. He let out a high-pitched yelp. She fought the urge to feel bad about it as he spasmed and bucked backward, retreating to a safe distance. Blood poured out of the fresh wound stretching across his left eye from his forehead to his snout. Jenny spun around to see the bear cub curled up behind her. It was in bad shape with a fresh paw injury in addition to the old wounds from the earlier encounter.

Jenny turned to face the coyote as he leaned forward on its front legs and bared its teeth, letting out a low growl. Jenny knew he was readying to lunge for her again and that her knife would be no match for him. Maybe she could scare him away. She mustered every ounce of her energy and imagined Gandalf standing up to the Balrog in *The Fellowship of the Ring.*

"*Go away!*"

There was a flash of lightning followed by a deafening boom. The coyote froze, but only for a moment. Then he launched at her, teeth baring, but this time Jenny kept her eyes open. In that moment, she decided it was better to go down fighting than resign to fate. If she could save the cub, she could die knowing she did something good with her short life. She opened her mouth to scream, but her voice was drowned out by a deafening roar.

The coyote froze and looked beyond her. Jenny slowly turned and faced an unimaginable sight: Standing in front of her on its hind legs was a full-grown American black bear. The beast towered above her, a massive being. It must have weighed at least five hundred pounds. Its dark fur reflected little light, but its eyes glowed with a fierce passion. Jenny knew, without knowing, this was the mother of the cub at her side.

For a moment, the only sound was the patter of rain. Everything else had stopped. Jenny couldn't help but wonder how humans had survived for centuries when they were clearly so weak in comparison to the fierce beasts in the animal kingdom. The moment passed as quickly as it came. The mother bear fell to her front paws with a thud, shaking the ground with her strength. She bounded towards the coyote, and for the first time, Jenny saw true fear in his eyes. She swung her gigantic paw at him, which he quickly dodged. He gnashed its teeth at her paw, but she swung at him with her other paw, sending him flying across the forest floor with her enormous strength.

The coyote quickly jumped to his feet and launched a counter attack at the mother bear, trying desperately to get at her neck. She swiped at it, but he dodged it and jumped to attack her from above. He landed a bite on her back, but she easily knocked it away, and he fell to the ground. She lashed out at the coyote, but he jumped out of the way.

The two animals stared each other down. The bear blitzed first and was about to bite him with her powerful jaws until he dodged to the side. Then he lunged for her neck, clamping down hard. She let out a roar and stood up on her back legs, lifting the coyote with it. Jenny couldn't believe her eyes. The coyote still held strong onto her neck. The mother bear gave a giant swing of her arm and hit him square in the chest, ripping his jaws away from her neck. He flew through the air and hit a tree with a wet crack and a yelp. He slumped to the ground and went still.

The mother bear fell forward onto her front paw and limped over to her cub. Jenny took a step towards them both, but the mother's head whipped around and she gave Jenny a glare of death, letting out a low growl. Jenny took the hint and walked to the other side of the clearing watching the mother lay down next to her cub. The cub curled into her chest and whimpered. Jenny could see that she was losing a lot of blood from the wound in her neck.

A twig cracked, and Jenny turned to see the coyote was gone. Somehow, he survived. At least for now. The sound of rain seemed distant and the air was heavy with moisture. Jenny suddenly felt old beyond her years as her adrenaline was replaced by exhaustion. Her arm throbbed with a dull pain and blood trickled down forearm from the bite.

She was simply too tired to care. She found herself collapsing into the base of a tree, watching the mother and cub. The idea of it all terrified her. Being this close to a wild animal bigger than a car was not a common occurrence for a girl from the Bronx. Jenny told herself that she would rest her eyes, only for a moment, and then she would leave the clearing.

CHAPTER EIGHT

Jenny woke with a start. Her heart thumped against her chest. She had somehow ended up in a cave. No memory of how she got here. Outside, a dense fog hung in the air. She could barely make out the nearby trees and not much else. She would need to survey the area. The thumping in her chest slowed and she relaxed. The cave was stuffy, warm, and dead quiet apart from a steady dripping sound somewhere nearby. The light coming in through the mouth of the cave was dim, but she could make out some details. Above, the ceiling was littered with stalactites. The cave was pear-shaped and smelled of rich pine and moss.

She slowly ran through the events in her mind, trying to remember how she got here, but the memories were fragmented. There was Eric, and the push that stranded her here in the Balsam Lake Mountain Wild Forest. There was the rainstorm, followed by the brawl with the coyote. How many people could say they saw a wild black bear fight a coyote? Then falling asleep in the clearing. That meant today was September 25th. Sometime in the afternoon. Still stuck here, alone, with next to nothing.

Jenny remembered standing over the mother bear, the injured cub nudging her paw, but she had stopped breathing. Then she remembered walking. Her memory was blurry. She remembered the injured bear cub following her. Her memory was such a jumbled mess that it was hard to say what was real, or how long she had walked, or how far. She didn't remember finding the cave at all.

As she sat up, her stiff muscles cried out in pain. Her body felt wooden and sore. The image of the cub nudging its dead mother's paw hurt like nothing Jenny had felt before. She flexed her forearm, where the coyote had clamped down, and felt a dull pain. The coyote wounded her, dried blood specking her torn hoodie confirmed it, which meant she could get rabies. Her father had always said to avoid raccoons and dogs in the Bronx because they could have rabies. And if you get bitten, you have a certain amount of time to get treated before it's too late. If she had rabies now, it would be a death sentence. Even if she didn't get rabies, the wound could get infected, and that could kill her.

It was time to stop dreading and just confront the truth. Jenny slowly pulled back the torn shreds of her hoodie and held up her forearm closer to the light spilling into the cave.

"Wow, this looks kind of bad," she said.

The bite tore through hoodie like paper, and had broken through her skin. The hoodie prevented some damage, but the wound was ugly. The bleeding had stopped and scabbed over. There was dried blood from her forearm to her finger tips. The bite had left a nasty laceration across her forearm. It would probably end up scarring, but it didn't look too deep into her muscle. Her arm ached, but if she kept the wound clean she might survive. Unless she died from rabies.

A loud snore startled her. To her left, there was a large furry mound. As her eyes slowly adjusted to the darkness, she could see the mound moving slowly up and down in a steady rhythm. Adrenaline surged, her face flushed, and her heartbeat picked up. The wild bear cub had followed her, and now it was lying right next to her. She felt frozen with fear. If she made a sound, the cub might wake up and attack her. Ideas of how to escape ran through her mind, each ending in death by bear. Only one option stuck out to her and it was by far the dumbest.

Hands shaking, she quietly felt around for her backpack. It was hard to see the floor in the dim light. Her hand brushed against sticks, tufts of fur and something smooth, like a bone. Immediately the image of bears munching on human bones flashed through her mind. Reaching far to her right, she felt the familiar texture of her canvas backpack and breathed a sigh of relief, mouthing *thank you* to the heavens. She tried to open the bag as quietly as possible. The zipper was painfully loud, each centimeter of grated metal screaming against her ears. When the opening to the bag was wide enough, she slipped in her hand and felt around. The bag was still damp from the night before, and the contents were wet as well. So much for water resistant. A problem to sort out later. Her hands brushed against the slippery plastic Ziplock bag. She slowly pulled out the sandwich triangle she had taken a bite out of it the day before. Or was that two days ago? They were blurring together already.

She took a big bite of her sandwich and pulled out the bottle of rainwater. She unscrewed the cap and took a long swig of water. The rainwater was cool, refreshing, and slightly sweet.

She fought the desire to eat the rest of her sandwich. It wasn't easy to part with, but if she could use the food to buy time to escape, it was a sacrifice she was willing to make. That's all she could do now: buy more time. If it was between eating her or the sandwich, maybe the cub would opt for the sandwich. It was a dumb plan.

She placed the last bite of the sandwich on the ground between her and the bear cub. Her last line of defense. She pulled her knees up to her chest and hugged them close, becoming aware of how damp her clothes were. Another problem to fix. Can't move, can't risk falling asleep, trapped in a cave with a wild bear cub. How had her life come to this? Anger bloomed inside of her. None of this was her fault, and she wanted nothing more than to watch Eric suffer for putting her through this. She imagined the coyote biting down on his arm and ripping it off. It seemed like a fair punishment. Her mind wandered to her warm bed back home. She longed to crawl into it where it was safe. Her eyelids grew heavy, she tried to keep them open but sleep overtook her.

Warmth radiated from her feet up to her chest. It was a pleasant warmth, and she didn't fight against it. She dreamed of a blanket that was as wide as a field. She snuggled under it with only her head popping out into brisk fresh air. Her eyes flickered open slightly, and she thought she saw a blanket. A real one. She reached out to touch it, but it was too coarse to be a blanket.

Her eyes opened all the way to see that the bear cub had snuggled up next to her. For one terrifying moment she almost screamed. Generations of survival instincts infused in her DNA begged her to run wildly out of the cave and into the forest, but she fought the urge. Surely, that would startle the cub and make it defensive. She took the moment of peace to examine its face. Its snout was short with a cute little black nose on the end. Its fur was light brown. *I guess black bears start off brown?* She thought. As terrifying as it should be, Jenny admitted that the cub was also slightly cute.

It was a moment before she realized the sandwich was gone. The cub must have woken up, eaten the sandwich, and cuddled up to Jenny. Maybe he didn't see her as a threat. If she could train the bear like a dog, he could be useful to her survival.

After all, they'd both survived an incredibly traumatic event together. Maybe it was the hunger and lack of sleep, but Jenny felt a bond with the animal. She watched its chest move up and down. They were both innocent bystanders in this mess. Eric and the coyote were wild beasts—predators out for themselves, hurting others for their own gain.

The idea of domesticating a bear felt absurd—more than absurd, practically insane. But then again, so was this situation. Here she was, miles away from civilization. Alone in the forest for two full days but still alive. Maybe, just maybe, she could train this bear not to see her as a threat. More than that, maybe they could become companions. This would likely end with Jenny as a snack in the belly of the cub. But if it worked, maybe they could survive together. If nothing else, right now she was warm and safe. She felt at peace—the first moment of calm she had in days. She let her worries float away. She closed her eyes and drifted off to sleep.

CHAPTER NINE

"Dad, why did Mom leave?"

His face froze. The sizzling bacon he stood over filled the silence. Jenny watched from the small linoleum table in their kitchen as a mixture of emotions washed over his face, but they were too complex for her to understand. She felt ashamed for asking the question. Did she say something she shouldn't have? The silence stretched as her father stared off into the distance. Smoke started to rise from the pan.

"I think the bacon is done," she said. Nothing happened. "Dad, the bacon is burning."

He snapped back to reality and yanked the bacon off the smoking pan with his tongs. More questions rose within her, but fell away at the fear of him returning to that quiet place again. Why did Mom leave them? Didn't she love them? He never talked about it and Jenny desperately wanted to know. Not because she wished things were different, but just to know. To understand.

She watched him divvy up the bacon strips and place them next to the eggs on her plate. The smell filled the kitchen and her mouth watered. She waited until he sat down across from her before she started shoveling the food into her mouth. She paused, mouth full, and looked across the table. He hadn't touched his food.

"I'm sorry, Dad. I shouldn't have said anything."

"No, kiddo, no. I'm sorry. You're a big girl now. Double digits, right?"

"Ten!"

"And big girls can talk about important things, right?"

"Right."

"Then I suppose it's time we talked. I just— you're still my little girl, you know that? You'll always be my little girl. I can't believe how fast you're growing. Soon you'll walk out that door to find your own path and leave me here, and I guess I just realized that all at once."

"I'm not going to leave you, Dad."

"No, you should. You'll understand someday, and by that time you'll probably want to." His laugh was deep, strong. She didn't understand what was funny but laughed with him anyway.

"Your mom and I met when I moved to New York. We fell in love very quickly and, well, when two people love each other, sometimes they decide to have a baby. And so we were blessed with you."

"But why did Mom leave?"

Her father tensed. The question clearly bothered him, but she had to know. "Well, your mother's father didn't approve of me. I wasn't successful enough, he said. So, your he forbade her from seeing me."

"That's unfair. Why would he do that?"

"Your mom and I had to communicate secretly. I mailed letters to a mutual friend, and he forwarded my letters to her so that her dad wouldn't find out. As it came closer to you getting born, we decided we wanted to raise you together, so we arranged for your mother and I to run away together."

"So, Mom wanted to stay?"

"Yes, she absolutely wanted to . . . at that time." He paused, and sighed before continuing. "One day, after her father left for work and her mother was out, she quickly packed a bag, hopped on the subway, and moved into my apartment. When she arrived, we were so happy to finally be together. She wrote to her father and told him we were going to get married and have you. She said they could only be in your life if they treated me like family. We never heard back from them and things were fine for a while. You were born, your mom and I got married, and we had our happy family together."

"But I don't understand. If everything was fine, why did she leave us?"

"Your grandpa refused to speak to us for years, and he convinced a lot of your mom's family to do the same. Your mom loved us, but she also loved her family. After a few years she said she felt like her soul was being divided in two. Then one day, she was gone. I tried to find her, but she didn't want to be found."

Tears were welling up in his eyes, and Jenny started to cry as well. She went to him and hugged him, and they stayed like that for a long time. After a while, she looked up at him. His eyes were red but he smiled.

"Do you think I could meet her someday?"

"Yes, someday."

She returned to her seat, and they ate breakfast in peaceful silence. Afterward, her dad pulled out a package of cigarettes and a lighter to have his usual after-breakfast smoke. She watched as he flicked the lighter open and tried to start the flame. He flicked it over and over, but the spark wasn't catching. He tried again. And again. And again. Then sparks flew and a flame erupted. He turned to look at her and was about to say something.

Jenny woke with a start. Metal plus flint equals sparks. Sparks means fire.

That's it. Her pocket knife was made of metal which meant she just needed to find flint and she could start a fire. It was day 3, September 26th, and she had a mission: find flint.

The dream nagged at her. It had been a while since she had thought about that conversation. A few years after that talk with her dad, she met her mother. Jenny struggled to understand her choices. After that first meeting, they had tried to connect a few times over the years, but the gulf between them seemed insurmountable. How do you connect with a mother who left? They never talked about why she did it and they were not friends, at least in Jenny's mind. Their meetings always felt forced and awkward. Sometimes the silences stretched on for minutes until the compulsion to talk just to fill the void took over. It seemed like neither of them knew what the relationship was supposed to look like.

Outside the cave, the fog had lifted and sunbeams pierced through the trees, illuminating the forest floor. Jenny felt a renewed sense of energy, and it all seemed slightly less hopeless than before. She struggled to shake the lingering feelings the dream had caused and missed her father desperately. She scanned the area around her.

"There has to be flint in this cave, right? Dumb question. There probably is flint, but what does it look like?"

She stood, but before she could look, the bear cub next to her sat up with a start.

Oh, right. That, she thought. They stared at each other for what felt like forever. The cub walked toward her, sniffing the air. Jenny held out the back of her trembling hand, like she would do to any dog in her neighborhood. The cub stiffened, and slapped the ground hard with a paw. Jenny let out a yelp. She held up both her hands and took a step back. The cub lunged at her, but stopped short, and let out a loud puff of air. Jenny's heart was pounding against her ribcage. Her hands trembled nervously in the air. Something about this was a show, she figured, because it hadn't attacked her yet. Maybe this was a show of dominance? She kneeled down slowly and sat on her feet. The cub watched her intently.

"Can we be friends?"

The small brown eyes stared back at her.

"Promise not to kill me? I'll give you the other half of my sandwich. It's cut in a triangle."

The cub turned his back to her and slowly retreated to the other end of the cave.

"I'll take that as a solid maybe," she laughed. "But what do I call you. Are you a boy or a girl bear?"

She looked down between its legs and quickly back up at its eyes.

"Definitely a boy. No question there."

She reached into her backpack and pulled out the last half of the sandwich. She split it into two pieces and tossed half to him. He licked it up quickly and swallowed it without a bite. Jenny nibbled at hers.

"You like PB&J sandwiches? There is a name in there . . . I can't call you Jelly. Butter sounds like a name Paula Dean would give her dog. So how about Peanut?" She tried to examine him for any injuries from the fight in the clearing. If there were, his fur hid it well, and he didn't appear to be in pain. Her stomach let out a low rumble. Peanut looked at her with indifference.

"I'm trying to start a fire Peanut. You wouldn't happen to know what flint looks like, would you?"

CHAPTER TEN

J enny gathered up as many different rocks she could find in the cave and laid them out in front of her. Peanut scratched himself and laid on his side, switching between napping and watching her with what seemed to be a general disinterest. He didn't trust her, but there weren't any further displays of dominance. So, progress?

The rocks might help create a spark, but she needed stuff to burn. Probably something small at first, like dried leaves or grass, until she could get a spark. It felt good to at least have a plan to carry out a goal. Made ignoring her other problems easier. Near the mouth of the cave, she got down on her hands and knees, and crawled through the narrow opening. It crossed her mind this would be the first time she had set foot outside of the cave in . . . how long had she been here now? The landing log was day one, the fight in the clearing was the morning of day two, wandering to the cave was probably in the afternoon of day two, and it was now the afternoon of day three. So yeah, a whole day spent in this cave.

"Hello, world. It's me, Jenny. Miss me?"

Jenny peeked her head out and looked at her surroundings. The cave sat at the base of a tall rock wall broken up by massive shelf-like slabs of stone. To her right, a thick tree jutted out of the rock face, its twisting trunk warping into a bulb-like shape at its base. To her left, along the front of the rock wall, a small climbing trail led upward, but foliage obstructed its destination. She figured it led up towards the top of the cliff, she made a mental note to explore that later. In front of her, the ground gently sloped downward, covered in dead leaves and small sticks. A large bear paw print led out of the cave. She placed her hand in it and felt very small by comparison. She looked back inside the cave and saw the small, furry brown shape that was Peanut. The last image of his mother flashed in her memory, and she saw her lying on the ground, wet, bleeding, and dying. Her heart ached for them both.

Jenny stepped out of the cave and searched the ground for sticks and dried grass, gathering them up one by one. Hard to believe it was now day three. Would a search party have been formed by now? What if they were already in the forest looking for her? Her stomach rumbled again reminding her that she hadn't been eating or drinking much. She would have to find more food and freshwater soon.

With a large bundle of sticks in her arms and a handful of dried grass, she made her way back to the cave. She set the bundle down near the mouth, crawled into the cave on her knees, and then pulled the bundle inside. She made her way to the back and found Peanut still on his side, but now he was snoring.

"Don't get up. I've got this."

Jenny set the bundle of sticks down next to the rocks she had found and set to work. She made a small pile of sticks, sprinkled the dried grass on top, and then grabbed a smooth black rock from the line she had laid out. She pulled the knife out of her pocket and flipped it open. She paused when she saw dried blood on the blade and flexed her forearm, remembering the fight with the coyote. Shuddering, she shook away the thought and set out to the task ahead of her. She held the rock over the sticks and hit it with the backside of her blade. Nothing. She tried a few more times. Still nothing. She set the rock aside and tried the next one. Nothing.

She tried rock after rock with no luck. Outside the cave, the sun casted a bright orange glow across the forest. Sunset. She was running out of daylight already. Another day with no fire, no food, and no freshwater. Despair overwhelmed her. She thought of her father's smile, the slight wrinkles at the corner of his mouth, the way his eyes lit up as if his whole face was smiling. She ached for home. Tears welled up in the corners of her eyes and her chest shook into shuddering breaths. Why had this happened to her? She was too young to die here, alone, in the middle of nowhere.

Peanut woke with a start, and looked around confused for a moment.

"Same vibes, Peanut, same."

He got up wandered toward the back of the cave and dug at something in the ground. Jenny returned to her project, and grabbing one of two remaining rocks. It was dark gray and waxy. She struck the back of it with her knife, and a small spark flew off toward the sticks.

"Holy crap."

She did it again. Another spark. Over and over, she hit the rock and sent small sparks flying. This time, she held the knife and flint over the small pile of dried grass and sticks she made earlier. With a firm strike a spark flew off and landed on the dried grass charring it. She did it again, making more sparks. Even though they were small, there were a dozen tiny sparks burning the dried grass. She blew gently on the sparks until they glowed a hot orange, burning a hole into the dried grass as the flame started to spread. She blew again, and this time lots of smoke came out.

Wow.

She blew again and again. With each breath, the flames spread and the smoke grew thicker. She took a deep breath and blew out in a steady stream as the small flame grew out of the dried grass. She grabbed more nearby sticks and placed them gently on top of the burning pile. The sticks quickly caught fire and the flame grew. She placed more sticks on top, and soon she had a small fire going. It warmed her face, and stung her eyes. Whether it was tears from the smoke or tears of happiness she didn't know, but she cried and laughed all the same. She started a fire all by herself.

"Does this mean I've evolved to the Stone Age now?" she said.

She looked over her shoulder at Peanut. He was still digging.

"Peanut, look at what I did." He didn't look up.

"Hey Peanut, look." She said louder.

Whether it was his name, or simply the loud noise, she got his attention. He turned slightly and let out a puff of air. He charged at Jenny and her heart stopped. She let out a short scream and scrambled out of the way just as he ran past her. He struck at the fire with his paws, causing burning leaves and sticks to go flying.

"No, no, no, no," Jenny said.

With fire completely extinguished, he turned and walked back to his digging spot.

"Peanut, why did you do that?"

At the sound of her voice, he turned and faced her. His small brown eyes gave away nothing. He slapped the ground again, and let out boisterous puff of air. Another display of dominance it seems. A strong flare of irritation filled her. She wanted to be mad at him, he clearly didn't trust her at all.

"Peanut, you ruined my fire. I need that. I guess I'll build it outside the cave if it bothers you so much."

The void in her belly ached and called to her. All the food in the world she could eat right now consisted of one small bag of Cheez

Doodles. It would hardly be enough. Plus, she worried about Peanut. When was the last time he ate? How would she take care of this bear cub and herself too? Her sense of accomplishment from creating fire was short-lived as her mounting problems rushed up to meet her.

She stood up and tried to shake off the negative feelings. There would be time for all that later. She stretched the stiffness out of her legs and walked to the mouth of the cave. Outside, the sun continued to set. Her mind wandered back to the bus ride that brought her here: Eric tossing her AirPods out of the window. It wasn't just the AirPods that she cared about; he scuffed her shoes too. Eric clearly lacked empathy. Pushing her off the cliff was intentional, but did he intended to kill her or just hurt her? He seemed to enjoy having power over others. Born with a silver spoon in his mouth, getting everything he wanted, but it still wasn't enough. Jenny hated his unfettered greed.

Orange sunlight spilled through the forest, bouncing off low plants and high treetop canopies. The air was fresh, earthy, and warm. Jenny breathed in deeply, taking in all of the smells, and it rejuvenated her. She may not have much, but she had shelter and the means to make fire. That was a start. Tonight, she would rest and eat the last of her food. Tomorrow would be a busy day. If she was going to survive this, it would take work. Her sense of despair had been replaced with something akin to hope, but with the sharp edge of caution that came with the knowledge that she was still lost in the middle of a vast ecosystem intent on killing her at every turn.

Jenny turned and walked to the back of the cave and sat down next to her backpack. She rummaged around inside of it, looking for the bag of Cheez Doodles. The sudden commotion caught Peanut's interest, and he lumbered over to inspect. His wet black nose sniffed Jenny's backpack. She pulled out the bag of Cheez Doodles, and Peanut sniffed those too.

"Hungry?" Jenny said.

She opened the bag and handed the first Cheez Doodle to Peanut. He sniffed it cautiously and then licked it out of her hand. His pink tongue felt rough like sandpaper. Jenny took one for herself as he slowly ate his. Then she had an idea.

"Peanut. Wait here."

She crossed to the other side of the cave and held out a Cheez Doodle.

"Peanut, yip-yip!" she cried. He looked at her and slowly walked toward her. She gave him the Cheez Doodle and rubbed his head.

"Good boy." Pavlov, eat your heart out, she thought. Just like training a dog with treats—reward good behavior to make it a habit. If a dog can, why not a bear? After all, treats were treats. She walked to the other end of the cave and held out another Cheez Doodle.

"Peanut, yip-yip!"

He swung his paw at Jenny's outstretched hand. She flinched and pulled her hand back, just missing his sharp claws. He retreated back into the cave, not turning his back to her. After a few steps he narrowed his muzzle let out a big puff of air.

"Sorry, sorry. I don't know what I did wrong. Was I too loud?"

Peanut sat down and yawned. Jenny watched him cautiously, not wanting to move or seem threatening. Eventually he went back to the spot where he'd been digging. Jenny pulled out Starfish and started reading from page one. What remained of the sun light disappeared quickly, so she didn't make it very far in the book. Peanut curled up in the little depression he had dug himself in the ground.

Did he make a bed for himself? It was curious behavior, and she felt there was a good reason, but the logic escaped her. As she wondered, her eyes grew heavy. She curled up on the floor and rested her head against her backpack, using her hoodie as a cover. The idea of a soft bed with blankets seemed like something out of a dream.

CHAPTER ELEVEN

Jenny woke early feeling rested for the first time since getting stranded in the Balsam Lake Mountain Wild Forest. She wandered outside and found a secluded spot to relieve herself. Then she set to work gathering sticks and piling them up at the back of the cave. Peanut was just waking up as she set the first pile of sticks down.

"Good morning, Peanut."

In response, Peanut made a clicking noise with his tongue.

"That's a new sound. What's that mean?"

Jenny continued adding sticks by the armful to the growing pile in the cave as Peanut watched her curiously.

"What are you looking at? I need sticks for fire. If I leave them outside, they might get wet if it rains again. Don't mess these up like you did my fire yesterday."

After half a dozen trips of gathering sticks and piling them in the cave, she switched to gathering dry leaves, which she piled next to the sticks. She figured these materials would last her a few days for fire. How much wood did it take to make a fire big enough to alert a park ranger? Were people still even looking for her? She reviewed the math in her head just to be sure because the days blurred together. Today was day four of being completely on her own. September 27th. How long did people wait until a missing person was presumed dead? She shook her head to clear away the negative thoughts and took a deep breath. There were more immediate things to worry about.

"Peanut, want to go out for a walk? We need to find water."

Peanut looked up at her blankly.

"Well, I'm going. You can join me or not."

She grabbed her hoodie and water bottle but decided to leave the backpack. No reason to spend more energy carrying it around. This was an exploratory venture—no gathering yet. She stood by the mouth of the cave and looked back at Peanut, who was still giving her a blank look. She patted her thigh a few times.

"Peanut, yip-yip!"

Peanut let out a grunt.

"Sorry, no Cheez Doodles."

Peanut gave a big yawn.

"Alright dude. Well, I hope you're here when I'm back. If not, it's been real."

She decided to hike up the thin climbing path trailing up the rock wall to see what was at the top of the cliff. The overgrown path proved difficult to navigate. Small trees barely a year old encroached the trail, and even smaller green-leafed plants littered the ground beneath them. And through them, Jenny could make out old bear tracks in the hardened dirt. She looked over her shoulder to check her progress, and surprisingly Peanut followed slowly behind.

"Hey, glad you decided to join. You and your mom walk this way before, Peanut?"

He sniffed at the ground. Behind him, the cave looked smaller amid the forest floor. The trail must have led them up at least ten feet above the ground so far. Nothing too precarious, but the trail continued to lead higher. She took her water bottle out and drank from it, tasting the now warm but sweet rainwater.

"I was thinking," she said to Peanut. "How about we name this pathway after your mother? We humans like to name things after other things to help remember. Like, for example, I'm from the Bronx. We have a big park there, bigger than Central Park, named after Stephanus Van Cortlandt, who was the first native mayor of New York City."

Images from the fight with the coyote flashed in her mind. Peanut's mother as tall as a tower in her memory. She died trying to protect them both—a sacrifice that Jenny promised never to forget.

"How about Virginia? One of my favorite writers is Virginia Woolf. She was a fiercely strong woman. Reminds me of your mom. Seems fitting. We shall call it: Virginia's Way."

The incline was steeper toward the top. When they reached it, Jenny had to pause to catch her breath. To her right, she could see below to the forest floor. It seemed far beneath her, at least fifty feet. Probably around the height of a five-story apartment in the Bronx. The rock face behind them was jagged, and a few trees had tried to take root but many looked scraggly and malnourished.

The path ahead turned to the left leading to the top of the cliff. It opened to a wide, flat clearing peppered with brown leaves and small leafy undergrowth. In the middle of the clearing sat a giant rotting tree carcass speckled with moss. Up here, the living trees were taller and more spread out while the younger, smaller saplings were low to the ground.

Peanut brushed against her leg and moved in front of her. He stopped at the big dead tree, scratching at it with his right paw. He climbed over it and continued forward, so Jenny decided to let him lead for a bit. It felt humid and the hike up Virginia's Way left her hot and sweaty, so she took her hoodie off and tied it around her waist. Ahead of her, Peanut slowed down and a stream of liquid shot down between his legs. Jenny's eyes widened and then she looked away.

"Wow. Next time give me a heads-up, Peanut."

After he finished, Peanut nibbled at some grass, and then took off running. He ran ahead toward a thick wall of trees and bushes. It was impossible to see what laid beyond, and there didn't seem to be an opening to the other side. Peanut dashed under a low-hanging tree near the edge, pushed his way through some bushes, and disappeared to the other side. Jenny's heart fluttered. What if he ran away? Would he come back?

She jogged to the edge of the tree where he'd crawled under. The bushes were thick but she could see a way forward. She used her hands to push against the branches and discovered they had sharp thorns. Probably not much of an issue if you were covered in fur. As she carefully crawled through, one branch scraped against the wound on her forearm, causing an intense flare of pain. She gritted her teeth and pushed through the dense branches into the clearing ahead. When she stood up her jaw dropped.

The scene was like a postcard, too perfect to even be real. Not more than two feet in front of her was a rushing river, its crystal-clear water rolling over stones and logs. Surrounding the river were huge pine trees with dense bushes of needles. And behind those were taller, thinner white trees just beginning to show touches of orange on their leaves. Large smooth stones at the water's edge crowded the riverbank. Jenny couldn't help but get a little emotional at the beautiful sight.

A warm tear slid down her face and she wiped it away, laughing. She never cried, save for one exception: Olympic opening ceremonies. Was it the lack of food and water that made her emotional? Whatever it was, she let herself enjoy the scenic view.

Peanut popped his head out of the river. Jenny let out a deep laugh.

Something about his cute little head popping out of the rushing river. He seemed happy.

"Having fun?" Jenny asked.

Peanut dove underwater. She untied her hoodie, and hung it up on a tree branch behind her. She took off her dirty Jordans and socks, and placed them near the tree. She walked to the edge of the river and stepped onto a large smooth stone that was half submerged. She dipped her toe into the river and pulled it back. The water was cold.

Having worn the same shirt and jeans for four days, her clothes looked like they desperately needed a wash. She looked around and then sniffed her armpit, pulling away quickly. It was clear that her clothes were not the only thing that needed to be cleaned.

Even though it was September, the air was warm enough to take a dip in the river. Jenny peeled off her T-shirt and carefully placed it on the rock. She looked around one more time just to be sure. Then she removed and piled the rest of her clothes next to her shirt. Then she took the hair ties out of her ponytail and let her thick hair fall around her shoulders. Even though she was alone, she still felt slightly embarrassed being completely naked.

Jenny stepped into the water and slowly walked until she was waist-deep, careful to only step on smooth stones. The river was cold but refreshing. The water was so clear she had little trouble navigating. She continued walking out into the river until it came right up to her neck. With her hands and fingernails, she scrubbed the dirt and grime away.

"I would give my right kidney for soap and a washcloth right now," she said.

The wound on her forearm needed cleaning, so she gently rubbed it with her fingers. Once it was clean, she dipped her head under the water and came back up, wiping her eyes.

Jenny swam for a bit while Peanut tried to catch fish. Swimming warmed her up, and the water didn't feel as cold after a while. She watched as Peanut swiped his paws at the river.

"I hope you're better at fishing than I am," she said.

Peanut looked at her and then back at the river. Jenny made her way back to the rock where she'd piled her clothes. She grabbed her shirt and jeans and walked back into the river. She threw her pants over her shoulder and submerged her shirt completely. She scrubbed it under the water and then wrung it dry. She did this a few more times, and then did it again with her jeans. Her father usually took care of the laundry at home. He was going to teach her before she left for college. Having no detergent or soap of any kind, she felt like rinsing them with river water wouldn't do much. Still, it was better than nothing.

She walked back to the shoreline and hung her clothes next to her socks on the tree branch. She grabbed her bra and underwear from the rock and put them on, and then her hoodie. She would have to come back and wash her undergarments later.

She walked to the shoreline and sat, leaning back on her hands and turning her face skyward, letting the sun warm her up.

As she soaked up the sun, Eric came to mind and a fresh wave of anger followed. Was Eric was feeling even an ounce of remorse right now? Probably not. If everyone thought Jenny was dead, did Logan tell the truth or did Eric shut him up? The odds of Logan lying to protect Eric were high, but how could he lie about something like that knowing how terrible the truth was?

If Jenny would ever make it back the Bronx, she promised herself she wouldn't stop until Eric was in jail. Or wherever they sent privileged seventeen-year-old boys who attempted murder. She bet Eric would scream and cry. His face would turn red as he was put in cuffs and hauled away to be locked up with other psycho kids. The world would be better off if he was dead. Jenny was already planning out counterarguments with her father. Surely, he would relax his "love everyone" rules with the guy who tried to murder his daughter if she could just think of the perfect argument.

Jenny stood up and walked out into the river up to her knees. She watched Peanut smack at the river with his paw. Still no luck. She looked down around her, scanning for fish. Between the rocks below and the rushing water, she couldn't spot anything. Too much visual interference. That and she had never seen a wild fish in its habitat before, so she had no idea what to look for. She stared for a long while and her stomach ached.

"I know. I'm trying here."

After what felt like forever, a long and narrow shadow in the river darted by her left leg. It was small, and the way the light hit made it hard to see. She shot her hand into the river and grabbed at it but came up empty. Peanut stared at her.

"This isn't easy, is it?" she said.

She tried to catch shadows until her arms ached. The groaning from her stomach intensified. She smacked the river hard, sending water everywhere.

"I'm so stupid. How am I going to catch a fish bare-handed?"

Peanut smacked the water with his claws and stuck his head under. When he pulled his head up, a silver fish was flopping in his mouth.

"Wow. You did it, Peanut!"

Peanut bent the fish in his mouth with his paw until it made a soft snapping noise and stopped flopping. He wandered over toward the river bank, near Jenny, set the fish down on a rock, and tore into it. He ripped at the guts with his teeth, and the fur around his mouth was bright red with blood. It was a powerful sight, watching him tear into the fish. He was only a cub, and already had formidable strength. Half finished, he went back into the river near the area where he'd caught the first fish, and stared into the water.

Jenny went to the rock where the dead fish laid. Peanut had eaten most of it, but there was enough left she could probably cook a few bites. She ran back to shore and pulled her pocketknife out of her jeans. She ran back to the rock and cut away the bits of meat near the head and tail, washed the blood off the glossy, translucent meat, and put three blobs of good fish meat into the pocket of her hoodie.

She walked back to shore and picked up her shirt and jeans. They had nearly dried, so she put them back on and tied her hoodie around her waist. She looked up toward the sun, which was nearly right over her head. Then she looked down at the ground. No shadows. It must have been around noon. Good time to head back. But one last thing.

She went back to the spot she'd crawled through earlier, thick with bushes. She flipped open her pocketknife and started to cut away branches. She'd worked up a sweat by the time she had cleared them away, at least enough to crawl through without scraping herself.

She stood up and turned back to Peanut, who was licking at the bones of a second fish. He took a few more gulps of river water, which allowed Jenny to inspect what he left behind. Not much meat left on that one. She took out her water bottle and drank it. Then she submerged the water bottle into the river until it was full, screwed the cap back on, and turned to Peanut.

"Hey. Let's head back."

He looked up from his fish, the fur around his muzzle a deep shade of crimson.

"Come on, Peanut. Yip-yip."

He bounded along, fish blood dripping from his mouth. Jenny reminded herself that Peanut was not some friendly pooch but a wild animal with enough strength to kill her.

CHAPTER TWELVE

When they made it back to the cave, Jenny gathered some materials to start a fire. She took a big swig of river water and tasted its earthy bitterness. Much different compared to the sweetness of the rainwater. It left a strange aftertaste in her mouth.

Peanut grunted from the back of the cave. She turned to see him scratching his back against the cave wall.

"Hey, what are you doing?"

Peanut paused to look at her, then charged at her. Jenny scrambled back, heart pounding. Was this it? He stopped short of her, and slapped the ground with his paw. He let out a big puff of air, and went back to scratching.

"What was that Peanut? Still don't trust me I guess."

Peanut ignored her. Jenny stepped out of the cave.

"Dad, I got lost," she said to the trees. "Sorry I didn't say something sooner. It's been hell here. I wish I could call you or write to you. That dick Eric pushed me off a cliff, and I'm lucky to be alive. At this point, I'm lost. I don't know how to find a trail, and I don't want to wander too far away from this cave. It's the first good thing I've had in a while. I figured out how to start a fire. You'd be proud. Bet you never thought I'd figure that out."

A breeze rustled the trees, and in her mind, she her the whisper of her dad's voice saying *good work, kiddo. I'm proud of you.* She took another sip from the water bottle.

"How do I get out of here?" she asked. "What would you do? I'm thinking of building a signal fire, but I don't want to scare Peanut."

The trees were still.

"I hope it works, Dad. I really hope so. I miss you."

Jenny dropped her fire materials on the ground and explored the area surrounding the cave. It was a gentle slope downward that opened up to a wide forest floor. The trees were tall, and the ground was covered with brown leaves and small ferns. There was a clearing in the tree canopy directly above, just enough to let smoke rise through.

"This seems like a good spot for a fire pit. I hope you will see the signal dad."

She set to work cutting down plants with her knife, careful not to touch any with her bare hands. Just the idea of poison ivy made her itch. She worked until she cleared out a small area about thirty feet away from the mouth of the cave.

After the area was clear, she gathered more sticks and a few fallen branches. A signal fire would take a lot of fuel to send enough smoke above the treetops, more than just some sticks and leaves. When she had gathered enough supplies, she hit her knife against the flint. It took her a few tries to get a spark going, but eventually the leaves caught, and she added sticks to keep it burning.

The fire grew slowly with every stick she tossed into it. A little too slowly. There had to be a faster way to do this. She snapped a few of the bigger branches in half and tossed them in. By now the fire was as high as her thigh, but it wasn't creating a whole lot of smoke. She looked up toward the tree canopy. Visible smoke was nowhere to be found.

"So I guess I can make fire, but not smoke Dad. I know you won't see this from a helicopter. I'll figure something out."

She sharpened the end of an extra stick with her knife, skewered it with fish meat that Peanut left her, and roasted the meat over the large fire until it was golden brown.

Back in the real world, she didn't much care for fish, but the aroma emanating from the roasting meat made her mouth water. She bit into it, and her mouth filled with the flavorful juices. It didn't take long to eat it all, and for once her stomach quieted down. A sense of wholeness washed over her.

As she stared up at the treetops, her stomach cramped up. It wasn't the usual kind of cramp. Even after stretching it out, it persisted. Frustrated, tired, and in pain, she let the fire die and returned to the cave.

Inside, Peanut was sound asleep, his snoring only slightly audible. The cramp turned into a dull throb beneath her belly button and radiated upward. She sipped some water and closed her eyes, hoping a nap would make the pain go away.

Sleep didn't come at first. The pain only grew worse over time. She faded in and out of consciousness until she drifted into a shallow sleep.

Her eyes opened. It was pitch black. Nausea washed over her in waves. She blinked, forcing her eyes to adjust. The sun was gone, so she must have slept for hours. It was a struggle to get to her feet, and she clutched at her midsection. She tried to stand up straight, but the pain was too intense. She shuffled to the mouth of the cave, doubled over like an old lady without a walker, and crawled outside.

She sat against the cave wall and tried to catch her breath. The cool air gave her some relief. Sweat drops formed across her brow.

Moonlight illuminated the forest. The sound of cicadas filled the air. She sat there for God knows how long, hoping the pain would subside.

She ached deep within, beneath her stomach. Suddenly, Jenny knew something bad was coming and was coming fast. She shuffled over to a nearby tree, hunched over and clutching her stomach. She pulled off her pants and squatted, leaning against the tree for support.

The moment passed as quickly as it had arrived. The smell was not pleasant, and she knew without looking there was no solidity to what had just escaped her. The pain in her stomach remained. Something was dangerously wrong, but she had no clue what was happening to her.

Jenny found her pants and carefully pulled them back on. As she wandered back to the cave, a fresh wave of nausea struck her and she threw up. She had the urge to puke again, but she was running on empty, so her muscles went through the motions but nothing came up.

An olive-colored plant sat nearby. She'd seen many like it everywhere on the forest floor. Its narrow-ridged leaves spread out from its stem. She tore off a few and used them to wipe, hoping it wasn't poison ivy. If she didn't bust out itching, she could continue to use it for this in the future.

When she limped back to the mouth of the cave, she fell to her knees, feeling like her battery had completely drained. Dragging herself inside took effort. Peanut was awake and sat staring at her. With no energy to make a comment, she crawled to her little spot and rested her head on her backpack, pulling her hoodie over herself like a blanket.

Jenny was terrified. Was she dying? This terrible sensation of nausea and pain hit her over and over. If she kept losing liquid out of both ends, dehydration would overtake her quickly. That was a death sentence for sure. She grabbed her water bottle nearby and drank more of the bitter river water. She closed her eyes and tried to sleep.

She thought a noise woke her, but the cave was silent. She tried to open her eyes but they wouldn't respond, as if her eyelids weren't her own. Her heart pounded faster. *Why can't I move?*

She screamed but her voice didn't make a noise. What was happening? She was damp with sweat, making her clothes stick her skin. Somehow, she was both hot and shivering at the same time. All sense of time left her.

Somewhere close by, claws scraped against rock. Her eyes felt like they were working, so she peeked one open. Peanut was sound asleep nearby. Toward the mouth of the cave there was nothing. The claws scraped again, and a chill ran up her spine.

There was something nearby. Something with claws. She couldn't move. She wanted to scream, run away, but she was frozen. Her body wasn't responding. She closed her eyes tight, screaming in her head: *Go away!* She counted backward from five. Four. Three. Two.

Her eyes shot open. Still, nothing. She looked at Peanut, but Peanut was gone. It was still dark out, so where would he go? Her only ally was gone.

With all of the will she had, she forced her hands to move. Surprisingly, they responded. She threw off the hoodie and rolled over onto her hands and knees. Her clothes were soaked with her own sweat. Her jeans were especially damp, and she looked down and examined them.

"I just cleaned these," she said.

Jenny crawled to the mouth of the cave, fighting against the waves of nausea and the cramps that came soon after. It took every ounce of energy she could muster, but she managed to pull herself up and lean her shoulder against the cave entrance. Her stomach wanted her to puke, but again nothing came up. When they finally gave up the effort, she looked up and scanned the forest.

There was nothing. Then, the sound of claws scraping against rock.

"What do you want?"

She was met with silence. The hairs on her neck stood up, goosebumps rippling across her arms. Something moved to her left.

"Stop, stop, stop!"

To her left, there was the sound of claws scraping against the ground. Jenny screamed and fell back into the cave. She curled into a fetal position and closed her eyes tightly.

At the entrance of the cave she heard the claws again. She pulled herself into as small a ball as she could, terrified at what would be there when she opened her eyes. Reluctantly, she turned to face her attacker.

Peanut stood, dripping wet in the cave entrance. Behind him, the forest was still. Her heartbeat settled back into a normal pace.

"Jesus, Peanut. You scared the hell out of me. Where did you go? For a midnight swim?"

Peanut sauntered over to his spot and curled up on the ground. Jenny returned to her own spot and pulled her hoodie over herself. She grabbed her water bottle and started to unscrew the lid but stopped.

The moon was just bright enough to cast some light into the cave. Jenny held the bottle up and illuminated the water within. For the first time, she saw little flecks of dirt floating around in the water. The image of Peanut and every other animal in the river came to her in a flash. Fish, deer, coyotes, and bears using the river, doing who knows what in it.

The water was dirty. Not safe to drink. It made her sick to her stomach that she was such an idiot. Death by water. *Here lies Jenny Woods: too dumb to survive.* Cruel Mother Nature cursed her again, this time with the elixir she needed to live. She set down the water bottle, trying to ignore her dry mouth. Her stomach cramped up again. Why could Peanut drink the river water but she couldn't? Darwin knew the answer. Probably something to do with evolution. *God, humans suck.*

Without water, she knew her days were numbered. Plus, she had just expelled all of the water she had in her system. If she couldn't figure out a way to purify that river water tomorrow, she'd be as good as dead.

CHAPTER THIRTEEN

Morning came but Jenny didn't feel much better. The cramps faded away but the nausea remained. Water was close but so far out of reach. Heat was the purifier. She knew that, at least. Once the water was hot enough, it would kill off the bacteria.

Back in the fifth grade, they were supposed to go over the basics of water purification using heat in science class. However, they first started with chlorine tablets, which did the work of purification without heat. Jax Holder, the class clown, ate one of the chlorine tablets on a dare and had to be rushed to the hospital, so the lesson was cut short before they could learn the ins and outs of using heat to purify water.

"Now I'm screwed because of you, Jax," she said. "Thanks a lot."

Her bladder was full, somehow continuing to work despite her lack of fluids. As she squatted against a nearby tree, she spotted another olive-colored leafy plant like the one she used to wipe yesterday. She hadn't gotten itchy from using it, so the plant must not be poison ivy. Thanks to this plentiful plant, she now had a steady supply of nature's toilet paper.

Jenny scanned her surroundings for water purification tools. She had fire but no pot with which to boil the water. The water bottle was plastic, so no good for anything beyond holding water. Nothing here could hold water and stand against the heat of fire without burning up. She pounded her head against the cave wall.

Is this how I die? She would survive a fight against a coyote only to die from dehydration. Next to a river. Jenny Woods, sixteen years old, good to laugh at and loved by few. Great obituary.

"Dad, what would you do?" she said to the trees. A breeze rustled the leaves above her.

I don't know kiddo, the trees answered. *This one is a pickle for sure.*

"I'm so lost without you. I can't do this."

That's not the Woods Stubbornness! the trees scolded. *We never give up, even when the going gets tough.*

Her dad's favorite motto. As if being stubborn was inherent to being a Woods. When he said it, he would use a silly sing-song voice and flash a smile. It always annoyed her, but now she missed it. Eventually, he would have to give up on finding her. She remembered from reading cheap paperback detective novels that police stopped searching for a missing person after seventy-two hours. Would he still be saying his motto once everyone stops looking for her?

Approach the problem from a different angle, the trees said.

"Yeah, what angle is that?"

The trees were still.

"That's what I thought. No help."

She touched the back of her hand to her forehead. Warm, so she was still running a fever. Her clothes were still damp from the night before. A low rumble in her stomach meant something bad was coming again. She slid off her pants and used the wall to steady herself as she stood up. She wandered toward her fire pit, picked a new tree, and squatted down, feeling the bark catch against her shirt. When she was done, she pulled up her underwear and shuffled back to the cave, taking her pants inside with her.

Peanut was still sleeping. She was freezing, so she pulled on her pants and then her hoodie, and lay back down, resting her head against her backpack. Peanut's light snoring echoed against the cave walls. She curled up on her side and tried to sleep. The floor was hard and cold.

Claws scraped against the cave floor. Her heart instantly started beating a mile a minute. The fear from the previous night came rushing back at the familiar sound. Something big thumped against the ground behind her. She peeked open her eyes and saw Peanut on his belly beside her. He looked warm and soft.

"Come to take care of me or waiting to eat me?"

He let out a low grunt, and made a clicking sound with his tongue. He looked at her, then back at the cave entrance. His eyes grew heavy. Jenny scooted back toward him and felt the warmth from his furry body.

A wave of nausea woke her a little while later. Light was still glowing from the cave entrance. Peanut had shifted with his back against hers, but the heat from his body radiated outwards. She rolled over and rubbed her face against his back. His fur was thick and had a sharp, earthy smell that reminded her of a blanket that needed to be washed. It wasn't a bad smell, just a well-worn one.

"Thanks, Peanut." she said. "I think it's time we washed off the grime of the day."

She gave him a double pat. He turned his head to her, his eyes scanning her face.

"Come on, lazy."

Jenny stood up and her stiff muscles protested against the effort. She stretched her arms out, but another wave of nausea brought her hands to her knees to steady herself. The stomach was such a fickle beast, one minute demanding food and water, the next rejecting it. She felt like her entire life solely revolved around nutrition.

Regaining her composure, she grabbed her hoodie and crawled out of the cave. She turned back to see Peanut staring at her.

"Come on. Let's go, kiddo."

When they reached the river, she took in the sight once more. The quiet beauty of it all made her nausea seem distant. The sun hung in the sky at an angle. She figured it was sometime after noon and that she had a few hours of light left before the sun would begin to set.

She stripped off her clothes and slowly waded into the river. Should be safe as long as she didn't ingest the water. It was cool and refreshing. She washed her sweat-soaked clothes and hoodie, and placed them on a nearby rock. She swam and watched Peanut as he batted the water, hoping to catch a fish.

Taking in the water around her, her mouth was dry like sandpaper. Her tongue stuck to the roof of her mouth. So much water, only to kill her if she drank it. She knew saltwater was deadly, but who would have thought freshwater would be too? The dip in the river helped her feel better, but there was a timer in the back of her mind that slowly ticked by the seconds until she was fully dehydrated.

"Have to heat the water up, but nothing to heat it up in. Is there a way to cook the water but not the pot?" she asked the river. "How can I drink you without killing myself? Tell me your secrets."

What did she have on her? She ran through the inventory in her head: clothes, a belt, shoes, her backpack, a book . . . nothing that could hold water. Her grandpa's lucky knife had saved her once already, but could it do it again?

A thought crossed her mind. If she found the right piece of wood, she could use her knife to carve out a cup or bowl. But wood burns up easily, so she couldn't cook with it in the fire. Close. So close. It nagged at her. The wooden cup idea, there was something to it.

She swam toward the rock where she'd left her clothes. They were still damp, so she sat on a different rock and took in the warmth of the sun. She mentally checked her stomach, and she realized she wasn't nauseous. The rest of her body ached like hell, but it was at least an improvement.

She stared out across the river watching as it curved up and down around the stones. At the bottom of the riverbed were more smooth stones, all various muted colors. They reminded Jenny of Fruity Pebbles. *That's it.*

The idea struck her so unexpectedly it almost knocked her off balance. Stones. That was the answer. That's how she could purify the water. At least she hoped so. If it didn't work . . . well, best not to think about that.

Jenny hopped back into the river and searched for the perfect stones. They had to be roughly the size of her palm. She collected five good ones and sat them next to her clothes.

Upstream, Peanut seemed to have given up on fishing. He walked downstream toward Jenny, scanning the river with his eyes, but Jenny sensed he was done. Something about the look in his eyes said as much.

"No luck with fish? Don't worry. I'll help tomorrow. Tonight, we're making water."

Her clothes were dry enough at this point, so she climbed out of the river and tried shaking herself off to dry. Peanut stared at her intently. She let out low grunt, and clicked her tongue like he did. He grunted back at her.

She threw on her clothes and slipped the stones into the pockets of her hoodie. Peanut took a moment to relieve himself in the river. She shook her head at him.

"You're the reason why I can't drink this water, you know that?"

Back in the cave, Jenny emptied her pockets. There were so many things to do, and daylight was running out. She was excited—a feeling she'd forgotten about. She had a purpose, something to do. It almost made her forget how depressed she was. Almost.

Outside, she searched the area surrounding the cave for the right piece of wood. It had to be big, thick, and dry. Plenty of logs and fallen branches scattered the forest floor, but she didn't have a way to chop them down into smaller pieces, so she had to find wood that was already the right size.

She circled her fire pit, growing her distance farther and farther with each round. On her fourth round, she came across a young fallen tree branch that looked fresh. No rot or bugs and not yet covered with moss. It was about as thick as her leg, nearly perfect, except for being about six feet long.

She dragged it back and left it just outside the cave before dashing inside. Peanut watched her curiously as she pocketed both the water bottle and her knife.

"Going to head back to the river, okay? Want to come with?"

Peanut huffed and rolled onto his side. Jenny huffed back at him.

"Have it your way."

Outside, she dragged the branch up the path. When she reached the top, she paused to catch her breath. Behind her, Peanut was slowly making his way toward her, his head swiveling lazily from left to right.

The effort it took to drag the branch to the river exhausted her. If she hadn't been recovering from her illness, she might not have felt so tired. She laid the branch across a large, flat river boulder near the shore. By this time, Peanut had caught up with her and was ignoring her entirely.

"You could help me, you know. Aren't bears supposed to be stronger than humans?"

Peanut huffed and walked past her to the water's edge, looking out to the river. Then he sat down and yawned.

Jenny paused to chuckle before scanning the shoreline for another sizable stone. When she found one, she stood with the branch between her legs, using her feet to hold it tightly in place. Then she raised the stone above her head and brought it down with all of her weight against the branch.

Peanut jumped at the loud crack it made. The sound echoed across the river. The branch had split but didn't break. She raised the stone above her head and brought it down again.

Crack.

And again.

Crack.

She was close. With one final strike, she brought the stone down and chopped through the branch. When the stone hit the river boulder, it vibrated hard in her hands. As much as it hurt, she had a big grin on her face. *It worked.*

She'd broken off about a foot of the branch. Perfect length. She stripped the bark off with her knife until it was soft and raw, revealing smooth yellowish wood underneath. Then she held the wood up to her nose and sniffed it. The smell was rich and reminded her of her father's chair in the living room.

Before she left, she made sure to fill her water bottle to the brim with river water. She stopped near the opening and turned back. Peanut was still staring at her.

"Come on, Peanut! We're almost there!"

She hurried back to the cave, and Peanut wasn't far behind. She sat down at the cave wall and pulled out her knife as Peanut looked at her with a sort of lazy curiosity. Kind of like when her dad watched her read a book.

"I'm going to make a mug. Just you watch."

She flipped open her blade and whittled away at the branch. She could only shave off a little at a time, strips no bigger than an inch or two. She sat carving away until her back and hands ached. Peanut shifted between watching her and wandering around the clearing, but she was happy to have the company.

When her hands ached too much to work any longer, she took a break. After gathering some dry leaves and twigs from her supplies in the cave, she started another fire in the fire pit outside. Once the fire was up and going, she continued carving enjoying the warmth of the flames.

The sun was low in the sky and the forest glowed a deep blue. That moment right after the sunset but before darkness came. It reminded Jenny of summers sitting on the porch of her house, reading until it was too dark to see the words on the page. Peanut retired to the cave, so she moved closer to the fire for warmth and light, adding a few more twigs.

The mug, if you could call it that, was starting to take shape. It looked nothing like a mug she would use to hold tea. It looked more like a mug that was squashed flat and stretched out. Like a Mancala board, but with one big hole instead of twelve small holes. She carved out the middle to make it as deep as possible.

Her hands had cramped up again, so she set down her woodwork and took a break. Inside the cave, she retrieved two of the rocks she'd taken from the river and tried to find two Y-shaped twigs from her pile of materials. When she couldn't find any, she made them by slowly snapping two sticks until they had the perfect shape.

When she returned to the fire, she tossed the two rocks in and watched as they darkened against the heat. Then she carved a small handle into the end of her wooden mug and set it flat on the ground. After filling it halfway with the river water, she used the two forked twigs to pluck out a rock from the fire and drop it into the wooden mug. The water hissed at the sudden heat, a plume of steam instantly rising from it. A smile spread across her face. She plucked out the other rock and did the same, creating another plume of steam.

Once the water stopped hissing, she removed the rocks from the mug. They were still warm, but not fire-hot. She held up the mug and examined the water. Small black flecks of ash floated around in it. She plucked them out with her fingers.

"Here goes nothing."

She tilted the mug into her mouth and downed the water. It was warm and tasted like smoke. She drank until the mug was empty. All she could do now was wait and see if it worked. If it didn't, she would be dead soon anyway.

CHAPTER FOURTEEN

The sun rose the next morning with a quiet stealth, Thin fog obscured most of the light. A steady breeze shuffled the leaves and birds began chirping in the distance. Jenny's back ached with a renewed stiffness. The cave floor offered little in the way of lumbar support. Next to her, Peanut lay on his side, snoring. She grew accustomed to sleeping next to him. He kept her warm, more so than her ripped hoodie. It seemed odd that they'd grown attached despite his initial reluctance. He hadn't performed his warning charge at her in a while. Perhaps it was the traumatic event they went through together, or maybe it was something deeper than that. She felt a bond to him unlike anything she'd felt before. Sometimes she forgot he was a wild animal.

A twig snapped. Jenny turned her head toward the entrance of the cave. Thankfully, it was empty. Outside, the fog hung low in the air and the forest looked gray. Inside the cave, the air was thick with moisture.

She stood up quietly to avoid waking Peanut and stretched her arms, trying to work out the stiffness in her shoulders. She didn't feel nauseous, she realized. Her abs were sore, but there wasn't an ounce of sickness in them.

"It worked!"

Peanut woke, startled. He looked over at her from the side of his eye. Almost as if to question why she was making so much noise this early.

"Sorry, Peanut. Go back to sleep."

He let out a low grunt, and Jenny grunted back at him. That seemed be enough for him to lay his head back down and doze off. But she was giddy with excitement. Her water purification plan had actually worked. *Live to fight another day*, she thought. *That is the Woods Stubbornness.* She made her rounds in and out of the cave, collecting her half-full bottle of river water, the wooden mug, an arm full of twigs, her lucky knife, two river rocks, and the flint.

Outside, the air was thick and heavy with humidity. She sat down near the fire pit and went to work. After a few tries, the dry leaves caught fire and she added twigs to keep it going. Then she tossed the river stones in, watching them darken as they heated up.

Up through the tree canopy was a sky full of gray clouds. Could mean rain. If so, that meant no signal fire today. Another day to survive. How many had it been now? She'd lost count. She ran through the days in her head. Eric pushed her down the hill on Day 1, which was September 24. The fight against the coyote was Day 2. This put starting the fire at Day 3. Day 4 she found the river, and Day 5 was her fight against nausea from the river water. That meant today was Day 6, September 29th. If she lived to see tomorrow, that would mean she'd been on her own for a week.

An unexpected wave of emotions hit her, forming a lump in her throat. The day after tomorrow was October 1st, a whole different month. Had they searched for her? Have they given up yet? Her poor dad must have been worried sick. She longed to see him. She stared up at the tree canopy, lost in thought.

"I'm sorry, Dad. Sorry for not saying 'I love you' enough. I'd give anything to see you right now." The trees rustled in the wind, but said nothing back.

Her stomach growled. She was famished. Over these past days, she had barely eaten any food. The waist of her jeans felt looser than they had been the first day. *Not good to be losing weight this fast.*

She poured the river water into the flat wooden mug. Using the same twigs from last night, she dropped the hot river rocks into the mug and watched the steam rise as the water boiled.

She mentally ran through her to-do list. The top priority was figuring out the signal fire. She could get a fire going, but she couldn't make one big enough to be seen above the tree cover. If she could somehow thicken or darken the smoke, maybe it would be visible enough reach above the trees and alert a search party.

When the steam stopped, she pulled out the two rocks and did her best to pick out the bits of ash from the water. If she could create a second wooden mug to clean the hot-rocks, it might help filter out the ash. Theoretically if she filled the first one with a little bit of water, dropped the stones in, and immediately moved them to the second one, the first mug should absorb most of the ash, leaving the drinking water cleaner. She sipped some of the warm water from her mug, pretending she was drinking tea.

Were they still looking for her? Even if they were, how far away had she wandered from where she'd first fallen? If she was nowhere nearby, would they think she'd been lost, or eaten? She pushed the dark thoughts away. Her goal was to survive long enough to be rescued. The Balsam Lake Mountain Wild Forest preserve was huge, but surely a search party would find her eventually. She couldn't have wandered too far from where she fell.

So, Priority 1 was a signal fire, but she needed time to figure that out. Priority 2: Food. She needed to find out what she could eat, and eat more of it. She didn't trust herself enough to start eating random plants. The river seemed to have a supply of fish that Jenny couldn't manage to catch. Priority 3: Learn how to fish.

The fire had died down to embers. She drank the rest of the water and put her knife, flint, and water bottle in the pockets of her hoodie. She hid the stick-tongs and river rocks under a tall moss-covered tree and tucked the mug under her arm. A few drops of water splashed against her head. Rain. She couldn't afford another day without food. And as unappealing as the thought of fishing in the rain seemed, starvation seemed worse. And she didn't want to resort to eating twigs and dried leaves.

She searched the area around the fire pit for more fire wood. Best to gather it now while it was still dry. She stuffed a handful of dried leaves into her pocket, gathered an armload of wood, and made her way back to the cave.

Inside, Peanut was awake and scratching his back against the cave wall. She dropped the leaves and wood in the pile of her fire materials. It should have been enough to last for a few days. Peanut sat on his back legs, watching her. She let out a low grunt.

"Want to try fishing?"

He sighed, his cheeks puffing with air. Jenny figured that was a yes.

She transferred the flint from her pocket to her backpack, and they set out to trudge up a damp Virginia's Way. The forest was quiet except for the lone twitter of a bird. Light rain pitter-pattered against the tree canopy.

The river looked chilly and uninviting among the gray haze of the day. The rain had stopped, at least for now. Peanut hopped right in after drinking a few gulps while Jenny struggled to remove her socks and shoes without falling over. It probably would have been easier to do this while sitting, but once she freed her left foot, it felt wrong to not take the same procedure with her right.

The Woods Stubbornness, she could hear her dad say.

"I know, I know." She said. Sometimes it was a great characteristic and sometimes it led to stupid choices.

With her jeans rolled above her knees, she waded into the river, only letting the water come up to her calf. It was cold this morning, so she had to take one step at a time and let her skin adjust to the temperature. She took out her knife, holding it firmly in her right hand, and flipped the blade open with a quick flick of her finger. Her hoodie was thick and warm, and she didn't look forward to putting her arm in the cold river water. She rolled up her right sleeve, and the cool breeze against her skin along with the cold river made her shiver. She waded out until the water was at her knees.

Downstream, Peanut stood as still as a statue, staring into the river. Jenny tried to do the same. The water rushed past her, but it was clear enough to make out some shapes. She mostly saw rocks, but after a few moments she saw other shapes appear. A small black-and-yellow head popped above the water a few feet away from her, and its beady eyes met hers—a turtle cautiously surveying the world above water.

Turtles were edible, right? Somewhere in her long-term memory was hearing something about turtle soup. They had meat tucked away under their protective shells. She slowly took a step toward it. She felt terrible for considering eating a defenseless turtle. It was probably young, had a mom and a dad. Wouldn't a fish have the same? Why does society think it's okay to eat some animals but give pause when it comes to others?

Jenny stepped on something sharp and she let out a yelp. After catching her balance, she again looked for the turtle. It was gone. She cursed under her breath.

"Focus, Jenny. Focus."

Downstream, Peanut had a large fish in his mouth. He bent it with his jaws until it stopped wriggling. Then he took it into his paws and made it a meal, teeth as sharp as blades effortlessly tearing through bone and guts.

As she turned back to her fishing spot, she caught a glimpse of something dart to her left. A long, thin shadow billowed back and forth, fighting against the motion of the stream but staying in place. It was a sizable fish, about as long as her forearm with a bright green back. Jenny slowly lowered the knife into the water.

The green fish darted left away from her, but only by a few inches. She held the knife in place. The blade was a few inches away, or at least appeared to be. The water warped what she saw beneath its surface, making it hard to gauge exactly where her knife was relative to the fish.

The fish darted back to the right, inspecting a rock. It was now or never.

She thrust the knife forward and watched as it cut the water right above the fish. The sudden lurch threw her off balance and she fell forward. She stuck out her hand into the water to catch herself.

As she regained her balance, she lifted her arm out from the water, the sleeve dripping wet. She felt hot, itchy, and annoyed, so she ripped off the hoodie and tossed it onto a nearby rock. She had misjudged the depth, and the knife cut at the water directly above the fish. It was long gone by now. Looking over her shoulder, she saw Peanut was back in the river, patiently waiting for more fish.

She let out a frustrated sigh and turned back. Since her spot was ruined, she slowly waded upstream. When she'd reached about ten feet forward, she took a few breaths to calm herself and stared into the water. Stillness washed over her. The only sound was the river. Her feet tingled in the cold water as if with pins and needles.

She caught a glimpse of a dark shadow darting to her right. The fish moved fast and didn't stay still for long. She leaned to her right and stretched out as far as she could manage, dipping her knife under the water. The fish was just a few inches away from her blade. It darted to the left, and then the right. For a moment, it stopped right in front of the knife. She thrust herself forward, but slipped on the rocks beneath her feet and fell face-first into the river. The water was cold and her knife was empty.

She burst through the surface of the water, screaming in frustration, and loudly stomped to the shore. Peanut watched her, a fish wriggling in his mouth. So close to catching lunch, but she was too awkward and unbalanced. The knife wasn't working at all. There had to be a better way. Haven't humans been fishing since the dawn of time? It should be easier than this. Then it struck her.

When she was twelve, her father had taken her to the New York City Natural History Museum. It was known for its lifelike displays of humans and animals, filled with information from the dawn of time to recent history. One exhibit she particularly enjoyed was the one on human origins. It had half-naked Neanderthals, surrounded by furs and bones, sitting atop a tall mesa. The alpha male had a large spear in his hand and a dead beast over his shoulder. She remembered reading that these primitive humans had carved spears from tree branches for hunting and fishing.

"Ahh, a spear. That's it. Thank you Museum of Natural History."

Neanderthals figured it out, all right. Hunt smarter not harder. They would be laughing at her falling face-first into the river with a puny little knife, starving as she tried to catch a meal. She returned to shore, grabbed her hoodie from the rock, and filled her water bottle with river water. When it was full, she walked across the stream toward Peanut, hoping he left a few scraps for the hungry human.

Peanut turned to face her; his muzzle coated in crimson blood. Bits of fish guts and scales stuck to the fur around his mouth. He looked into her eyes as she stared back into his.

"You leave anything for me?"

He let out a low grunt, and she replied with her own. She explored the rocks around them and found the remains of the two fish he'd caught. The front half of one fish was all that was left. Its eyes were glossy and there wasn't much meat. She rinsed it in the river and stuffed it into her pocket anyway. Maybe she could cook it and nibble. It was better than another night on an empty stomach.

The second fish was in worse shape, with even less meat. She tossed it into the river. Her stomach groaned. Jenny put socks and shoes back on and unrolled her pants.

She crawled underneath the tree and into the forest on the other side. Exhaustion caught up with her, likely due to the whole starving thing, so she sat for a moment to catch her breath. Peanut sauntered past her towards Virginia's way, looking content. She envied him; his claws made for great fishing tools. Her stomach let out another low rumble, and he turned to look at her.

"Mind your business."

CHAPTER FIFTEEN

Halfway down Virginia's Way it started to drizzle again. It was a light rain, but still annoying. Once she was in the cave she collapsed into a sitting position and let out a big sigh. Peanut walked up to her and licked her face.

"Thanks, buddy."

He shook off the river water, spraying Jenny in the face. She glared at him as he innocently looked around the cave.

"Peanut! I came in to stay out of the rain."

Outside, the rain was picking up. She transferred her water bottle to her backpack and paused. Maybe she should drink the rainwater. But given how sick she'd been from the river water, she decided not to risk it. Peanut circled around her and plopped down beside her. With nothing to do, she pulled out Starfish and picked up where she left off, letting the gray light from outside illuminate the pages.

The pages of the book flew by as she read. She found herself relaxing, pushing away the worries of the day. The soothing sound of rain combined with her exhaustion made her drift into sleep mid-page. When she woke a while later, the rain had stopped. She didn't remember falling asleep. Her neck was stiff from sleeping at an awkward angle and her mouth was dry. Peanut was still snoring away, so she quietly grabbed the flint and water bottle from her backpack, tucked her mug under her arm, and took a handful of sticks and dry leaves.

When she stepped outside, the air was hot and thick with moisture. The sun peered through the clouds above. It had to be somewhere around 3:00 or 4:00 p.m.

She sat before the fire pit and began working at her knife and flint to start a small fire. It was up and going in no time. Then she found a two-foot-long stick nearby, carved it to a point with her knife, and used it to pierce the fish through the mouth. Then she pushed the other end of the stick into the ground so the fish head hung over the low fire.

She found a knob jutting out from a mossy tree nearby, so she hung her hoodie on it. It reminded her of the coat hangers her dad had installed in her closet back home. He was very proud of his handywork, but once she hung her coat, the hanger fell out of the wall. It turned out he had completely missed the studs behind the drywall. She found herself laughing as she remembered the look on his face.

The heat from the fire warmed her up. She used her stick-tongs to place the river rocks into the fire. The fish head looked half cooked, so she turned it, the raw side sizzling in the heat. Still a bit of time until her meager dinner was ready.

While she waited for her food, she explored south of the fire pit. She found a fallen tree covered with moss, termites working away at the rotting wood. Circle of life. Beyond the fallen tree, the forest floor was flat and wild with competing overgrowth. Patches of grass struggled to find sunlight among the taller, big-leafed plants. The trees here were young and thin, with an occasional thick tree towering over them all. To her right was a small rock outcropping where a long tree branch laid, as thick as her arm and covered with patches of dark-brown bark. It must have been ripped from a taller tree during a storm. The branch was too twisted to work as a spear, but with some work she might be able to put it to use. She dragged it back to the cave.

The fish head looked cooked, so she plucked it up and tore through the meat with her teeth. There was hardly enough for a meal, but maybe her stomach would quiet down for a few hours. She used the hot-rocks to make more water.

The surrounding area yielded five more branches, but once again they were either too twisted, knotted, or thick to turn into a spear. One by one she dragged them all into the cave. By the time they were all inside, she was sweating and breathing heavily. It felt good to be productive.

The sun was setting, so she gathered up her supplies from the fire pit, hid the tongs and rocks under the moss-covered tree, and grabbed her hoodie off the knob. Once she kicked dirt onto the embers to douse the fire, she heaved a big sigh and looked around.

"Dad. I really, really miss you. I don't know how the hell I'm getting out of here."

This entire situation was unsustainable. She collapsed and sat down as anxiety overwhelmed her. Her heart was beating fast, and dizziness made her head spin. It took her a moment to recover. Anger rose from her chest.

"Eric, if I ever find you, I will kill you."

In her mind she imagined putting the knife to his throat and watched as his eyes widened in surprise. Then Peanut charged him, knocking him to the ground. Jenny stood over him and laughed. Somewhere in the back of her mind, her dad's voice said something about love and forgiveness, but she pushed it away. She made a vow to fight and survive this ordeal so that she could get revenge and make Eric suffer.

CHAPTER SIXTEEN

Jenny felt an unmistakable shift in awareness as soon as she set foot outside of her territory. In fact, she hadn't even realized she had a "territory" until she left it. Some innate sense deep within her had clicked on and felt the shift. There was her and Peanut's little spot they had carved out for themselves, and then there was everything else. The moment she stepped foot into everything else, her senses instinctively went on high alert.

She had decided early in the day to take Peanut on a journey upstream along the river to find a branch that she could use as a spear. Peanut trailed behind her, stopping every once and a while to drink from the river. Jenny kept her eyes on the tree line and lost track of time as they walked.

The river here was narrower and quieter than the river she was used to, with more twists and turns and less rocky rapids. The tree line was footed with low bushes that fought for sunlight. Everything was different. She had the strong urge to turn around and return to something familiar: her corner of the cave, her section of the river, her patch of the forest. She looked toward Peanut, who was inspecting a shrub for berries. Two lone survivors.

She pushed away the feeling to run back to the cave and hide. Now was not the time for cowardice. Her stomach wouldn't allow it. With the spear, she could fish. With fish came food. Plenty of opportunities to hide in a cave once she had a fully belly.

"Hey, Peanut. Let's cut in and see if we see anything," she said.

She climbed over a low bush, through the tree line, and into the forest. Peanut followed close behind.

The forest here was beautiful. The leaves had started turning, so the ground was covered in a fresh layer of yellow and orange leaves. The occasional mossy rock or fallen tree peered through the carpet of leaves, texturizing the otherwise flat ground. The trees were tall and sparse, so it felt very open and spacious. And eerily quiet. The only sound was the crunch of leaves beneath their footsteps. She looked back, mentally noting the two tall white trees with yellow leaves. That was her key to finding her way back to the river.

Looking ahead into the distance, a bright red tree caught her eye. It wasn't until she moved closer that she saw just how tall it reached, and how wide the trunk expanded. She picked up a red leaf from the ground. It reminded her of the Canadian Flag.

"Maple tree," she whispered.

She held the leaf to Peanut, who sniffed it. Once he figured out it was not food, he lost interest. Jenny pocketed the leaf and looked up beneath the tree's branches. Not a single branch had fallen to the ground, a testament to the strength and resilience of the Maple tree. A perfectly straight branch stretched up to the top, about seven feet long and not too thick—no twists, no knots, no splits. This was the one. Had to be.

Just the thought of climbing this tree made her glutes sore. Still, the potential spear was too good to pass up. She hadn't found any branches as good as this one around her cave. This was her first real shot at getting the perfect spear. A groan from her stomach reminded her of the urgency of her mission.

She dropped her hoodie at the base of the tree. No use in making this harder with added weight. She stood under the lowest branch and stretched her arms as high as she could. It was just out of reach. She cursed under her breath and took a few steps back. Then she burst into a sprint, jumped, pushed off the trunk with her foot, and caught the branch. Arm muscles straining, she swung her legs forward, hooked them around the branch, and pulled herself up to straddle it. She took a moment to catch her breath.

Below, Peanut was digging at the ground. He stuck his nose into the fresh hole and ripped out the root of a plant. He turned toward Jenny, the root sticking out of his mouth. She couldn't help but laugh.

"You look like an old-time prospector smoking a cigar. You just need the hat. But then you might look more like Smokey the Bear."

Peanut just stared at her.

"You know, the bear from all of the National Park ads? You must know him. He is super famous. Although now that I think about it, is Smokey an appropriation of bear culture?"

Peanut turned away and started digging away at a nearby tree. "Good talk."

Jenny climbed her way upward, carefully sinking her weight into the branches that looked the steadiest. Thankfully, they were all close together. But while these branches were good for climbing, the perfect branch was still a long way up.

She remembered back in the seventh grade when she had begged her dad for months to take her to the Empire State Building. She had read about it in *James and the Giant Peach* and desperately wanted to see peach's famous final location. He finally accepted, and even rode the elevator with her all the way to the top, but refused to walk out to the viewing area, choosing instead the safety of the elevator lobby. That was when she learned of her dad's fear of heights. Or, as he put it, fear of falling.

Halfway up the tree, she leaned against its trunk, carefully balancing herself just below the perfect branch. She looked down at the ground. Peanut looked small from her vantage point, but she tried not to think about the distance too much. He pulled his front leg out from the tree, revealing a paw full of bugs. To Jenny's horror, he started eating them. She wondered if bears normally ate bugs, or if this was just an oddity. A strong gust of wind swayed the tree for a moment and her gut leaped into her throat. Look at that, she had a fear of falling too. Who would have guessed it would have taken a swaying tree thirty feet in the air to discover? She was her father's child after all.

She swallowed her fear and focused on the task at hand. With a flick of her finger the knife blade was out. She reached it toward the perfect branch with one arm and clung to the trunk with the other. She had to stand on her toes to get the right angle to cut it. Back and forth she worked the blade. It was slow work because the knife was smooth with no teeth to saw with. Her right arm started going numb, so she pulled it back to rest. There was no progress. This wasn't the type of blade to saw a tree with.

Once the feeling returned to her arm, she tried again. It was frustrating work. The blade kept getting stuck in the wood. It was like trying to cut through paper with one of those fake plastic scissors for kids. She threw her entire body weight into the sawing motion, the tree swaying with her movements. Her hand was falling asleep again, so she gritted her teeth and pushed harder.

For some reason, her frustration made her itchy. It scratched in her arms and ribs, but she didn't stop sawing, even with the tree shaking hard. Her hand was throbbing. The blade got stuck and she couldn't rip it free. She let out a scream directed at the stupid knife.

The blade was less than a centimeter deep. She had made virtually no progress. The knife stuck out at an odd angle, practically mocking her.

"Why can't you do your job?"

She smacked the knife, and it popped out of the branch. Her mouth hung open as she watched it fall to the ground below.

"Brilliant."

CHAPTER SEVENTEEN

Sheer stubbornness took over. The branch was hers and not a damn thing could stop her. She climbed her way up the tree until she stood on top of the perfect branch. Gripping a slender limb above her, she pushed down on her branch with both feet and watched it bend beneath her weight. It gave even more when she did a few jumps. She jumped over and over, increasingly with more force, but the branch would not break. She jumped up and down like she was on a trampoline, the upper half of the tree thrashed violently in response. Leaves rained down on Peanut.

The branch finally gave in with a loud crack. She froze so suddenly that her pounding heart physically shook her ribcage. Near the base of the tree branch, there was a small explosion of yellow wood splinters. The perfect branch had split off, and was dangling from the tree by a thin strip of bark. Her grip tightened on the slender limb above as she hung dangling like a cat on a motivational poster, feeling just as useless. Swinging herself forward, she wrapped her legs around the tree and hugged it with her arms. She slid down until she was on a tree limb below.

With one strong tug, she pulled her branch free from the maple tree, sap sticking to her hands. The coast was clear below, so she let go and watched her branch fall to the forest floor, landing with a soft thud among the red leaves. Her hands were sticky, so she licked off the sap. It was surprisingly sweet, like caramel.

Climbing down was easy. Finding her small knife in a pile of leaves was harder. Peanut sniffed around with her, mostly in solidarity. She found it near the base of the red maple, hidden under recently fallen leaves. The blade was open, defiant; reflecting her scowl in its metal.

Knife in hand, she grabbed her branch and sat under the red maple tree. First, she cut off all the leaves and small twigs. Then she paused as she debated: To strip the bark or leave it? Leaving the bark was less work, plus it could act as a protective coating. This last part seemed like a smart thing to say, but what really sold her was that it was less work. The bark shall remain, she decided. Next, she cleaned up the end where it broke from the tree. It was splintered, fractures of wood poking out in different directions. Working her knife, she cut away piece by piece until it was smooth and rounded—raw yellow nub against the thin brown bark.

Last was the business end. She flipped over the branch and snapped off the tip with her hand, leaving only the thick part of the wood. Jenny did not rush carving the point, instead focusing on each slice of her knife. Creating a weapon, no matter how crude, demanded attention. It used to provide shade and caramel-tasting tree sap. Now it would take life.

The finished spear was about six feet long, the point itself as long as her hand from fingertip to wrist. She admired its weight in her hands. It was light, strong, and firm. She gave a quick jab at the air in front of her, then another. With practice, she could get faster. Maybe even catch a fish or two. She spun it around in her hand, like a ninja, but it slipped out and fell to the ground.

"Need to practice that."

She hopped to her feet and set off toward two tall white trees with yellow leaves, Peanut following behind. Starvation gave everything a sense of urgency, she discovered. It was time to fish and she had to catch something.

"Peanut, I'll be honest. Fishing for sport never made sense to me. It seems like frustration sandwiched between boredom: a macabre sport that glorifies maiming fish for the sake of it. My dad has sat on a boat all day, walked away with nothing, and felt happy having done it. Makes no sense."

But now, with starvation bearing down on her, catching fish was not a sport but a necessity, because the alternative was much worse.

At the river she forgot which way was home: Right or left? Panic rose in her chest. But then she remembered: she had walked upstream, so home was downstream. The panic melted away and was replaced with a strange new feeling. She just called the cave "home" in her mind. That was the first time she had ever labeled her cave as home. But wait, why would she do that? The goal was to escape, right? She reminded her self that home was in the Bronx, but felt weird doing that. Why did she need the reminder?

Spear in hand, she shook off the conflicting thoughts and set off walking downstream. Then she realized something. She didn't have to walk to a familiar territory in order to fish. She could start fishing right now if she wanted to. But the desire to be in her own territory was too overwhelming. Emotion replaced logic.

Better to fish somewhere familiar, she tried to convince herself. But the thought rang hollow in her head.

The sun was high in the sky at an angle. She guessed it was after noon. Daylight would start running out soon, and if her earlier foray into fishing was any evidence, this would take a while. Walking away empty-handed was not an option this time. Her pants weren't as snug as they used to be. She never thought of herself as a skinny person, but this kind of rapid weight loss was dangerous.

Jenny's anxiety melted away when she looked into the distance and recognized her part of the river. The large rocks jutting out from the shoreline, the tall and bushy pine trees, the low underbrush. She was home.

Not wasting any time, she peeled off her shoes and socks and waded into the river. The water was cold. It took her skin some time to adjust. Peanut bounded into the river upstream, splashing with each step.

"Must be nice to have fur," Jenny remarked.

The spear felt awkward in her hand. She wasn't sure how to hold it— Left hand back and right forward? Vice versa? She went back and forth. The most comfortable position was with her right hand toward the base of the spear, and her left hand toward the middle, supporting from underneath. She took a wide stance and practiced a few thrusts in the air. She didn't lose her balance, so that was an improvement over the knife.

The one issue that still remained was the light refraction. She dipped her spear under the river, feeling the resistance of the rushing water. The light made the spear appear to bend at an angle. How could she stab a fish without knowing where the fish was? Clearly the Neanderthals figured this out somehow, so it couldn't be that hard.

Her feet started to numb in the cold water, so she focused on her breathing, trying to ignore the sensation. She scanned the river for movement. Peanut was doing the same upstream, still as stone as he stared into the water. In a way, he was a terrible standard to compare herself to. He survived off of roots, bugs, and fish. He could drink any and all water he came across. He was built for this environment, and she clearly wasn't.

Just then, a shadow darted against the river stone below. She scanned the rippling water and found a medium-sized fish swimming erratically within reach of her spear. She shifted her feet slightly so that they were in a stable position.

She tried to slow her breathing to calm her heartbeat, but it had little effect. Her heart was pounding, and even more surprising, her mouth watered. She craved the flavor of the fish morsels she'd tasted a few days ago. But she pushed it all away and focused on the fish in front of her.

The tricky part was that she needed to kind of stab it in the side, She took two small steps forward so she was perpendicular to the fish. She dipped her spear into the water and carefully studied the illusion of it bending at an angle. She was only inches away from her next meal.

With a strong thrust, her spear missed the fish and hit the river rocks beneath as the fish shot upstream. Jenny sighed, the frustration that rose in her chest made her itchy again. *At least I didn't fall in the river like last time*, she thought. As she slowed her breathing, she replayed it all in her head to find out where she went wrong.

Clearly, she'd overcompensated for the refraction and went too low with her thrust. So, aim higher next time. Approaching from behind was good. It seemed to be a blind spot for fish.

It's okay that I missed the fish, she lied to herself. *I'm learning.*

She walked upstream a dozen steps. No use staying put; the commotion had probably scared all the fish away. Peanut was busy bending a fish in his mouth until it stopped moving. Every time he caught a fish, she would watch him go through that strange procedure and wonder if there was a reason for it.

Something darted to her right. She froze, watching the river, letting its motion wash over her. Through the current, she could make out a large fish, bigger than the one she'd just missed. She took her stance. This one was a slow mover, probably due to its heft. If she caught this, it could feed her for days. Images of fireside cooking floated through her mind. She dipped the spear into the water and prepared for the kill.

Approaching it from the side was harder. She guessed too much motion would scare it away since she was in its field of vision. Maybe she should approach it from a different angle. But this thing was big, so it would move more slowly.

Close enough for the kill, she emptied her lungs of air and counted the seconds as they passed. She thrust downward and felt the spear graze the big fish. It dashed upstream and out of her reach. She pulled the spear out of the water, its empty point mocking her. She smacked the spear against the river.

"Fuck!" she screamed.

Peanut had stopped to watch her. There was almost a look of admonishment in his eyes, as if he were saying, *Don't lose your cool, kid.*

She took a deep breath and tried to calm herself down. She replayed the scene step by step in her head, studying what went wrong. First, she didn't approach from behind. How arrogant of her to assume the large fish would move slowly. Not only was he fast but he'd seen her coming and moved at the moment she grazed him. At least she had good aim. But if her aim had been just an inch ahead of the fish, she might've had a meal on the end of her spear right now.

Peanut was still watching her with that look in his eye.

"I hate this. Why do people do this for fun?"

He didn't respond. She took a few more steps upstream and tried to clear her mind. Anger would only make this harder. She should just focus on what she knew. Come from behind, don't aim too low, strike ahead of the fish in case it moves. Simple stuff in theory, harder in practice. That and her feet had nearly lost all feeling. She didn't know when they'd stopped throbbing in pain, but she wasn't sure if it was because she was comfortable, or something else. She hoped it wasn't something else.

As she waded through the river, she saw clear as day a green fish swimming only two feet in front of her. Spotting three fish in one session was rare. Peanut smacked the water loudly and pulled out another fish in his paws. Rare for her anyway.

She planted herself firmly in place and readied her spear. The fish was facing her, which would make this extremely difficult. An idea crossed her mind. It was risky, but it might work. Squatting down in the water, without taking her eyes off the fish, she reached into the water and grabbed a small pebble. With a quick underhand toss, she threw it slightly upstream of the fish. When it splashed, the fish turned to inspect the commotion.

Not wasting any time, Jenny took the spear in hand and lowered the tip into the water. She took aim and exhaled slowly. With both arms, she thrust the spear forward and felt it hit. When she lifted it out of the water, it was heavy. She laughed uncontrollably. On the end of her spear was the fish, wriggling and bleeding. It had worked. The stress had all paid off.

"Peanut, I did it! Look!"

She held the spear straight up with one hand as Peanut stared at her. She knew she looked crazy, but it didn't matter. She caught her dinner. The stress and fear melted away because tonight she would finally eat.

She was back on dry land within a few steps. As the fish squirmed on the end of the spear, she had the thought: *What do I do now?* She tried to pull the fish off the spear. It came out a little, blood pouring over her hand and down her arm. She pulled the fish clean out, and more blood gushed out of the wound. The fish squirmed more intensely, clearly in a lot of pain. But then Jenny lost her grip and it slipped out of her grasp.

"No, no, no, no!"

It dropped onto the ground and flopped desperately as it tried to return to the river. Jenny dropped the spear and went down to her knees, grasping for the fish with both her hands. But because they were covered in blood and water, the fish once again slipped from her grip. She searched the area, desperately looking for something to kill it with. Her hand stumbled upon a rock, so she planted a hand on the fish's tail and smashed it's face hard with the rock. The fish violently contorted and tried to slip away. She struck it again and again. By the time it went still, she was pissed off and sad. This wasn't how it was supposed to happen at all.

She sat back on her knees and stared at the fish's mangled corpse. Her hands were covered in blood. The fish died in pain, suffering until the end. Peanut's odd routine all clicked into place, and she knew why he bent the fish in his jaw until it snapped: If they died quickly, they were easier to hold. Dying quickly also meant its suffering was brief. She made a promise to herself: From now on, she would not let a dying animal suffer.

CHAPTER EIGHTEEN

The fish had a sweetness to it that surprised Jenny, but she ate it with little enjoyment. As she gutted it, all she could think about its final moments of suffering. She felt the broken bones, saw the giant hole where the spear had pierced through its side. It was a subdued meal, accompanied by the sound of crackling fire.

As she sat, letting the flames hypnotize her, she thought back to when she'd watched her dad gut a fish for the first time. Had to be when she was around ten years old. He had gone out fishing with his buddy Pedro, which they did once a month in the summer. Jenny loved fishing days because it meant she had the whole house to herself. She would grab a book, sit on the couch, and read all day. He came back one evening with a huge fish, and she watched him clean it, half in fascination, half in disgust. He cleaned off all the scales, which looked like little paper jewels. Then he cut it down the middle from tail to belly and slid out the guts with his finger. The smelly entrails fell out of the fish with little resistance, which had made Jenny shudder. If only he could see her now, putting his teachings to use.

The cooked fish coupled with her purified hot-rock water was the best meal she'd had in a week. Which was an incredible thing for so many reasons. On one hand, she did it all herself with nothing but a pocket knife. On the other hand, she shouldn't be doing it at all in the first place. She shouldn't be here.

Jenny sat back on her hands and looked at the bright orange sky above, enjoying the soft heat from the fire. It was a peaceful evening. It struck her that for the first time since she fell down the hill, she was content. Homesick as hell, but that aside, things were stabilizing. She could focus all her attention on the signal fire now, and maybe she could get out of here soon. The thought of leaving Peanut behind was a problem she wasn't ready to face yet.

She stood up and kicked out the fire. The wooden mug had some water left in it, so she downed the rest.

Inside the cave, Peanut was fast asleep. She took *Starfish* out of her backpack and used the bag as a pillow. She read until there wasn't enough light to read any further.

The next morning, she woke feeling rested. She sat up and scratched her head. It was itching a lot for some reason—probably needed to wash her hair today.

Outside, the sun was just starting to create an early morning glow. The air was cold but full of moisture. She made a small fire and heated up two rocks. While they were cooking, she circled the perimeter and gathered up as much dry wood as she could find. Today was the day she would make the signal fire, and it was going to be freaking huge.

"So, today is my eighth day here, which makes it October 1st if I'm right." She said. People had survived for longer, so maybe the forest rangers or police or whoever haven't given up on her yet. Her dad wouldn't give up, that's for sure.

Hopefully, he was taking care of himself. Sometimes he forgot to do that, and Jenny would have to take care of him. There was the time he was so focused on making Jenny dinner that he forgot to cook enough for himself, so she declared she would make him dinner in return. However, she didn't know how to cook yet so she made him a grilled cheese sandwich that was simultaneously burnt on the outside, and cold on the inside. He ate it anyway. Who knew such a simple thing could be so hard to make? Or there was the time he had forgotten to get his usual haircut and missed the appointment two weeks in a row. So, Jenny sat him down at the kitchen table and gave him a haircut. Thankfully, he enjoyed short hair, because she had accidentally taken too much off the sides and tried to even it out by taking more off the top and created a vicious cycle of cutting too much off trying to balance it all out.

She dropped the wood near the fire and went back to making water. Having a warm cup of water every morning had been a great way to start her days. Almost like having tea every day, if that tea was bitter, smoky, and had flakes of ash floating around in it. Not a flavor that would be getting popular at coffee shops anytime soon.

After she finished drinking her water for the morning, she did another loop around the perimeter and added more wood to the pile. She was going to need a lot. Might be worth checking out the cliff above the cave.

As she was thinking about this, a new idea struck her: Why not build the signal fire up there? It was at a higher elevation, which meant more chance of visibility. She nodded to herself; it seemed like a good plan. No reason not to try. Probably best to build it around sunset, or later, so the fire and smoke would be more visible.

Back in the cave she scratched Peanut's back. He jumped at her touch and let out a loud huff. He twisted himself around to look at her.

"Hey, sorry buddy. What did I do wrong?"

Peanut opened his mouth widely and yawned. She stared at his sharp teeth and imagined the destruction they could cause. Something as simple as a yawn made him seem so innocent. The memory of his mother, Virginia, reminded her that he could always become a fierce and violent creature. Peanut let out another loud huff.

"Ok got it. I'm going to go fishing, you're welcome to join."

She arrived at the river first. Peanut arrived awhile later, looking tired. It was starting to warm up, so Jenny dropped her hoodie and backpack by the shore and rolled her pants up to her knees. Before she started fishing, she undid her ponytail and dipped her head under the water. It was cold and nearly took her breath away. She used her fingers to scrub her head, trying to wash out all the dirt and filth. She loved her hair, but cleaning it was no joke. Her thick hair took a long time to fully clean under normal circumstances, but these abnormal circumstances made her beautiful hair feel more like a liability. How did Indigenous people maintain and clean long hair back before colonizers showed up and wrecked everything? Did they stand in rivers like she was doing right now with nothing but water and vibes? She whipped up her head out of the water and shook off her hair to dry. The cold water felt refreshing to her senses.

Spear in hand, she started to fish. It only took her four failed attempts before she had speared her first fish of the day. It was another green one, which seemed like the common fish in this river. She placed the tip of the spear against a large rock so the fish couldn't wriggle free. Without hesitating, she grabbed a hand-sized stone and smashed its head. It stopped moving instantly. She took it off the spear and placed it in her backpack. The smashing stone was effective, so she put it in her pocket.

Peanut chose a spot downstream and seemed particularly focused today. She wondered what was going on in his head. He was still young but seemed independent enough to fend for himself. She had to remind herself that he was a wild animal. It was easy to forget that and anthropomorphize him. The earlier incident was a good reminder that he could just snap and kill her. It was a strange juxtaposition of emotions to feel a strong connection to him, feelings of love and compassion, but also to experience moments of deep, almost ancestral, fear and panic. As if all her ancestors' collective experiences are screaming *RUN. BEAR.* In her mind, her compassion had overshadowed her fear. They were now forever connected in a profound way.

Peanut smacked the water with his claws lightning fast and pulled out a fish. Its silver scales flashed, reflecting sunlight. He put the fish face-first into his mouth and the fish squirmed inside it. The image of the wriggling fish sticking out of his mouth made her chuckle. He bit down and the fish went limp. A sobering reminder.

Jenny turned back to the river and looked for another one. If she could catch two, then she wouldn't have to come back out for dinner. That would mean two whole meals in a single day. Her belt was on its last loop, so she needed to put on some pounds if for no other reason than to fit into her pants.

She spotted a decent-sized fish close by. It swam low to the ground, its dark head camouflaging with the dark water. Its middle was a bit lighter in color, so she focused on that. The dark fish twisted and turned, searching the riverbed. It was hard to find an opening, so Jenny waited still as stone.

The dark fish paused to inspect a rock less than a foot away from her. Jenny stabbed her spear straight down through its back. A red cloud bloomed around the fish and washed downstream. She pulled her catch out of the water and placed her spear against a rock. The impaled fish wriggled and convulsed as it tried to escape, but its efforts were fruitless. In one quick swing she smashed it with her stone, and it instantly went limp.

She pulled the fish off the tip of her spear. Something sharp punctured her hand and a sharp pain shot up her arm. She gasped and dropped the fish into the river. When she examined her palm, there was a small puncture near her thumb, trickling with blood. The limp fish body slowly floated down the river. She threw her spear toward the shore and splashed after the dead fish. She felt ridiculous. She needed huge strides to run fast enough against the water resistance. When the dead fish was within reach, snatched it by the tail. She pulled the mysterious fish out of the water and examined it.

Its underside was white, its back dark, and its flat head had two long whisker appendages. A catfish, she realized. After carefully feeling around the fish, she found that its fins had a sharp spiky point, which is how it punctured her hand. Her father had talked about them but, evidently, she missed the part about the spiked fins. As she waded through the water toward the shore, she made a mental note to watch out for these little jerks. She flexed her hand. The bleeding had already stopped, as the wound was quite small, but her hand felt swollen and sensitive. It was the last time she would make that mistake.

She dropped the fish into her backpack. Spear and hoodie in hand, she turned toward Peanut.

"I'm heading back if you want to join me."

Peanut stared at her, perfectly still. As she waited for him, she filled her water bottle with river water to purify it later. Peanut hadn't moved, and while she didn't want to leave him behind, she had things to do.

"Suit yourself. See you later. You know where to find me."

She crawled through the bushes under the tree and into the clearing overlooking the cave. Behind her, she could hear water splashing. Grinning, she turned and faced the hole under the tree. Peanut popped out and scratched at the ground to pull himself through, nearly getting stuck in the process.

"Someone's been eating too much fish." She said. "Soon you won't be able to fit."

Back at the cave, she dropped off her backpack and spear and gathered up her fire supplies. Peanut curled into his spot let out a tired grunt. She wanted to go over and give his back a scratch, but after the indecent this morning she decided to give him space instead. She let out an equally tired sounding grunt, grabbed the fish, mug, and water bottle, from her backpack and made her way out to her fire pit.

The fire didn't take long to get started. The heat of the flame warmed her face. She wanted to just sit and enjoy it, but there was more work to do. A strong twinge of loneliness hit her, but she ignored it. At this point she felt like if she thought too much about her father it might send her into a deep depression, so better just to avoid it all together.

Having gutted only one fish, Jenny stared at the catfish in her hand, unsure of what to do. The previous fish had scales. This catfish was all skin, no scales, and pointy fins. She cut along its back slowly, making a line above the fins toward its head. She pulled the slimy skin back, and beneath was delicate white meat. She cut it out, carefully pierced it with a small stick, which she stuck into the ground near the fire. She did this with a half-dozen more globs of catfish meat. By the end of it all, she had seven sticks of meat cooking, and one hollowed-out fish carcass that looked like a gruesome game of *Operation*. She dropped the remains near the fire.

The other fish was much easier. With her knife, she scraped away all the scales, made a line down the belly from tail to jaw, and slid the guts out with her fingers. They fell out with no resistance and smelled terrible, which caused Jenny to shudder. It still disgusted her. She placed the guts next to the catfish remains. Then she put the edible bits of fish on three sticks, and sat back and surveyed of all her hard work. Two fish turned into ten sticks of cooking fish meat. It felt like a feast.

She dropped the two river stones into the fire and stood up, stretching her legs. She scratched her head, trying to satisfy an intense itching feeling. It was odd. She'd scrubbed her hair in the river, but for some reason the itching remained. What if something else was causing her head to itch?

Oh God, she thought. *Another problem.* She slipped the two hair ties off her wrist threw her hair up into a tight ponytail, promising to figure this problem out later.

The wood pile from the morning was looking small. For this signal fire to be noticed, it would have to be huge. Jenny began gathering armfuls of sticks and branches and dropped them off at the wood pile. The fish meat was looking half done, so Jenny rotated all of the sticks to cook the undersides and went off to find more wood. The wood pile looked better, but carrying it up Virginia's Way was going to suck.

A thin layer of sweat had formed across her forehead. The fish meat looked golden brown, so she plopped down near the fire, picked up a stick of catfish meat, and tore into it with her teeth. It had a strong fish taste and an oily texture. She chewed it, enjoying the warmth and flavor. She ate four more sticks of the catfish, and stick from the other fish.

She quickly filtered an entire mug of water. Better safe than sorry when it came to beating dehydration. She sat sipping the from the mug, enjoying the quiet sounds of the forest. It struck her that the mug, the spear, and all the cooked fish had all been created by her. With only a small pocketknife, she had managed to survive for eight days. Brian in Gary Paulsen's *Hatchet* had nothing on her.

Peanut was snoring away, so Jenny softy crept to her backpack, trying not to disturb him. She put all of her cooking supplies, and the rest of the cooked fish, in her backpack and grabbed a handful of dry leaves for fire starter.

It was hard work, bringing all the wood she had gathered up to the top of Virginia's Way. She had started with her hoodie on, but after one trip up the hill it was too hot, so she took it off. By the time she had finished, she was uncomfortably warm in the cool October air. A thin layer of sweat and dirt covered her bare arms.

After surveying the top of the area, she guessed that the best place for the large fire was in a clearing near the cliff edge that overlooked the mouth of the cave, south of the large rotting tree. There were fewer trees surrounding the spot, so the signal fire might have a better chance of shining through the canopy of leaves above.

The question she struggled with was how to make the fire huge. Smaller cooking fires were easy because all it needed was sticks and leaves. There wasn't really any rhyme or reason to it. A large signal fire required more organization. So, she went with what she knew.

In *Lord of the Rings*, the Beacons of Gondor were basically huge signal fires. In the book they were more of a footnote, but in the movies they were an important plot point. So, she opted to build it like she remembered from the movies: large and square with a hollow middle for the leaves and smaller twigs.

Jenny gathered as much wood as she could find. She used the biggest branches as a base, laying them out in a square shape. She laid down the smaller branches on the inside of the square, working toward the middle until only a small area in the middle remained, which she covered in dry leaves.

Once the foundation was laid, she started building the next layer, and then the next. It was slow work, but she found the automatic motions oddly soothing.

Her wood pile was running out, but the beacon was only up to her waist. She was hoping it would be at least as tall as she was, so she set out in search of more materials. Her shirt was soaked with sweat at this point, and the orange glow of the sky meant the sun was starting to set. She was running out of time. If there was a plane or helicopter looking for her, she figured they probably only searched during the day. The pressure to complete this task was giving her anxiety.

She stepped through some low bushes on the north end of the clearing. Here the leafy plants were thicker, so it was hard to see the fallen branches and twigs on the forest floor. Odds were that poison ivy was around, so she resisted the urge to touch the green plants with her bare hands.

She continued walking north, and the greenery around her was now up to her waist. To avoid touching the plants she had to stick her arms up, looking like a swimmer wading through water. The ground was uneven here. It didn't look much better up ahead. Just more tall plants and no wood in sight.

Defeated, she turned back. When she returned to the clearing, she searched her surroundings for a solution. Her eyes stopped on the giant rotting tree in the middle of the clearing.

"Well, isn't that's a ton of wood?" She said. "Why not use some of it?"

She dashed toward the river and crawled under the fallen tree. When she reached the other side, she scanned the shore for a large rock like the one she used to chop the wood mug branch. She spotted one, half in the river, half out. She carried it back to the giant rotting tree, raised it above her head, and brought it down hard. The entire tree shook on impact, bark splintering off. The plan was working.

She smashed the rock against the tree again, watching more pieces split off. After a few more times her arms were getting tired. But there was no time to rest, so she took a break by gathering all the wood that had broken off the tree and adding it to her beacon.

"Still not enough. Need more if this thing is going to be big."

It only came up to her chest. She smashed the rock against the tree again, but this time from the side. A huge sheet of bark slid off. She shook her head. Should have started with this.

She worked her way up and down the tree, chopping all the dry bark off but avoiding the parts with moss. Probably wouldn't burn as well.

When she added the bark to the beacon, it added enough height to reach her shoulders. She added one last sheet of bark to the top and stepped back to marvel at her little structure.

With no time to waste, she grabbed the flint and knife from her hoodie and made sparks until the leaves caught fire. She blew air onto the flame to help get it going, and then she sat back on her hands and finally allowed herself a moment to rest.

The twigs crackled in the fire. They'd caught surprisingly fast, and the inside of the beacon was already glowing orange. She could feel the heat against her face, so she stood up and stepped back. Above, a steady stream of thick smoke streamed into the sky.

Pride blossomed inside of her. It worked. The plan had worked. Now all she could do was hope someone, somewhere saw her signal and came to rescue her. But then she felt a pang of guilt. Inside the cave below was her only friend in the world. She would be leaving him alone forever. How would he feel waking up to an empty cave?

The beacon fire was in full swing, and she could feel the heat ten feet away. It burned an afterimage into her eyes. She tried to blink it away, but still saw the purple-green shape when she looked away. Hopefully, that meant it was bright enough.

Her stomach growled and, with nothing to do but wait, she grabbed her hoodie and made her way down to the cave. She stood below at its mouth and paused to marvel at the fire above.

Inside Peanut slept, oblivious to the world around him. It made her sad for him. He had no idea she was fighting to leave him. They had grown close; she felt an attachment to him. They had experienced mutual trauma. That had bound them together. Or at least her to him, she felt. Hard to know if he felt the same way.

The grimy layer of sweat coating her exposed skin combined with the coolness of the cave forced her to put her hoodie back on. She quietly pulled out *Starfish* and some fish meat out of her backpack, and sat next to the mouth of the cave with her back against the rock wall.

She ate the bits of fish. They were cold and tasted like fishy smoke. She looked out into the clearing. This had been her home for just over a week. She found herself strangely attached to it all. There had been painful moments here but also personal triumphs. Maybe someday she could come back and visit. Would Peanut be here? Would he remember her?

After she ate the last bite of fish, she tucked the Ziplock bag into her pocket. She opened *Starfish* and started reading.

CHAPTER NINTEEN

A stiff and sharp pain in her neck made her eyes flutter open in disorientation. It was dark. She couldn't remember where she was, and her memory was slow to recall. She had been reading. Had she fallen asleep?

Starfish lay open in her lap. She shook her head, clearing away the fog of sleep. She had fallen asleep sitting just outside the cave. Then she remembered—the signal fire. She sprang to her feet and looked up towards the top of the cliff. The signal fire was dark. The forest felt still.

Jenny sighed. It would have been ridiculous to expect the cavalry to come running. For all she knew, no one saw her fire. Still, she'd hoped it would lead to a more noticeable result, like a low-flying airplane or helicopter. Surely, she would have heard the noise of an aircraft in her sleep. But the forest was silent. Not even the sound of a bird or cicada.

How long had she been out? She tilted her head, and once again felt the pain in her neck from sleeping at the wrong angle. She grabbed *Starfish* and crawled into the cave.

Peanut was wide awake, staring at her. It was oddly discomforting.

"Something wrong, Peanut?"

She walked over to him and gave his head a rub. He continued staring behind her toward the entrance of the cave. Jenny looked over her shoulder, but there was nothing.

"Can't sleep?"

Her throat felt like sandpaper. She felt around for her water bottle, but it was empty.

"Peanut, I'm going to make a quick run to the river. Stay here. Keep keeping watch, or whatever it is you're doing."

She patted him on the head and crawled out of the cave, empty water bottle in hand.

The forest at night was full of shadows. The sky was incredibly clear up away from all the light pollution of the Bronx. The moon illuminated the forest floor, and Jenny discovered that walking without tripping was easy once her eyes adjusted.

At the river, where there was no treetop canopy obstructing the view, the night sky was a sight to behold. Thousands of stars twinkled with tremendous clarity. As she dunked the water bottle into the river, she stared upward and let her eyes wander. For a moment she could make out the haze of the Milky Way. The immense beauty of the universe made her feel small and unimportant. How had she not taken notice of this until now?

Once the water bottle was full, she screwed on the cap and crawled back through to the clearing. It was much darker here, stars and moonlight obscured by the thick tree canopy above. Shadows danced as the trees swayed in the wind. The darkness made Jenny a bit anxious, so she quickened her pace.

She stopped to inspect the signal fire. The large square structure had collapsed in on itself, and a large pile of embers glowed on the ground beneath her. The embers looked like puffy Cheez Doodles, and she had to fight back the desire to reach out and eat one.

A strange sound emanated from below, something between a yelp and a growl. It was Peanut. Her stomach dropped—something was wrong.

She ran down Virginia's Way, trying not to slip and fall. As she ran past the fire pit, she noticed that the fish guts and catfish carcass she had left by the fire were gone. The smell. It had attracted something to their cave. She cursed under her breath. What a stupid mistake.

At the cave entrance, the sound from inside grew louder: grunting and the clacking of teeth. A succession of dull thuds, like punches, made Jenny's heart pound in her chest. She dropped to her knees and started toward the cave mouth but stopped. *Am I really about to put myself in danger?* After a moment's hesitation, she pushed the fear away and crawled in. Peanut was in trouble and needed her.

Once inside, she paused and allowed her eyes to adjust. A narrow beam of moonlight provided a little illumination. She could only make out rounded dark-gray shapes. As her eyes adjusted, the shapes developed sharper edges. Her fire materials were scattered across the floor, and her backpack was in a different place than she'd left it, its contents strewn on the ground.

Peanut was against the back wall, frozen. His fur near his right paw was matted down with dark wet splotches. Directly in front of him was a large four-legged shadow. The shadow turned its head toward Jenny. It stepped into the beam of moonlight that illuminated the cave. Her eyes widened when she saw the familiar scar across the coyote's face, the one her knife had left in their last encounter. Time felt like it stopped, and all Jenny could hear was the pounding of her heart against her ribs.

The coyote lunged. Adrenaline kicked into overdrive and her mind went blank. She was in pure survival mode now. A full body dive away from the coyote sent her flying to the ground. She seized an armful of fire materials, and threw them as hard as she could. Sticks and twigs bounced off his wiry fur, and he bared a sharp-looking set of teeth.

Jenny scrambled backward, pushing with her feet and hands. Did she leave her knife in her backpack or hoodie? She jumped to her feet and dove for her backpack, which had been tossed against the wall.

Before she could yank it open, she heard the scratching of claws against the cave floor approach her. She screamed and swung her backpack reflexively. There was a soft thump, but the empty backpack only bounced off the coyote.

Two heavy paws pressed against her chest and pinned her down. A jaw snapped above her. Somehow her hands were at the coyote's throat. She didn't remember how they got there. Every ounce of strength pushed against the coyote's neck. She felt his hot breath against her face.

"Get the hell off of me!" She yelled.

There was a low thud and a high-pitched yelp as the weight bearing down on Jenny lifted. She blinked and saw the coyote against the stone wall. Across the cave, Peanut stood on three paws, the last one bloodied and cradled up against his side.

The coyote got to his feet and bared his fangs. Peanut charged, as best he could, limping along and letting out a loud bellow that sounded almost human. They both collided and tumbled out of the mouth of the cave.

Fear was replaced by white-hot rage. This damn coyote, which should be dead, was set on tearing apart everything Jenny had built. Eric's face flashed in her mind and she saw no difference between them. Both were wild animals attacking, unprovoked. Enough was enough. It was time to make a stand.

Jenny stood up and frantically searched for her spear. Hands trembling with adrenaline, she tossed aside her fire making supplies until she found her spear underneath the pile. Then she scrambled through the cave mouth and into the night.

Peanut and the coyote were fighting near her fire pit. They had squared off and charged at each other, teeth bared. They collided. It was a tangle of teeth and claws. Peanut let out a yelp as he fell back against his injured paw.

The coyote took advantage of this moment of weakness and charged. He clamped onto the injured paw with his teeth. Peanut let out a loud pained growl.

Jenny was already sprinting before she knew what she was about to do. She brought the spear around and swung it hard at the coyote, hitting him across his backside. He let go of his grip on Peanut and jumped back, baring teeth at Jenny. The two froze.

Peanut tried to stand, but failed and crashed forward. He scraped at the ground with his one good paw, trying to move, but only flailing around in a circle. He was delirious. Something was wrong. Her heart ached to see him in pain.

She took the spear in both hands and pointed it toward the coyote. She thrust forward, but he jumped back. She tried again, and he dodged right. Then he clamped down on the spear with his teeth and shook violently. Jenny's grip loosened at the strength in his jaws. She stumbled forward and nearly fell.

Once regaining her balance, she thrust the spear downward, straight into the dirt. The coyote held on, just as she expected, and she kicked right at his jaw with every ounce of strength she could muster.

Her foot connected, and the coyote yelped and let go of its grasp on the spear. She pulled it from the ground and held it in both hands. They stared off again and, in that moment, Jenny realized this was a fight that would only end in death. Her versus the raw power of nature.

The coyote leaped at her suddenly, headbutting her in the chest. They fell to the ground in a tangle of limbs and teeth. Jenny, pinned against the ground, fisted the spear in both hands against the coyote's neck to push back against his powerful jaws.

Saliva flew from his mouth, gnashing his teeth inches from her nose. She pushed hard against its neck but felt her strength waning. She yanked her knee up to his stomach, hard. The coyote didn't see it coming and flinched. She used the moment to twist her spear and push the wild animal off her.

The coyote rolled onto his side as she slipped out from underneath him. Before he could get back on his feet, she smacked its head hard with the bottom of her spear. Another loud yelp from the mongrel. He contorted his body to get to his feet. She hit its legs over and over until she heard a loud crack.

At first, she thought she broke the spear. She paused to look at it, but it was solid. Then she looked back down at the wild animal, where he was trying to drag himself away, his back legs bent at a strange angle.

"You're not getting away."

A deep anger welled up inside her. Eric's laughing face sprung forward in her mind, and then she was falling down the hill all over again. Somewhere in the back of her mind, she remembered the promise she made not to make an animal suffer. She made a choice and pushed the thought away. Jenny figured she may have been powerless to stop one bully, but she could stop this one.

The coyote growled at her as she took a step toward him. She stared down at the animal and felt nothing. No remorse or pity. She brought the spear high above her head and, with both hands, brought the point down hard into the coyote's ribs.

He let out a noise unlike anything she had ever heard before. A deep growl mixed with a pained, piercing yelp. He kicked, trying to get away from her, but she pushed the spear in farther, feeling it work its way through bone and viscera, until it came out the other side with a dull pop. She continued pushing until the spear had fully impaled through the coyote and into the ground. He struggled, barking and scratching, but the spear pinned him in place.

She watched as he squirmed and still felt nothing. He let out a long, deep howl. The creature that had caused her and Peanut so much pain. Shouldn't those who cause suffering be met with equal or greater suffering? As the coyote let out a low whimper, she turned her back on it and went to Peanut.

Peanut had managed to twist himself around and crawl toward the cave with his one good front paw. A trail of blood followed behind him. Jenny looked at him and didn't know what to do. Tears filled her eyes, and her entire body was shaking until she fell to her knees. The adrenaline rush was coming down and, in its place, a deep sadness took over. Watching Peanut, with his twisted, blood-soaked arm, it felt like she seeing a friend suffer. Anger boiled up. She was going to save him. He'd saved her, so she had to save him.

She gently took his head in her hands and looked him deep in his eyes.

"I need you to trust me. I'm going to take care of you, okay?"

Peanut stared back. It wasn't until now in the moonlight that she noticed there were golden flecks in his brown eyes. He was a beautiful creature. Jenny grabbed his good paw and pulled him toward the cave. He was heavier than she thought he would be, but thankfully he put up no resistance. She dug her feet into the dirt and pulled with every ounce of her strength. She screamed as tears of anger fell down her cheeks.

It felt like hours before they'd made it to the mouth of the cave. The light in Peanut's eyes looked dim. He had lost a lot of blood. The coyote must have nicked an artery. She had to stop the bleeding. But first, get him inside the cave.

Jenny became aware of a distant thumping. She ignored it. She ran around behind Peanut, dug her feet into the earth, and pushed his backside feeling like Sisyphus and his boulder. Peanut feebly tried to help with his one good paw, but his movements were uncoordinated and lazy. The blood loss had made him delirious. Her muscles ached and screamed for rest, but she couldn't give up yet. The thumping grew louder by the moment. Was it her heart in her ears? Jenny gave a mighty push, and they crossed the threshold into the cave.

She undid her belt, whipped it out of the loops, and pulled it tight around Peanut's mangled arm, holding it with all of her strength. She prayed this would stop the bleeding.

Outside, the thumping grew even louder until it was all she could hear. The trees shook. Jenny's mind raced to find out what was happening, and then she saw the spotlight flick on.

A helicopter. The signal fire had worked.

She almost stood to her feet but stopped. The realization hit her hard: If she didn't hold the belt and keep pressure applied, Peanut would bleed out and die. Tears welled up in her eyes and she screamed, her voice drowning amid the steady pulse of the helicopter blades.

The bright white searchlight pierced through the forest canopy, scanning for signs of life. She let out another scream and pulled the belt tight around Peanut's arm. She buried her face in his fur and sobbed.

"I'm sorry, Dad. I can't leave him yet," she whispered.

Eventually, the thumping of the helicopter blades grew distant. Outside, the low howl of the coyote continued. After a time, it stopped, and all she heard was the sound of trees rustling of in the wind.

Part Two

CHAPTER TWENTY

A month had passed since the incident, which made today November 1st. Or Day 39 of surviving in the Balsam Lake Mountain Wild Forest. The forest had shed its remainders of fall and given over to winter. A blanket of snow coated the ground, and thousands of leafless trees rose out of the smooth white surface. The branches of tall pines bent as small green needles clung to heavy snow. The lines of the hills and valleys against the horizon were visible through the sea of trees.

Jenny stood motionless behind the trunk of a tall evergreen; the only movement were her eyes scanning her surroundings. About fifteen feet away stood a young buck, sniffing the ground cautiously. He was scrawny and didn't have any antlers. Less than two years old, she guessed.

The buck popped its head up, and she ducked behind the tree. She had been tracking the buck for two days now as it searched for small morsels of food. Two days away from Peanut. Not about to try for three. The buck had not reunited with its herd, which she thought was odd, but meant it would be less hassle to take him down. She scratched her head and felt the spot where her ponytail used to be.

Cutting her hair off was one of the hardest things she had to do since arriving here. At first, she thought the itchiness was simply because her hair was dirty. Then the itchiness became intense. After feeling her scalp, she had discovered it was covered in clusters of bumps. Without a mirror it was hard to see, but then they spread to her ankles, and that was when she knew she had a flea infestation.

Her lucky pocket knife had served as the instrument of destruction. She stood over the river, using it as a shoddy mirror, and cut off chunks one by one. Each cut felt like the destruction of years of hard work.

Hours and hours lost cleaning it. Hundreds of dollars in appointments to keep it healthy. How ugly would she be without it now? Her father probably wouldn't recognize her. When she first saw her new reflection in the river, she cried. Her patchy hair looked like something out of a horror movie. The girl who was Jenny had died in this forest, and the last remnant of her had floated away down the river. Who was the woman that remained?

Ever since the river froze over, she had been forced to expand her search for food. Subsisting on fish meat alone had nearly killed her desire to eat. Thankfully, she had expanded her menu to rabbits and squirrels for variety. Though they were easy to hunt, they provided little in the way of meat. She had managed to take down a fox once, but the meat was tough and greasy. Eating it reminded her of *Fantastic Mr. Fox* by Roald Dahl, which had made her feel guilty. Whenever she managed to get back to the Bronx, she promised she would go vegan for at least a year to atone for killing all of these innocent animals.

Ahead, the buck perked up and moved forward slowly, scanning from left to right. Her grip tightened around the spear in her hand. If it moved a little closer, she might find an opening. Her stomach growled loudly, and she covered it with her hand. The deer looked in her direction and she froze, holding her breath.

When the buck looked away, she exhaled and slowly crept out from behind the tree, crouching low to the ground. Her footsteps were silent, thanks to the rabbit pelts she had tied around her shoes. Turns out, a pair of old Jordans weren't all that great in the cold snow. Her feet would be numb and frostbitten, but she had come up with a quick and dirty snowshoe solution: she'd pulled the shoestrings out of her Jordans, poked holes in the rabbit pelts, and tied them around her shoes. She couldn't sprint in them, the force would tear the whole thing apart, but at least the fur deadened the sound and kept her feet warm.

She crouched and inched closer to the buck, staying low to the ground, and hiding behind the wiry branches of dead bushes. It was looking in the opposite direction, and she had positioned herself in its blind spot. Trouble was, these young bucks were quick, so she had to move slowly.

Yesterday, she had come within striking distance, but when she raised her spear, it had brushed against the coyote pelt that she wore around her neck, and made just enough noise to scare the buck. It had jumped off without even looking back at her.

In *My Side of the Mountain*, she remembered reading about how furs needed to be stretched and dried so they could be used for clothing.

However, the book had not prepared her for how disgusting the process turned out to be. After the coyote was good and dead, she decided to try and skin it to keep its fur as something to keep her warm during the cold fall nights. Skinning the coyote had been a gross process and she regretted trying it. After leaving the hide out in the sun for a few days, it had turned into a wearable covering.

She had cut a hole in the middle of the pelt and wore it around her neck and across her shoulders just like she'd imagined the wildling Ygritte would have in the *Game of Thrones* books. Jenny felt a lot like the "Free Folk" in that book, living in a desolate winter wasteland with nothing but animal furs to keep her warm. The way the snow made everything quiet meant she had to take extra precaution against noise, so she tucked the coyote pelt into her hoodie and wore it around her neck like a scarf instead.

She crawled around the bush and under the low-hanging branches of a tall pine tree. The branches hung low under the weight of the snow and provided a decent place to hide. If she didn't move, she was practically invisible to the buck. She watched him. He was just on the other side of the low branches, inches away now, and she was right behind him still in his blind spot.

He dug at the snow with his hoof, dropped his snout to the ground, and sniffed. This was the moment. Jenny felt her body surge with adrenaline as she leaped out from under the pine and thrusted the spear just behind the buck's ribs. She felt the hit of its soft hide, and she watched the red droplets sprinkle the snow.

The animal mechanically jumped upward. The momentum knocked Jenny off balance, and arms flailing, she fell flat on her back, making an imprint like a snow angel in the soft ground. The buck dashed away, the spear bouncing up and down stuck in its side, until it fell to the ground. She grunted in frustration.

She hopped up to her feet and hurried toward the spear as quickly as her shoes would allow. The buck was out of sight, but it had left a bright red trail of blood. She knelt and examined it.

"Should bleed out and die," She said softly.

The blood trail was bright red against the snow, and easy to follow. As she tracked it, the splotches grew bigger and the trail grew more sporadic. A good sign. One spot had a large, dark patch of blood. It had stopped here to rest.

Up ahead, a patch of blood seeped beneath a tangle of dead bushes. *Looks like he got tripped up here*, she thought. *He is growing disoriented.* The scratches and hoof prints showed signs of a struggle, confirming her theory.

Behind a tall nearby tree, she found him. He lay on the ground, his chest rising and falling slowly in the snow. She knelt by his head, looking deep into his eyes. They looked distant, glassy, but there was a dim light in them. She flicked open her pocketknife and slit his throat. A pool of blood spilled out from his neck, and she watched the light in his eyes go out. She stood over the dead animal, taking notice of the fact that she felt nothing.

There wasn't enough sunlight left to wait for the buck to bleed out if she wanted to return to the cave today. She grabbed its back legs and hiked them over her shoulders like a backpack. The spear fit snugly under its legs, held against her back by the deer's weight.

"Damn, you're heavy," she said.

Each step took concentrated effort. The buck's head flopped back and forth on the ground, leaving a trail of red. It wasn't long before her breathing grew heavy and sweat dampened her clothes. She continued trudging through the snow, feeling the full weight of the buck on her back. Eventually, she reached the frozen river. She stopped to catch her breath and examined the sky above. It was glowing orange. She estimated about two hours of daylight left. She hoisted the buck up and made her way downstream.

"Almost to the cave," she said. "Almost home."

CHAPTER TWENTY-ONE

The sun had fallen beneath the horizon by the time Jenny arrived at her spot in the river. The last burst of twilight illuminated the sky, giving the forest an eerie blue glow. The frozen river still and reflective like a mirror with snow-frosted edges.

Jenny dropped the deer by the river and planted her spear in the shoreline. From her hoodie she pulled out the water bottle, long empty from her two-day hunting trek. Her dry mouth a reminder of this fact. Filtering water and saving it in the water bottle for later was a relatively new idea Jenny discovered. Usually, she just drank it right away. Building up a stock of fresh water was a tricky balance of available resources. Rather than go back and forth to the river every time she needed a drink; Jenny made a bucket to hold all the river water so her one sealable bottle could be used to store purified water.

She hated the bucket. It was ugly, misshapen, and had taken a week to carve. The calluses on her fingers were proof of the effort. She had visualized the bucket perfectly but had completely failed in actualization. Now she had to stare at her failure every day. Once she found the time to make another one, she would burn this one. The hardest part of it all this was keeping Peanut hydrated. With his injured leg, he couldn't make the trek to the river every day, so she had to make sure he had enough water to drink day to day. Despite being a monument to her failure, at least the bucket had two functions.

She broke through the river ice, carefully filled the bottle with water, and tucked it back into her hoodie. Then she hoisted the buck on her back once more, feeling her cold, sweat-soaked shirt press against her skin, and trekked back through the entrance of the river.

It had taken two days to clear out the fallen tree and underbrush surrounding the entrance, but the result was well worth it: No more crawling on her knees, but the real reason was that it made it easier for Peanut to hobble to the river.

Clearing the fallen tree that blocked the entrance was surprisingly tricky. When she had decided it was time, she grabbed her wood-chopping stone and started hacking away at the tree. The first strike of stone against wood had shaken her hands so violently she'd dropped the stone on her foot. The combination of toes and hands in pain had instantly flared her anger.

Jenny tossed the stone aside, stomped down to the cave, and gathered fire-making supplies. It was only in hindsight that she realized her plan was stupid. But in the moment anger fueled her choices. She started a fire under the log and kept it going until the log started to catch. Her next idea, equally stupid in hindsight, was to smash the burning log with the stone. Logically it made sense to her. The tree was weak now, the stone was strong, smash it and be done. What she didn't think about was where all of the embers would land.

It took hours to contain the fire. She hadn't considered how remarkably dry the trees nearby had been. The embers scattered and started a dozen mini fires. The snow helped douse some of the flames, but for a while it seemed all but certain she would burn the entire forest down. After the smoke settled, she had burned most of the surrounding trees, and the spot had widened considerably. From the river she could stand and see through to the cliff top of Virginia's Way completely unobstructed.

She dragged the deer through the entrance and across the familiar cliff atop the cave. The pile of black burnt wood that had been the signal fire sat covered in snow. The remnants of the rotting log poked up through its white cover. Her frequent treks had carved a footpath through the snow to follow.

At the top of Virginia's Way, she stopped and looked down at the cave. *Home.* Two days was a long time to be gone, and she was happy to be back. Exhaustion nagged at her, but her growling stomach reminded her there was still more work to do before she could rest.

She stopped outside the cave, dropped the buck, and stood under the small shelter she had built. It wasn't much, just a small roof over the cave's entrance. Four tall branch posts poked out of the earth to support a small square of log crossbeams. A thick blanket of pine tree branches laid on top of the cross beams to keep out water and snow. Vine-like plants she'd found held it all together. She had discovered them on one of her survey runs, and figured they could be used like rope. With the shelter over the entrance, she could build a small fire under it and not have to worry about snow or rain.

She pulled the buck through the cave. It was dark, and little light spilled in from outside, but at this point she felt familiar enough with the layout to navigate blind. She let the buck drop in the middle of the cave and felt her way toward the back wall. When she reached the warm lump of fur, she clicked of her teeth. Peanut popped his head up and turned toward her.

"Hey, Peanut. Sorry I was gone so long."

She put her hand against his chest. His brown eyes looked back at her. He had lost a lot of weight. Ever since that night, he had been virtually immobile because his paw had been injured so badly. He still couldn't put weight on it, so she figured at this point, a month later, it must be broken. He struggled to the river to drink and couldn't catch a fish to save his life. Without her, he would have been dead already. Now she had to hunt for two. He could eat five fish a day on a good day, which meant she spent a large chunk of her time fishing.

The part that worried her the most was that he would need to hibernate soon. That had changed everything. She didn't know a thing about what bears needed to do to prepare, other than eat to build up fat to last the winter. But Peanut's round belly was gone, his full cheeks looked loose on his face, and worst of all, his playfulness had dwindled.

She had no idea when hibernation started but if she could get him to that finish line, then maybe she could leave the forest and come back in the spring when he came out of hibernation with a veterinarian or a park ranger to fix up his leg. If she left at all…

"Hungry?" she asked.

It was too dark inside to start working on the deer, so she grabbed her fire-making supplies and made a small fire outside the cave. The yellow light bounced around inside the cave. She could see her home more clearly now and took a moment to appreciate what she had made of this small cave.

In the back corner was her stock of dry wood for fire. It stretched from the floor to well above her head, filled with twigs, sticks, branches, and wood she chopped with her rock. She spent days building up the supply, and only used as much as she needed.

Next to the woodpile was a large stack of river stones, her pride and joy. She had created a little dugout for the stones and on particularly cold nights she would warm up the stack of river stones in the fire and put them in the dugout. It was like a low-tech space heater, keeping a small part the cave warm.

Off to the side was the tanning rack she had built. Using more of the vine plants as rope she created a small square structure where the animal skins could be stretched out, scraped clean, and hung to dry. This was hugely still a trial-and-error process that she was figuring out. The coyote skin had turned out alright, but she didn't have luck with much else. The smaller furs would either turn out gooey, or dry and stiff to the touch. Out of all of dozens rabbits she had killed, only two pelts turned out to be usable.

Next to the rack was the squat and ugly little bucket. She hated it. She took out the bottle from her hoodie and dumped the river water into the bucket to use for later. Then she tossed the bottle next to her faded green backpack.

She propped her spear up against the cave wall and hung her hoodie on it. She unwrapped the coyote fur from around her neck and set it near the bed.

Jenny, the young girl from the Bronx, would have felt disgusted by the idea of gutting a deer. Now it was just more work that needed to be done. Feelings didn't matter out here.

Cutting through the skin was an odd sensation. Not like sliding through butter, more like a tearing through a burlap sack. She cut a line from the ribs to the back legs. The smell was horrible. Like rancid trash mixed with vomit. She had to cover her mouth with her arm just to hide the warm sulfur odor. This next part was her least favorite. Doing this to rabbits and squirrels was bad enough . . .

She took a deep breath and plunged her hands deep into the buck. The first thing she noticed was that he was still warm on the inside. It made the next sensation much worse. She pulled out the slimy body organs without much resistance. She cut the esophagus and the lower intestine, as they were attached to both ends. The "pile of eternal stench" she called it. Horrible, smelly, and full of calories for Peanut.

"Peanut, dinner," she said.

Peanut limped his way over, putting next to no weight on his broken paw. The shallow outline of ribs from under his fur made Jenny's anxiety spike. He had lost so much weight.

Jenny brought the rest of the deer over to the tanning rack. She had never skinned an animal as large as a deer before. More making it up as she went, it seemed.

She flicked open her knife and grabbed a leg. The fur was soft to the touch. She placed her knife on the back of the hoof where it met the fur. The dull blade went in with a strong push. She carved a bloody circle around the ankle, a few red drops falling to the floor. By the last leg, she'd gotten the hang of how much pressure to apply and cutting went faster.

Next, she carved out long red lines along the back of each leg. Those lines connected to the major incision in the center of the stomach, where she had pulled out Peanut's dinner. From there, it was like peeling off the outer layer of an onion. The skin stuck to the muscle and sinew beneath it but came up easily with a little applied pressure.

It stopped being easy once the leg skin was done. The front and back end of the deer were a bit more complicated. Jenny wasn't quite sure how to tackle the back end, so she started at the front. The buck's eyes were glassy and clouded. At some point, during the trek back to the cave, the buck had become an object to her. Not a former living creature. The glassy eyes might have been why. They looked like fake marbles attached to a trophy head that might be on a wall in some bar.

She cut an incision in the neck. The blade was so dull it took a lot of sawing back and forth to get through all the layers. A trickle of blood flowed out of the new wound. She hacked away at an incision around the neck, attempting to make a circle. When she came back around to the first incision, the lines didn't match up. She sucked her teeth, trying to figure out if this was a problem. After a moment, she decided whether it did matter, there wasn't much she could do now. A carved diagonal line brought the two ends together, forming a jagged red band around the neck.

From there, she hacked a line down the neck to meet the incision she'd made in the belly. Her hands ached. The dull blade made the work arduous. Nearly done. The only trouble now was the ass of the damn thing. Dread welled up in her chest.

Gross things sucked. It had taken her practically dying twice to soften her feelings in this regard. She knew that who she was before the forest wouldn't recognize the young bald woman kneeling over a deer with a dull knife. In some strange way she felt proud of that. Still, dealing with the ass-end of a dear grossed her out. That was her old self coming out again.

Jenny pushed the feelings away. With a firm grip on the knife she shifted toward the lower half, mapping out the strategy in her head. Start with the incision she already made, trace it back further to the bum hole. Cut that all away, maybe save the tail, and then start peeling. Seemed simple enough.

The first obstacle was the tool kit that made this buck a male. After cutting from the belly southward, she met this little furry obstruction and had no clue what to do with it. Not wanting to emasculate the poor guy, she cut around it. At least his manhood would remain intact.

Moving southward was harder than she expected. Her knife was so dull she had to saw back and forth like cutting through a tree. At one point she pushed, but it didn't cut. So she applied more pressure, and still nothing. Her cheeks were hot and she was getting frustrated. She put all of her bodyweight into it and pushed as hard as she could until something popped. Before she could think about the weird sound, a stream of cold shit shot out of the deer and hit her in the face.

CHAPTER TWENTY-TWO

Jenny smashed through the ice with a rock and plunged her head face-first into the freezing river. It nearly took her breath away. Her skin tingled with pins and needles and her nose started to go numb. She used both of her hands to scrub the deer poop off her face. Her entire body was shivering by the time she was done. It felt like no amount of icy water would be enough to feel clean again. She had never wanted a warm shower more than this moment.

As she walked back to the cave, the sequence of events flashed through her head like a stop-motion animation. First the knife getting stuck, then the strange pop, then the explosion of cold shit, then she vomited all over her pants. If Peanut could laugh, he would be laughing at her misery right now.

The inside of the cave was exactly how she'd left it: Peanut sleeping away in the corner, his dinner gone, all her stuff where it should be, and a poop-covered deer carcass laying by the tanning rack.

"Great," Jenny said. "Just... Great." She sighed.

She was as clean as she was going to get, so back to work. Freezing to death wasn't how she wanted to go. It was November which meant the possibility of below-zero nights. Her warm river stones could only do so much. The deerskin would be the perfect blanket to keep her warm.

What came next was like watching herself in third person. Clear the mind, establish the objectives, move from one task to the next. She threw some more kindling into the fire under the shelter in front of the cave and set to work.

The shit-covered deerskin needed cleaning. Clear objective. It was coating the back half of the fur she would use to make into a blanket.

She grabbed the bucket of river water and dumped it on top but quickly realized her mistake. Now there was a small pool of water on the floor of her home.

She dragged the deer carcass outside, just past the fire. She grabbed some snow and scrubbed the fur. Not great, but at least not inside. When her hands got too cold, she warmed them up by the fire. Back and forth she worked until the fur was as clean as it would get. Then she dragged it back inside.

Jenny sighed. Another late night in a long line of late nights. Exhaustion begged her to just put it all off one more day and sleep. But she knew she couldn't do that.

She flicked open her knife. It was dirty, and she couldn't see herself in the reflection of the blade. She pushed the tip into where she'd left off, and slowly cut away toward the tail, curving around the not-so-glamorous areas. *Disgusting.*

With aching hands, the cuts were completed, so she peeled off the rest of the skin. Some spots were more difficult, partially frozen, so she used the knife to cut away the bits that clung to the fur. She pulled the fur away from the carcass and smiled. Nearly done. With the pelt finally in hand, she stretched it out on the tanning rack, tying the four legs to the corners of the rack until it was all taut. It looked like a bad rug she had seen at Ikea.

The pink-and-red carcass that remained had a strange sense of fakeness to it. Like it didn't ever exist as a living breathing creature. Speaking of, what the to do with the head? Would Peanut eat it? Worth a shot. With her knife she sawed at the meat and cut through the bone. When she was finished, she picked up the deer head and turned it to face her.

"Sorry, buddy. No hard feelings."

She tossed it back toward Peanut and hoped it would be gone in the morning.

Her legs were stiff and the dull knife felt heavy in her hands. She desperately wanted sleep but pushed on. With her little knife she cut away slab after slab of thick red meat. The buck was young, but not without some muscle. When there wasn't much left to the carcass besides bone, she stopped.

Her eyes blinked long and slow. Her hand felt stiff from holding the knife. She flexed it, open, closed. Open. Closed. She caught herself staring mindlessly into the distance. She shook her head and took a quick breath. *Not done yet.*

She hopped to her feet and grabbed some sticks from the fire pile.

Outside, a few feet down from the cave entrance, she started another fire. It had to be big, so she took a few trips to the cave, until the flames reached as high as her shoulder. Not wasting any time, she dashed into the cave, grabbed a dozen sticks in one arm, and a few slabs of meat with the other. After this, she could finally rest.

Once she had everything by the fire, she started making deer meat kababs. She sliced off chunks of meat with her knife and did the same procedure she'd been doing since the fish all that time ago. Soon, all of the deer meat stood roasting on multiple sticks in a large meat circle around the fire. Jenny stepped back and took in her achievement.

After a short time, she started the process of orbiting around the meat circle to rotate every stick. Pink juices dripped onto the snow below, creating a pleasant-smelling steam. When she had finished with the last stick, it was time to rotate the first one again. She lost count of how many rounds she'd made. There wasn't anything else to do but this, and if she sat down she would fall asleep, so she pushed herself to keep going.

Once the meat was all cooked, she brought as much as she could carry into the cave. First, she stuffed her backpack full of meat. It filled up after one trip. Next, she piled the rest of the meat on top of her fire making supplies. It was high enough where Peanut couldn't reach it and eat it all. She could ration the meat out as long as he didn't get to it. It took two more trips to bring it all into the cave.

She dropped a few clumps of cooked meat next to Peanut. It would be a good late-night snack and breakfast for him. A brief bout of dizziness made the cave wobble. Jenny blinked hard, trying to steady herself. Time to wrap this up and sleep.

She threw snow on the fire, grabbed the stick of meat she had left behind, and took a big bite. The deer meat was incredible. It was smoky from the fire, but a richness unlike anything she had tasted. She ate the whole thing standing up, not pausing for anything except air.

A loud burp punctuated the meal. With the warm food settling in her belly, the desire to sleep overwhelmed her. She grabbed her hoodie off the cave floor, threw it on, and collapsed next to Peanut. It felt comforting to be next to him after two days away. She drifted off into a deep, dreamless sleep.

CHAPTER TWENTY-THREE

The deer hide ended up being an extremely warm blanket. It had taken several days to dry out to a point where she felt comfortable wrapping it around herself. She knew that if a hunter saw it, they would probably laugh at her crappy attempt to tan the hide. It was good enough to keep her warm and that's all she needed. Despite multiple trips to the river it was still flecked with blood and feces., but it had a rich, earthy smell to it, which Jenny found comforting in an odd way. It kept her so warm that she didn't need to sleep in the hoodie, which felt like a luxury.

A week after returning from the deer hunt, early in the morning, Jenny found that the food supplies running low again. Jenny had been rationing the deer meat to make sure that Peanut got the bulk of the calories. It bought them a week, and Peanut even seemed to have more energy than usual. Squirrels and rabbits simply weren't enough to get him ready for hibernation. She would need another large kill to buy more time, which meant preparing for another hunt.

Fear and worry clouded her thoughts.

"How am I going to another deer when this one had been so hard to track in the first place?" She said to Peanut. He huffed back in response, and she clicked her teeth at him.

She spent the day prepping for another long hunt: Making hot rock water, preparing the spear, cleaning up the cave a bit, restocking fire supplies, and fixing up her snow shoes. That night she packed her bags, stowing away enough meat for two days. The rest she gave to Peanut. Hopefully he could survive another few days without her. She wrapped herself in the warm deer skin and slept soundly.

Early the next morning, she drank a full mug of hot-rock water, refilled the water bottle right away, gave Peanut a grunt goodbye, and left the cave without looking back. It was not easy, but looking back would make it even harder. They had been through a lot together, and it broke her heart to leave him there alone, injured and vulnerable.

She hiked up Virginia's Way toward the river. It was another cold morning but the sun was shining. The air was still and the silence was deafening. The only sound was her rabbit-fur Jordan snow shoes and the spear she used as a walking stick, crunching into the snow. Her breath was visible, and the cold air froze the hairs inside her nostrils.

The forest seemed livelier at the river. The muted sound of water running below the ice added to the postcard scene before her. A perfect layer of snow, untouched by any living creature, coated the shoreline. The frozen river sparkled as the sun reflected off its surface like the reflection of a mirror.

A foggy memory from a science class told her that somehow the sun and the stars could orient you to true North, like on a compass, but she didn't remember how that worked. This was a problem, because she needed to eventually figure out how to find South so she could escape back to civilization, while Peanut was hibernating. She knew that they had taken the bus North, away from the Bronx, so the city had to be roughly south of where she was.

After Jenny walked for a bit, she came upon a familiar location and decided this would be a good place to start the hunt. Two tall pine trees reminded her of the journey to find the spear. She walked through it, pushing aside some dead underbrush, looked ahead, and saw the familiar branches of the old maple. Its beautiful red leaves were long gone, but the bones of the tree were still there. She stood at its base and looked up. It was from this tree that she had cut her spear. Toward the top, the scarred stump of a branch jutted out and her grip on the spear tightened a little. It was a proud memory for her.

With practiced ease, she climbed halfway up the tree and found a solid branch to sit on. The plan was to wait and see if anything walked through this area. *Just like fishing,* she thought. *Sit and wait.*

The quiet morning was peaceful. Sitting in the tree and staring down at the world below was strangely relaxing. The only sound was her breath, so she held it and enjoyed absolute silence. For as long as she lived, she would remember this active sound of nothing. It felt otherworldly, and yet comforting. After counting to thirty, she exhaled.

Jenny hadn't thought about her "day of arrival" in weeks, mostly because she didn't want to. In moments like this, when she was sitting, waiting, her mind always wandered back to the push. Without fail.

Almost like a curse. Eric's face full of anger and hatred intruded her mind. Then she remembered the terrifying feeling of falling. Her heart rate jumped and it felt like the start of a panic attack. She had run through this memory so many times, she had come up with a script of what she would say to him if she ever saw him again.

"Hello, Eric," she would say, most likely catching him off guard.

"Oh. Hi, Jenny," he would say back. Probably try to act innocent.

This next part, Jenny had been working on for a while. She would deliver it cold, without emotion.

"You tried to kill me. I will never forgive you for that. You're a terrible person and don't deserve to live on this planet."

Then she would take her knife and cut his throat before he could respond. In one version, Jenny had her spear in hand and stabbed Eric through the heart with it. The best version, and most impractical, involved Peanut chasing him down the hallway at their high school, and mauling him outside of Mr. Blumfit's classroom. Running through the scene in her head, she felt her heart rate settle down. That feeling of panic went away.

Jenny knew she could make it back to civilization. She had survived long enough out here on her own that she felt confident in her skills to mount an expedition south. But she couldn't leave Peanut here, not while he needed her. Despite the bad times, she felt proud of how well she had faired thus far. There was almost some small part of her that enjoyed living out here, away from the hustle and bustle, surviving solely off the land. No way in hell Eric would survive out here. That stuck up rich kid would be long dead by now.

The biggest thing she missed was her father, so much so she had to stop talking to "imaginary" him. The reminder became too much to feel. He probably thought she was dead. It had been weeks since she disappeared, and anyone looking for her would have stopped long before the first snow. If she could just contact him, let him know she was okay, it would make surviving the winter much easier.

What confused her, though, was that the helicopter never came back. She had been so close to escaping. The helicopter had hovered right over the cliff above the cave. But she couldn't run out because she needed to stop Peanut from bleeding to death. They saw her signal fire, but why didn't they come back? A small part of her mind blamed her dad. If he was the man she thought he was, he would have insisted they go back the moment they saw the fire. Something about the Woods Stubbornness mandated returning at least once. Why didn't he make them come back for her?

Up ahead, behind a tree line, a twig snapped. Her back stiffened and she stared ahead to track any movement. The brown colors of the trees and dead undergrowth blended together.

There was some movement, but it was small. Could be a squirrel or rabbit. Her eyes were on bigger prizes today. According to the math, if a small buck could last her and Peanut a week, she only needed four more to get them through to hibernation season. She guessed in about a month, in December Peanut would have to start hibernating, but without knowing the process it was just a guess in the dark. She made a mental note to do some research on this when she returned to civilization.

Morning gave way to the afternoon and sunlight lit up the forest. It was a clear day, few clouds in the sky. The snow sparkled like a smooth sheet of crystals. The stillness of the world felt ghostly. Her muscles had grown stiff, so she decided it was time to move to a new spot. This one wasn't having any luck.

Jenny dropped her spear, climbed swiftly down the tree, and snatched it up again from the snow. Wandering in the unfamiliar parts of the forest increased her risk of getting lost. She decided to walk back to the river. That was her north, the guide that gave her direction. If she could find the river, she could always find her way home.

Once she reached the river, she tested out the ice with her spear. It seemed solid enough. With some trepidation, she walked out onto the ice. It creaked under each step. It wasn't the fear of falling that made her hesitate—the water was shallow enough—it was trying to hunt while she was soaked in ice water and freezing to death. Falling in would mean going back to the cave to dry off, and she couldn't afford to start over.

She shuffled across to the other bank of the river, using her spear to balance. The rabbit fur didn't give much traction on the smooth surface. Less than five feet from the shoreline, she lost her footing and fell to one knee. The ice cracked under the impact of her weight. She dashed forward into the snow bank and landed face-first with a soft thud.

Jenny hopped to her feet and walked upstream, munching on a cold chunk of cooked deer meat. When it started to get dark, she stopped and surveyed her surroundings. A large sheet of stone peeked out of the ground and cut into the river. Ahead of her, a series of large rocks stacked on top of each other were completely encased in ice. In the warmer months, this area would probably be a series of small waterfalls crashing against the surrounding granite.

To her left, one of the large stone shelves looked ice-free and led deeper into the forest. It was hard to see ahead, the shade from the surrounding trees cutting out the already minimal light.

"Need to make camp for the night soon. Not much sunlight left in the day. Someplace quiet, out of the way should do."

She walked across the large stone shelf and found that it led quite a way into the forest. The trees here were skinny and gray. The stone shelf gave way to a more slanted rock patch, with thin sheets of rock layered one on top of the other. There was no path into the forest here, only the rock path ahead that eventually bent up at a steep angle and around a corner out sight. A large dead white pine stood at the bend in the path, its scraggly roots sticking up out of the ground.

Jenny slowly climbed the steep sheets of rock, trying not to fall. At the dead white tree, the path bent around to the right, and up ahead, she could see a huge stone wall at least twenty feet high, with a narrow path leading to the top. A large boulder at the bottom created a step as tall as she was, and above that was a steep but climbable incline. With some work, she could make it to the top; and it was above the tree line, so she would have a fantastic view of the ground below when the sun came out. Could be a promising place to camp.

She slipped off the rabbit's fur around her shoes and took the laces out. Traction was more important than warmth right now, and her old beat-up Jordans still had some useful rubber on the bottom. With the rabbit furs tucked away in her backpack, she laced up her Jordans.

After both shoes were tied, she walked up to the large step-like boulder. She tossed her backpack and spear onto the flat surface above and hooked her hands on the edge. Her arms cried out as she pulled herself up, but she pushed through it. Even without the backpack, the furs added some weight. When her chin was above the edge, she swung her leg up and over, using the leverage to pull the rest of her body up. She snagged her backpack, fastened it tightly around her shoulders, and slid the spear underneath it so that she didn't need to carry it. Now that she was closer, the climbable incline didn't seem as climbable as she first thought.

At her feet was a series of small stone slabs, and at eye level was a rockface bulging outwards and continuing up. It was smooth as a cue ball, apart from one small indent that cut across the bulge like a scar. She stepped onto the small stone slab and stretched her hands up, feeling around for a finger hold. Her face pressed against the cold rockface, but she didn't find anything solid to grab on to.

Jenny stood back and stared at the cue ball boulder.

"How do I climb you rock? Tell me your secrets."

She put her hands against the small indent. It was at chest level and had some solid finger holds. She stretched her right foot as high as it would go and placed her toes at the low end of the indent. She pushed off the ground with her left foot, and used her right to push herself above the bulge. She felt around the surface for a finger hold but didn't find anything to pull herself up. Her toes started to cramp, and she felt herself slipping downward. She frantically felt around the top of the boulder. Her right hand brushed against a small fingerhold, but not soon enough, and she lost her footing and fell backward.

"Found your secret."

She looked for a flat surface above to toss her backpack and spear, not wanting to put her spear at risk again, but found nothing. She placed her foot in the indent, gave herself a few practice hops, and then pushed up hard with every ounce of strength. Her right hand felt for the fingerhold she'd found earlier and gripped it. It was so small she could only fit three fingers in it. Her left foot searched for a hold in the indent but failed to find one.

"Come on rock, you really going to make me do this the hard way?"

Her strength was failing, so she pulled up hard with everything she could muster, fingers screaming out in pain, carrying her full weight and the backpack. She swung her left leg around the boulder, the rubber of her shoes catching against the stone surface, and managed to pull herself up onto the top of the boulder.

She stood up and flexed her right hand. It hurt. She steadied her breathing and continued upward. The path ahead was steep, but there wasn't any more rock climbing as far as she could see, and the top of the rock wall was just ahead. A few small saplings had tried to grow on this path, but they all looked dead in the snow. She pushed through a thick bunch of trees into a wide open clearing and the sight stunned her.

"Wow."

Tall white-and-green mountains covered the horizon in the distance. Snow-coated trees covered every inch of the hills, and they looked tiny from a distance. The last of the sunlight gave it all a bluish glow.

Before she could take it all in, the sound of Velcro ripping to her left startled her. The spear was in her hand instantly, and she turned to face the noise. A bright blue dome stood in the snow. A middle-aged woman with long curly hair popped her head out from the tent flap.

"Oh, hi," the woman said. "You scared the hell out of me. Nice spear."

CHAPTER TWENTY-FOUR

Jenny didn't move. This didn't feel real. It had to be a dream. Her mind struggled to process the human face before her. It had been so long since she had seen one. Her grip tightened around the spear. The woman in the tent stared at her.

"Is . . . everything okay?" the woman said.

"What's your name?"

"What's *your* name?"

"I asked first," Jenny spat back.

"I was here first."

Jenny looked down at the spear, and then back at her.

"I have a spear."

"Fair point. My name is Rebekah, with a K."

"Jenny."

"Good to meet you, Jenny. Nice animal skins, are you cosplaying or something? You look familiar. Do I know you?"

"No."

"I don't really like how you're pointing that spear at me, Jenny. Mind pointing it somewhere else?"

"Why are you here?"

"I'm allowed to be here. I'm minding my business. You should try it, instead of threatening people."

Jenny flipped the spear into her left hand, so that the point was facing upward, and walked up to Rebekah, extending her right hand.

"Sorry. Can't be too careful. Pleased to meet you." Jenny extended her hand, and Rebekah shook it, but stayed in her tent. "I'm hiking."

"It's late to be hiking, isn't it?"

"Yes. It is."

"Well, Jenny, I can't say this conversation has been particularly engaging. Do you want something? Or can I go back into my tent?"

"Uh . . . can you talk for a bit?"

"Why should I talk the strange woman covered in dead animal skins, who pointed a spear at me?"

"I didn't know who you were."

"So, your first thought was to threaten me? Not helping your case, Jenny."

"Fine." Jenny turned to walk away.

"Wait. I'll talk. Just let me throw on some warmer clothes. Want some tea?"

Jenny paused and turned back. "You have no idea."

Tea and another human being. This had to be a dream. Her mind struggled to process this unexpected turn of events. She felt bad about pointing the spear at her, but now she had thoughts racing through her head. Rebekah might know a way out of here. What about Peanut? Does Rebekah know about Jenny's class field trip, and if anyone got in trouble? If they were still searching, or when they gave up? A thousand questions to ask. While Rebekah got dressed, Jenny built a small fire near the tent. Spear close by, Jenny sat down next to the fire and let the heat warm her face. Rebekah emerged from the tent in a thick green flannel shirt.

"Nice fire. How'd you start it?"

"Flint and a pocketknife."

"Wow, that's really impressive."

"Thanks."

Rebekah took out an aluminum camping teapot. In the light of the fire, Jenny could see her features more clearly. She had a long curly hair that fell past her shoulders and bright blue eyes. There were a few wrinkles in the corner of her mouth from smiling. When Rebekah pulled out a Ziplock bag stuffed with tea bags, Jenny's jaw nearly hit the ground. Rebekah put snow into the teapot, along with two tea bags, and put it right into the fire. It struck Jenny that Rebekah could be homeless, living out here because she had nowhere else to go.

"I haven't had tea in a while," Jenny said.

"I know you, Jenny. Your hair looks different, and you seem like you haven't had a proper shower in a while, so it took a moment to remember, but I recognize you from that photo they put on the news. You're the girl that everyone thought died out here, aren't you?"

She said it so casually. Everyone thought Jenny was dead. It all clicked together. No more search parties, no one wondering where she was, they all thought she was dead. Did her father think so too? It seemed impossible to believe, but maybe he did.

"Yeah. That's me."

"So . . . are you hiding from someone?"

"Can I ask some questions?"

"Ask away, Jenny. But then I get to ask some more questions."

"Deal. How long did they look for me?"

"About a week."

"You said I was on the news?"

"Oh yeah. Big time. National news coverage for about a week. Then they moved onto the next thing."

"I can't believe they just gave up."

"So, did you fake the suicide? Was it to get away from someone? You owe some money?"

The air went out of her lungs. Jenny felt anger bubble up in her chest. "What are you talking about? I didn't fake anything. I would never do that."

"That's not what your best friend said."

"What are you talking about?"

"I think his name was Eric."

Jenny jumped to her feet. Instantly, all she felt was rage. It was like she had been transported into some evil alternate universe.

"What the hell are you talking about? Eric is not my friend."

"Well, Eric went onto *Good Morning America* claiming to be your best friend, and said that you had been acting weird on the hiking trip. Evidently, you told him that you were depressed and then you threw yourself off a cliff. He tried to stop you, but it was too late. They searched for your body to confirm, but never found it."

Rage gripped her, rushing through her veins. She was beyond upset, beyond outraged. It was clear to her in that moment that Eric had to be a sociopath. Logan might be worse because he knew it was wrong and stayed silent. Eric knew what happened and lied to the world about it. Her father gave up because he thought she gave up.

"Eric is not my best friend. Far from it. He pushed me, trying to kill me, and lied about it all. About everything. I'm going to kill him!"

"Woah, woah," was all Rebekah could squeak out. "Don't shoot the messenger. I'm sorry that happened. You've been out here alone this entire time? How did you survive?"

Jenny sat down by the fire and told her everything, from the moment she'd stepped off the bus until now. Everything except Peanut. Her gut told her that Rebekah wouldn't understand. The entire time Jenny talked,

Rebekah listened. It felt good to talk, to have someone to talk to. To share a connection. Midway through the story, Rebekah pulled out two blue tin mugs. She picked up the teapot in a gloved hand, poured the tea into a mug, and handed it to Jenny.

She took it and watched the steam rise in a thin white trail. The warm, earthy aroma filled her senses. By the time she was done, her voice was sore from all the talking, but the tea helped.

"It's been so long since I've had tea. Thank you."

"Incredible what you've managed to do, you know. Survive out here this long. Most people starve to death."

"I can't believe Eric would lie about me like that on national television."

"You can't?"

"True, he's privileged guy, used to getting what he wants."

"That's not what I mean."

"What do you mean?"

"Well, first, Jenny, let me tell you what I see. You're a privileged young woman who . . ."

"Excuse me. Privileged?" Jenny interrupted, nearly spilling her tea at the audacity.

"You go to one of the best private schools in the Bronx, plus AirPods, Jordans, the newest iPhone."

"I'm a Latina in America. Need I say more?"

"How much money does your dad make?"

"What does that matter? Are you really going to lecture me on privilege?"

"I let you speak. Want to let me finish what I was trying to say?"

"Fine." Jenny crossed her arms.

"This conflict with Eric started with AirPods. Expensive, but also just headphones. What did you do when he tossed them out of the window? Escalate the situation by lying to Eric about that viral video. You lied about it to inflict pain. Here is my first question for you to think about: Why did you want to make Eric feel pain? And further, what did you think it would get you? Let's fast-forward a bit. You're free, you get out of here, and you confront Eric and kill him? What does that get you?"

"Whatever point you're trying to make, it's not working."

"Answering pain by inflicting more pain only begets further pain."

"Oh, so the classic eye for an eye and the whole world goes blind crap. Got it. So, I just let Eric get away with attempted murder."

"Did I say that?"

"Isn't that what you are implying?"

"Hell no, Jenny. I want to be very clear here: What Eric did is abhorrent. Hurting you and then lying about it. He sounds like a repulsive, repugnant, hateful young man. You said you can't believe he could do it."

"Ok. Fine."

"Part of you knew that inflicting this pain would cause him to react. Did you seriously think he wouldn't?"

"You're saying I shouldn't have intentionally tried to hurt him."

"I'm saying if you provoke a bear, you'll get mauled."

The analogy was too on the nose for Jenny to handle.

"Sure, whatever. So what do I do with this anger I feel towards him? It's not fair he treated me this way."

"Forgive him."

"Then he gets away with it."

"That already happened, Jenny. He caused the pain and he hurt you. But now? You are the one who is hurting you. You're out here all on your own surviving. Hell, thriving, yet holding onto so much hate and anger. Why? It's going to warp you. It may have already. This anger, this feeling of revenge, it doesn't hurt Eric. It only hurts you. It lives in you like a parasite, stealing your joy. It's like you're taking poison hoping it will hurt him."

"What about justice? Is there no such thing as justice in your point of view?"

"Justice and peace are two different things. Plus, you should know that true justice is rare."

"So, give up on justice, and just forgive him, move on, and let him get away with it."

"The truth about Eric will come out, Jenny. It may take much longer than you want, and you may never see it, but the truth always manifests itself."

"Such wise words from a homeless looking woman." Jenny said the words before her mind could stop them. Rebekah's blue eyes winced from the painful insult. It was clear Jenny had hurt her, but she was boiling over with so much anger it didn't matter. Jenny stood up and grabbed her spear.

"Jenny, wait."

"I'm sorry. I have to go. Thank you for the tea."

Jenny wanted to get away and clear her head. The guilt of saying those words was almost too much to bear right now. She turned and tried to walk away, but Rebekah had sprung up and grabbed her wrist.

"Please, Jenny, wait."

"Let go!" Jenny felt another flash of anger and swung the spear upward. It connected with Rebekah's wrist, and she flailed her arms, falling backward onto the snow-covered ground. Rebekah's blue eyes opened wide with a look of pure fear. A horrible thought crossed Jenny's mind: she could just kill Rebekah right here and now. Take her gear, and no one would ever know. Fear and adrenaline were pumping through her veins now. No one would miss this homeless person. Jenny wanted badly to do it, to focus all her rage against this woman on the ground. A little push into her throat with the point of her spear and it would be over. Then Jenny would have a tent and a teapot. The world wouldn't notice. This feeling of pure power over another human felt good. Briefly. Disgust and guilt came quickly after it. Jenny didn't feel like herself. Worse, it felt like it affirmed what Rebekah said about Jenny.

Jenny's hands started to shake. *What just happened?* she thought to herself. *Was I really considering killing this woman? Did I like that feeling?* She looked into her blue eyes and saw fear. Jenny dropped the spear and fell to the ground. Confusion and adrenaline swirled around inside her mind. She couldn't erase Rebekah's look of fear from her mind. That rush of raw power she'd felt scared her. Complete control over another human's life felt sickeningly powerful. All she wanted to do now was puke. Killing people isn't who she was. Tears blurred her vision. Who was she becoming? Jenny knew there was some sick part of her that would have enjoyed the power trip. That's not who she wanted to be.

"I'm sorry. I need to go," Jenny said. Rebekah didn't move. Jenny stood up, and before she could take a few steps, she heard a sound behind her.

"Wait, please." Rebekah said.

"I have to go."

"Don't you want to go home? I can help you."

"I don't need anyone to save me."

"I can send help."

"I can save myself."

"At least let me give you something. To help."

"I can't take anything from you."

"I know, but take this."

Jenny turned. Rebekah was holding out the teapot and baggie of tea bags. "It wouldn't feel right, letting you go without this. You need it more than I do."

"I hurt you."

"No, the hate and anger you are holding onto hurt me. I don't think Jenny is the kind of person who would do that. But hate can turn anyone violent."

"Why are you helping me?"

"A great man once said that darkness cannot drive out darkness; only light can do that. Hate cannot drive out hate; only love can do that. You have been greatly wronged, Jenny, forced to be in this situation against your will, and yet you thrive. The justice system may or may not punish Eric for what he has done, but don't expect the justice system to heal your pain. You will be disappointed. You must find a way to forgive Eric for what he did. Not for him, but for yourself. That forgiveness will release this anger that has its hold on you. Trust me. Or else you will be forever changed by holding onto that hate."

Forgive Eric. For weeks, Jenny fantasized about all the different ways she would kill him. Yet Rebekah was telling her to forgive. It seemed impossible to even comprehend.

"I . . . I don't know." She took the tea and teapot and put them in her backpack. As she zipped it up, Rebekah held up a finger.

"Wait, one more thing." She stuck her head into her tent and quickly popped back out. She held a small, round metal object in her hand and extended it toward Jenny.

"What's this?"

"A compass." Rebekah popped it open. Inside, a red-and-white needle slowly moved around until it pointed north.

"Won't you need this to get back?"

"If you follow it south, at this degree"— she pointed to a small millimeter-sized mark—"you will eventually find a small town. From there, you can find your way home."

"I don't deserve this, Rebekah."

"Everyone deserves compassion. Compassion is what separates us from the animals. Which side will you choose?"

"I'm so sorry, Rebekah. For everything . . . Goodbye."

"Goodbye, Jenny Woods."

Jenny picked up her spear, turned, and walked away without looking back. Carefully, she retraced her steps back down the rockface, and across the stone path until she was at the frozen river. Guided only by moonlight, she crossed the icy terrain and found a small place near the trunk of a tree to settle. She fell to her knees, dropped her spear, and started sobbing.

CHAPTER TWENTY-FIVE

For the first time in years, Jenny dreamt of her mother. They were sitting at a kitchen table in a room that seemed unfamiliar. Her mother was talking but she couldn't understand the words. She tried rubbing her ears but that only made it worse. Then her vision started to blur. She blinked hard to focus but suddenly she grew bigger. Like *Alice's Adventures in Wonderland*, growing nine feet in the blink of an eye, but her mother didn't seem to notice. A strong feeling of vertigo made the room seem like it was spinning.

When she woke up, the world was spinning. She felt nauseous and cold. The tree she was sleeping against was stiff, the sun hidden behind clouds painting the morning gray. Jenny got to her feet as her stiff muscles protested.

As she folded the deerskin blanket, she thought about one of the few positive memories she had of her mom. They were going to spend some time together on a random Saturday, seeing a movie at the Magic Johnson movie theater in Harlem and grabbing a bite to eat after. Midway through the movie her period came, and Jenny remembered feeling extremely embarrassed and a bit confused. It was her first. Her father never really had the talk with her. Luckily, her mom was prepared and took her to the bathroom. She showed her how to use the pad, how to make sure it stayed in place—thankfully, the problem was solved before it could get worse. They went back to the movie and had a wonderful dinner together after.

Reflecting on that moment sparked a new realization in Jenny's mind, she hadn't had her period yet. She did some rough math in her head, and concluded it should have happened two weeks ago. The lack of food plus all the stress had to be the explanation..

Thinking about her mom reminded her how isolated and alone she felt right now. Even seeing her mom would be a welcome relief. Rebekah's blue eyes flashed in her mind. Disgust was the only word Jenny could use to describe how she felt about her actions toward this woman. That moment of pure rage, where Jenny felt like killing the woman simply because she challenged Jenny's views, was something she would never forget. Forgiving Eric seemed impossible, so Jenny pushed the thought away.

"Hey mom. I know we don't talk as much as we should. I think I need you right now. Are you worried about me? Have you reached out to Dad?" The trees gave a slight rustle in response. Jenny resolved to reconnect with her mother if she had the chance.

No matter how she looked at the situation in her mind, it all pointed to the same conclusion: head to the cave and figure out the next steps. Process what happened. Make a plan. But could she afford coming home empty-handed?

Jenny's feet were ice cold, and when she looked down she realized she still hadn't put the rabbit fur back on her shoes. She removed her shoelaces and grabbed the rabbit's fur from her backpack. Lacing the rabbit's fur with numb fingers was slow business. Her shoes looked beat up and worn down. When she got out of here, and got Peanut help, she would get a brand-new pair of Jordans.

As she came out from under the tree, she followed the stone path back down to the frozen river. The path home was near. She needed to get moving. She started off, heading downstream, staying to the left bank of the river.

As she was walking and reflecting, the compass came to mind. She took it from her pocket and looked at it. The needle inside the little metal circle was lazily spinning between south and east, shifting with each step she took. When she stopped walking, it settled on one point. Turns out the path back to the cave faced southeast.

At midday, when the sun was high in the sky and the shadows were at their smallest, she found a log to rest on. Her mouth was dry and her stomach was rumbling. She took a swig of water and gnawed on a chunk of deer meat.

The previous evening felt unreal, almost like a dream about someone else. The look in Rebekah's eyes after Jenny had knocked her to the ground would haunt her for a long time. That desire to kill her, the adrenaline and excitement she'd felt, made her sick.

Right now, everyone thought that not only was she dead, but that she had killed herself. Yet Rebekah said she needed to forgive Eric, who went on national TV and lied about her. What was her father thinking right now? What would he do?

Anger bubbled up inside her. Her chest tightened and she started to hyperventilate. The thought of Eric sent her spiraling into a familiar circle of hatred and jealousy. He always got what he wanted, even if it was to get away with attempted murder.

"How am I supposed to just forgive? It doesn't make any sense."

Jenny wished she'd asked Rebekah more about forgiveness. Does it mean letting Eric get away with this? That didn't seem fair at all. Why should he be allowed another free pass?

The hate and anger overwhelmed her, so she forced herself to stop thinking about it. Instead, she took in the beauty of the forest. It was quiet. The aches and groans of trees shifting far off in the distance added to the silence like soft background music. Her heart rate slowed, and calmness washed over her.

During the time she'd been here, she had found a new respect for nature. It was a harsh, unforgiving place that punished every mistake. If you weren't careful you could wind up dead. There was beauty in the struggle. It was refining, like a crucible to metal ore, and the creatures that succeeded in this environment were stronger for it. Jenny wondered what returning would be like. The girl who fell into this forest was shy and timid, afraid of many things. Who would be the woman that walked out?

Peanut needed her, so leaving was off the table until he was strong enough for hibernation. Not to say the idea of leaving wasn't tempting. She struggled every day to justify staying. The hardest question to answer was that of her own safety: At what point would it be ridiculous to endanger her life for Peanut's?

Her stomach growled, reminding her again that she was coming home to him empty-handed. Her mind began searching for other ways to find food, but she couldn't think of anything. No wonder bears hibernated. Finding food in the winter was difficult.

The forest around her shifted and changed as she wandered, lost in thought. Problems kept mounting. Her chest tightened as anxiety built in her mind. Food was low, she couldn't hunt for at least two days—preferably five—and yet through it all she couldn't get Rebekah's eyes out of her head. The way she looked at Jenny, after Jenny had knocked her to the ground. It was the same way the coyote looked at her. That's when it clicked in her mind: It was the look of fear toward a stronger beast. Had she become an animal and lost all empathy?

The sun was low in the sky when she arrived home. Standing outside the mouth of the cave, she looked at the orange sky above and knew it would be dark soon. Inside, things were how she'd left them. At the back of the cave, Peanut had curled into a small brown ball. He had a half-eaten rodent next to him. An unlucky animal that had wandered into the wrong cave.

Her hands brushed against his fur, and she felt him stir beneath her. When he popped his head up, he clicked his teeth. She clicked back at him. There was still light in his eyes. He was looking a bit more energetic. All the calories from the buck had been good for him. If only she had returned home with another one.

"Sorry, Peanut, no food. Bad hunt," she said.

In response, he yawned and rolled over to face her, looking into her eyes. They enjoyed each other's company for a while. She couldn't shake the gloomy cloud that had been hanging over her the entire day.

Jenny was shocked to watch as Peanut stood and wandered around the cave. His limp was painfully present, but he had an energy she hadn't seen in a while. He did a lap around the cave, sniffing and exploring, scratching at the ground as he pleased. It was like he was a different bear than the one she'd left in the cave. The broken one with thin ribs, a gaunt face, and a useless leg.

Then an idea crept into her mind. Slowly at first, and she rejected it outright because it was full of holes. Then she kept thinking about it, watching as Peanut hobbled around the cave. It seemed wild, but so was the current situation by any standard. If she was going to sit around a cave for five days, it could be a fun game thinking about it. Planning it. So, she said it out loud to see if it sounded as crazy as she thought it did.

"Peanut, want to come back to the Bronx with me?"

CHAPTER TWENTY-SIX

Peanut stared at Jenny. Of course, it sounded crazy. Could a bear and a woman walk hundreds of miles through harsh winter terrain and reach the Bronx? No way in hell. And yet, the thought excited her. This could solve all their problems. Peanut could visit a veterinarian that could fix his leg, she could see her father again, they could eat all the food they wanted—Oh God, she could take a warm shower.

Of course, a lot could go wrong. One, they would need to hunt food on the journey. How would hunting with Peanut work? Two, finding shelter every night, finding dry wood for fires, crossing dangerous terrain, staying warm—this would take a lot of luck. Plus, Peanut still had a limp, so that would slow them down. But if he could keep up this energy, then maybe they could make it. It struck her as odd that she was trying to convince herself that this plan would work.

Let's say it all worked out. Then what? There was no way Peanut could move in with her and her dad and stay in the backyard. Some law would probably dictate that he must be returned here. She decided not to focus on the after. It was too big to figure out.

Her hands were shaking with excitement. *Home.* The word had changed so much in the past few months. Yet her first home, the one she grew up in, could be hers again soon. She needed to sleep on this. Maybe there was something she wasn't seeing, and once she figured out what it was, her plan would fall from the sky like a popped balloon.

The deer skin was stiff from the cold. It crackled when Jenny unfolded it and wrapped it around her shoulders. It smelled rich and pungent, like sweat and leather. Her face was cold against the frozen air. Behind her, Peanut had laid back down and curled up. The aroma of fresh deer hide and stale unwashed-bear filled her nose. A weary smile spread across her face as she closed her eyes and dreamed of home.

A strong cramp in her leg brought Jenny out of her sleep. It came on slowly, so she tried to ignore it and fall back asleep. It grew until it was too much, so she opened her eyes and sat up, letting the deer skin fall away. Her entire body felt hot and damp. Taking deep breaths, she tried to force the cramp to pass. Eventually it went away, but she was wide awake now.

Outside, the morning was gray and gloomy, which either meant it was early in the morning, or it would be like this all day. Jenny hoped it was just early.

She desperately needed to clean herself but was dreading the ice-cold water. Once the river had frozen over and she'd cut off all her hair, she'd stopped caring about her personal hygiene. When she would catch a whiff of her body odor, it would rejuvenate her need to figure out a way to clean, but plans never materialized. It was hard to care about that when she and Peanut were slowly starving to death.

Today seemed like a good day to figure it out. She dreaded the cold water. Her eyes went wide and she scrambled for her backpack. How could she forget? She pulled out the teapot along with the tea bags and practically wept she was so happy. Not only would she be able to make hot tea, but she could also make hot water to clean her clothes and wash herself. The possibilities were endless.

Shame soon replaced the joy. The look of fear in Rebekah's eyes flashed in her mind. The memory of how, for a brief moment, she'd seriously considered taking an innocent woman's life. Some small part of her had enjoyed the power trip and she regretted it.

It only took a few minutes to get a fire going outside the cave. The teapot was sitting near the fire, slowly heating up. Her wooden mug already had a tea bag in it. She could hardly wait. When the water was hot enough, she grabbed the kettle with the cloth of her hoodie sleeve, careful not to burn her hand, and poured the hot water into the mug. Steam quickly rose from the water. She lightly blew on the tea and took a sip. It was heavenly and filled her with warmth.

Planning the trip gave her a sense of purpose. It was something to dream about, and she could obsess over the tiny details. Like which hot-rocks to bring, how much emergency fire supplies she should pack, and which pocket was the best one for quick knife access. Having purpose felt exciting.

Food was the constant issue. She had been ignoring the fact that her pants no longer fit. Her belt had to have some new notches carved out, because she had lost so much wait. The last time she looked under her shirt—and it had been more than a few weeks ago—her ribs were more visible than they had ever been. Even with hunting and fishing she had only caused the starvation to slow, with every bit of food only pushing back the inevitable. There simply hadn't been enough food, and eating a meat-only diet had adverse effects.

She needed to find food soon, and that meant hunting. Maybe she could find a squirrel or a rabbit, even though they were hard to catch. She needed pure calories now.

Once the tea was gone Jenny doused the fire with a few kicks of snow. She gathered up all of her supplies and crawled into the cave. Quiet snores were coming from the back. Jenny carefully stuffed her materials into the backpack, trying not to disturb Peanut, who needed to rest. She grabbed her spear, slipped on the rabbit's fur around her Jordans, and headed back outside.

Hunting around the cave had never yielded much. Jenny assumed animals had a sort of sixth sense when avoiding predators. They somehow knew she and Peanut were in the area, and so they avoided the cave. She climbed Virginia's Way and hiked toward the river. It was a quiet morning. The trees stood motionless in the frozen forest.

Jenny found a spot hidden behind some dead bushes where she could sit and watch the frozen river without being seen.

She sat still for hours, waiting and watching the world pass by. This small corner of the world was hers and she loved it. It was home. And for the first time, Jenny realized that when she left it—even if she came back—it would be different. It wouldn't be hers. The thought made her melancholy. She had grown attached to this place, the quiet woods and soft rolling river. It would be a beautiful place in the spring, teeming with life. Hopefully, once Peanut was all fixed up, he could return here.

Somewhere nearby, a twig snapped, and Jenny's senses went on high alert. Looking out over the river, she softened her focus, using her peripheral vision to try and spot movement.

A few feet away, near her side of the river, she spotted a furry brown animal, digging at something in the ground. It was too big to be a squirrel, but she wasn't exactly sure what it was. Didn't matter. It had meat, so that meant food. Moving slowly, she sat forward and inched out from behind the bushes.

Just like spearing fish, she figured approaching from behind was the best tactic. *Take advantage of the blind spot.*

Each step was a momentous amount of effort, slowly shifting her weight from one foot to the other, careful not to make a sound in the snow. When she was a few feet away, the animal popped its head up but didn't look behind. She took her spear in both hands and moved it forward. Two more steps and she was ready.

She sprang forward, thrusting her spear at the animal. The point struck between the shoulder blades and the poor creature let out a dying screech. Pinned beneath her spear, it kicked at the ground, trying to escape. She flicked open her knife and slit its throat. The kicking stopped.

Standing over the carcass, she recognized the animal for what it was: a beaver. She pictured Mr. Beaver from *The Lion, the Witch, and the Wardrobe*. He would probably be disappointed in her right now.

"Sorry, dude," she said back. "But I'm literally going to die if I don't eat you. Nothing personal."

What surprised her most was the beaver's tail. It had a strange texture that reminded her of leather shoes. It hardly seemed practical. Millions of years of evolution had led up to this tail, the primary feature for a beaver, and it looked like an old Italian shoe. Peanut would eat it, so it had its use.

Heavy white snowflakes began to fall around her. She looked up at the sky, now laden with gray clouds that slowly covered the sun. It almost seemed pleasant, the quiet snow falling to the ground. Like a painting that might hang in a museum. But as the clouds completely covered the sun, the world went gray and a cold wind cut through all of her layers. Jenny hurried back to the cave. A snowstorm was about to hit.

CHAPTER TWENTY-SEVEN

The blizzard lasted three days. High winds and thick snow battered the world outside the cave. Jenny spent most of the storm wrapped in the deer skin, reading *Starfish* for the millionth time, and ignoring hunger pains. The beaver managed to last them three days, but it was miserable rationing it out.

The first day she skinned it, gave Peanut all the guts, and roasted the edible meat. She ate only a few bites and found it to be hard, tacky, and flavorless. Not at all appetizing.

The second day a strong wind knocked over the shelter she had built over the cave entrance. The beaver meat remained remarkably unappetizing, so she only ate a few more bites and gave Peanut the tail, which in her mind was like bear-sized beef jerky. Unfortunately, Peanut's stomach didn't think the same. He puked the tail out after eating it. Then he started to lick at the vomit, which nearly made Jenny throw up.

The third day she didn't want to eat. The meat had become hard and cold. Without her shelter outside of the cave building a fire impossible, so she couldn't warm up the meat. But her stomach demanded substance. She tore off a few pieces of meat. Chewing them felt like chewing a rug. She tossed the rest of the beaver to Peanut, and he ate it all without remorse.

On the morning of the fourth day the world outside was quiet. Jenny woke slowly, her eyes working to adjust to the darkness. At first she thought it was still night, but near the mouth of the cave a tiny beam of sunlight streamed in through a white hole. It had snowed so much that it blocked the entire entrance to the cave. She scurried up to the wall of snow and cleared it out with her hands until they were numb. It fell into the cave like white sand.

As she peeked her head out, the forest was quiet and thick layer of snow coated everything. The sun shined bright and the sky was a brilliant shade of blue. She estimated that the snow was four feet high. There was no way she could crawl out of the cave. Somewhere buried underneath it all was the shelter she had built.

Today was supposed to be the day they set out to journey south toward civilization, but this snowfall looked to make that very difficult. They were out of food, and in rough shape, so it was either stay here and slowly rot, or look for home.

It took a few hours to clear out the snow at the mouth of the cave. She used the misshapen bucket to bring a load of snow into the cave and pile it near the fire-making supplies. Now that they were leaving, it didn't matter if the supplies got wet. When the entrance to the cave was clear, , she tossed the bucket into the cave, hoping never to see it again. Then she started a fire and put on some water for tea.

While it was heating up, she walked over to a tree and squatted against it to relieve herself.

The fire wasn't quite up and running yet, so she started packing. She slipped the flint into the front pocket of her backpack for quick access. *Starfish* went into the bottom of the main pocket, and the tea bags on top of it. She put in a few of the hot-rocks as well, as keepsakes. The little stones had saved her life and gave her clean drinking water for weeks. Worth holding on to, she figured. The rest of the backpack she filled with fire-making supplies. Dry wood would be important in the days to come. She left room for her mug and the tea kettle.

The spear needed sharpening, so she grabbed it and brought it out by the fire. The tea was warm, relaxing. Every sip spread warmth through her chest. Around her the forest felt still, the only sound her breathing. She closed her eyes, basking in the peaceful sound of nothing. She smiled to herself, because she knew once she was back in the city, she wouldn't be able to experience this level of quietness.

She opened her eyes and flicked open her knife. Shavings flew off as she sharpened the tip of her spear. It felt like sharpening a large, deadly pencil. This tool had helped her through so much. It was like a third arm. She remembered the first time she tried fishing. It was mostly stumbling around in the river. It was interesting, at some point, she couldn't place when, she had grown more relaxed with it. She stood up and rested the spear against the cave entrance.

Inside Peanut was stirring. A wave of panic and guilt washed over her. If things went badly on their journey for him, it would be her fault. She was leading Peanut away from his habitat. Sure, he might die here, malnourished and unable to hunt. But somehow this felt worse. Like she was endangering him without his consent.

It was time to leave. The sooner the better. They needed the daylight to make some progress. It was best to walk by day and find shelter at night. She didn't want to run into unsavory characters in the middle of the night.

She downed the rest of the tea from her mug and grabbed the cool tea kettle, bringing them both inside the cave. She looked around the cave one last time. This would probably be the last time she saw this place. Why did this make her feel so sad? Shouldn't going home feel better?

She stuffed the kettle and mug into the backpack, folded up the deer skin, and stuffed it on top. She pulled the coyote skin over her hoodie so that it rested on her shoulders, keeping her upper body warm. She made sure the compass and knife were in her front pockets for quick access.

This place had been her home. It had taken her and Peanut in when they needed it. They struggled and managed to carve out a life here. Grew to know every inch of this place.

"Come on, Peanut. Yip-yip."

He perked up his head and slowly trudged toward her. He rubbed his head against her thigh, and she scratched him back. Jenny left the cave followed by Peanut. Neither looked back.

Spear in hand, they set off, slowly hiking through the snow up Virginia's Way. The rabbit-fur covers for her Jordans kept her feet warm, but they added a lot of work. Each step sunk deep into the high piles of snow. Pulling her foot back out took a lot of effort. Behind her, Peanut didn't seem phased. He limped his way through her tracks.

By the time they reached the river, Jenny was breathing heavily. The snow was so thick near the shore it came up to her waist. Jenny took out the compass and watched the needle as it moved back and forth. Southeast was downstream. If what Rebekah said was true, the little marker on the compass was all she needed to follow, and eventually they would reach town.

Jenny paused, taking one last look. The river was a frozen sheet of ice. covered in snow. Behind it, acres of dead looking trees laden with snow. Even now she knew that her memory of this place would always be what she stumbled upon back in September. That picturesque, postcard-perfect image of a rushing river, with crystal-clear water rolling over multi-color stones. The green pine trees, the brown cedars and oaks with leaves that had been touched orange with a hint of fall. That feeling of the cool, crisp water against her skin. Upstream, Peanut with a fish in his mouth. That would be how she remembered this place, and it would always be her little part of the river. Someday, she would come back and take a picture of it.

Peanut's head popped above the snow, and he sniffed at the air. Jenny turned her back to the river and headed south, Peanut following behind. Each step in untouched snow was an exercise in caution. Without knowing what lay hidden beneath, she had to walk carefully to avoid stepping on a stray stick or rock. If she twisted her ankle, this would be an even more difficult journey.

The snow ahead looked like a thick white blanket, undisturbed. If you didn't know there was a river here, you could easily walk out onto the ice and fall below. Snow coated the branches of the trees, and one side of their trunks, uniformly.

They trudged along for hours. By the time the sun began to set, her feet ached from walking. Peanut's limp had grown worse. She worried the walk might be worsening his leg. But what concerned her most was that the river was starting to bend more eastward, which meant they would need to cross the river and walk through the forest on the other end if they wanted to stay headed in the right direction.

The riverbank did not offer much in the way of shelter. Thick, snow-covered fallen trees crisscrossed with tall living ones, making it impossible to navigate the shoreline. It would be best to find a clear, hidden place to create shelter for the night, but there wasn't anything to be found. So, either they set up camp here or journey into the forest on this side of the river and hope they found something.

Peanut found a spot near a tree that had broken in half. The top had fallen backward to the ground, but the stump still stood tall. He scratched his back against it.

"We'll camp here," Jenny decided. As if on cue, Peanut slumped and sat with his back against the tree. He stared out over the river, looking quite stately.

Jenny dropped her backpack and cleared the area around the tree stump. She moved the snow with her hands until they were numb, kicked out a dry patch of land, and snapped some dry bark from the dead tree for firewood. Peanut had wandered toward the tree line. Jenny kept an eye on him to make sure he didn't wander too far.

Using as little of her fire supplies as she could spare, she made a small pile of dried twigs and leaves. With practiced ease, she made a small fire. After slipping the knife and flint back into pants pocket, she peeled off another few strips of bark from the tree and added it to the fire. It was difficult to find wood that wasn't wet or covered in snow. She stripped the rest of the dry bark from the stump.

After she had enough wood to last a few hours, she sat near the fire and allowed herself to relax with some melted snow tea. With warm tea and a steady fire, the cold was more bearable. She hoped Peanut would lay next to her for warmth.

As the fire crackled, she pulled out *Starfish* and her deer skin blanket. Leaning against the stump, she wrapped the skin around her legs and opened to a random page. On her twelfth read a few weeks ago, it dawned on her that she and the main character of the book, Lenie Clarke, had a lot in common. They were both trapped in an unfamiliar world, both adapting to their environment, and both very lonely people. The difference that mattered most was that Jenny had Peanut. She guessed that without him, she would be dead by now.

The fire had grown low, so she tossed a few more strips of bark onto it. Orange sparks flew up to the sky. Peanut wandered back and walked cautiously around the fire, watching it closely.

Jenny had thought a lot about the first book she would read when she got home. At first, she wanted to read the sequel to *Starfish*, something she had meant to do for a while. Though, after reading *Starfish* so many times, it seemed criminal not to get into something new. Lenie Clarke would have to wait a while. She had no real desire to read any survival stories for a long time. There were two Stephen King books she had been thinking about reading but couldn't decide which to read first: *Cujo* or *The Shining*. Of course, there was the *Guns of August* too.

The sun had just fallen behind the horizon and the sky was darkening. Around her the river land glowed in a deep blue twilight. Peanut made his way toward Jenny. He sat down with a huff, curling up next to her.

She tossed the last pieces of bark into the fire. If they could get an early start tomorrow, they might be able to make more progress. But without food, they would struggle to find the energy to move forward, which meant stopping to hunt. Jenny wasn't sure how she would keep track of Peanut and hunt at the same time.

As her mind explored these problems, she lowered her head to her backpack she used as a pillow. The ground was cold and hard, but Peanut and the deer skin were warm. The stars in the night sky twinkled like millions of jewels on display. All around her the forest felt still and quiet, as if humbled in the sight of such grandeur.

CHAPTER TWENTY-EIGHT

Near the tree line, Jenny spotted two little glass disks reflecting the early morning sun. A small gray shadow appeared, and Jenny recognized the black bandit mask across its eyes. A raccoon. It sniffed around at the perimeter of their small camp, looking for food most likely. The river land around them was quiet. The only sound was Peanut snoring next to her. Most animals avoided the bear. This little racoon boldly defied those natural instincts. When Jenny moved her hand towards the spear, the raccoon dashed away.

At some point she fell asleep again. When she woke again her energy felt renewed and she stood ready to face the day. She adjusted the coyote fur around her shoulders, and packed up their makeshift camp. Together they continued the journey downstream.

Hunting was going to be tricky. As they walked together, Jenny wondered about the best way to hunt with a loud, injured bear at her side.

He was too large to hide, too loud to sneak, and too slow to help. Any way she looked at it: ball and chain. She couldn't hunt with him. But that wasn't what worried her. What worried her was the thought of losing him. He could wander off and never come back. Jenny couldn't part with him. Not yet. Not until she fixed his injured paw.

So that meant hunting with him. Or at least near him. Within eyesight. Was this how moms felt?

While she pondered this, she noticed the river had become both bigger and wider. The other side of the river was farther away than it had been yesterday. The thought briefly crossed her mind that now might be a good time to cross the iced over river, but it would really slow them down. Plus, the river could curve back south and then they would need to cross it again. Better to wait, she figured.

Something behind them brushed against a branch. Jenny gave Peanut a look, and dashed off into the thick tree line to chase the sound.

A flash of brown fur skirted under a fallen tree. Jenny sprinted after it and shifted the spear into her hand. She vaulted over the fallen tree, using her free hand to glide across. Not an ounce of momentum lost. The furry brown creature dashed ahead but stumbled over a stick and smashed against a tree.

As Jenny cornered it, the little brown ball of fur froze in spot, stunned in fear and disoriented from smashing into the tree. Jenny took advantage of the moment, planted her feet and, with two hands firmly around the spear, thrust it downward. She felt it crunch into the ground. Jenny looked at her spear and saw the small brown squirl impaled.

The squirrel twitched at the end of the spear, dead. The spear had blown a hole through its entire chest.

It wasn't much meat, but it would feed them. She swung around. Where was Peanut? She stuffed the squirrel into her backpack and set off to find him. Everything around her was unfamiliar. Her sense of direction was thrown off in this new environment. She pulled out the compass. This feeling of being lost was not one she'd had in a while.

The needle slowly spun until it pointed toward north. She turned until she was facing southeast. That was the direction the river was running.

"If I take a forty-five-degree left at the river, that means I'm running northwest," she said to herself. She turned around again. "If I go southwest that should lead me back."

With a direction in mind, she walked. After a while she started to jog. When she reached the fallen tree she'd hopped over before, she knew she was going in the right direction. She fell into a sprint, hoping Peanut was still around. The thick tree line rushed to meet her and when she dashed through it, Peanut was sitting on the other side, licking his paw.

Jenny fell to her knees and burst out laughing. Peanut was so shocked he rolled onto his back and then let out a low grunt when he saw her. Jenny smiled, and let out a matching grunt.

After they both recovered, they set off downstream. A few hours of walking sailed by without issue. Jenny noticed that the shoreline on the other side was farther away than before.

"The river will be deep here," she said, "too deep to risk crossing. Better to wait until we find a better spot later."

CHAPTER TWENTY-NINE

Around sunset Jenny decided a better spot to cross wasn't coming, and it was time to walk across the frozen river. In truth, she had been dreading it. The snow made it hard to see the ice. It could be slippery, or thin, or cracked and the snow made it impossible to tell.

The river had been growing wider as they journeyed downstream, and started twisting to the east, away from the southern direction Rebekah had recommended. It was huge compared to her little section of the river back north. At least five times wider, which also meant deeper. If they walked across a thin part of the ice, their weight could plunge them under the surface into the deep cold of the river.

Peanut was heavy, despite the malnourishment he was still a bear, so she somehow needed find the thickest ice through the layers of snow. She ran through her entire inventory of tools but couldn't think of anything that would be useful to help here.

Staring out over the river, she pondered, trying to ignore the slowly sinking sun, which was only a reminder of how little time they had. Either they cross now or wait until morning. Peanut was tired. How much longer could he hobble on that leg?

There was no time to waste. They needed to cross the river today. She looked at Peanut's furry face, his brown eyes with gold flecks looked back at her.

"Stay here until I say 'yip-yip,' okay?"

He stared into her eyes. Hopefully the message was received.

She swung her backpack over her shoulder and stepped out onto the river. Her legs trembled as she slowly slid her feet across the ice. It was solid underneath her, but that could change at any moment.

Then a thought popped into her head. She took the spear in both hands and held it out far in front of her, tapping the ice and feeling the vibrations in the spear. Slowly twisting herself around in a circle, she tapped the ice as she went. Near the coastline, the ice was thinner. One area broke under the pressure of her tap. After tapping around for a while, she had a rough sense of how thick the ice would feel and sound.

This new information filled her with confidence. Nature wasn't so hard after all. It just took some thinking and creative problem-solving.

Jenny walked more confidently, tapping the ice in front of her. As she made her way outward, she noticed a small shift. The ice was getting thinner. It was gradual but noticeable. When she had made it about halfway across, she turned back toward Peanut.

"Peanut, yip-yip," she said. He perked up and trotted across the ice toward her.

Jenny turned and resumed walking to the other side, tapping the ice with her spear. It seemed thicker in this area, judging by the feel and sound. Over her shoulder she could see that Peanut was catching up to her, so she quickened her pace to stay ahead of him. Best not to stand too close and have all of their weight in one spot.

The far shoreline grew closer, and she knew the ice was thick in the middle of the river, so Jenny sped up her pace without tapping. At about three-fourths of the way across, she looked back to check on Peanut. Her right ankle twisted at a bad angle and she slipped. The world spun around her and she felt herself falling backward.

Her backpack hit the ice with a loud crack, and the air rushed out of her lungs. She gasped trying to catch her breath and orient herself all at the same time. Another loud crack, and then the world shattered around her. She plunged below the ice, and into the cold dark river. Any air in her lungs had been instantly sucked out by the cold water. Her lungs screamed for air. She felt an urge to gasp but held her mouth shut with every ounce of will she could muster.

Jenny forced her eyes open. The ice water stung like pins and needles. She tried to swim toward the light, what she assumed was the surface, but her arm movements were restricted by her backpack. She fought hard against the bag and could feel her strength rapidly draining. This wasn't working.

She pulled the straps loose and let the backpack fall to her right hand. She kicked hard and fought to swim upward, flailing in the water. As she was kicking she felt her Jordans fall off her feet. The backpack made it impossible to coordinate everything, and it felt like she wasn't moving at all. Her lungs ached for air and she knew what she had to do. She let go of her hold on the backpack and allowed it to sink. She wanted to mourn the loss, but there wasn't time. Without wasting another moment, she kicked and swam harder than she ever had. Her chest felt like it would burst. Her head broke through the surface and she gasped for air, breathing it all in.

She turned and saw Peanut running toward her. He was moving too fast. He tried to stop suddenly, but his right paw bent, holding no weight under the injury. His left paw found no traction, and he fell onto his shoulder. His momentum carried him forward and he crashed into Jenny, and together they tumbled below the ice.

Her world spun around in a dark and silent blur. With Peanut knocking her back into the water, it was hard to know up from down. She forced her eyes open again ignoring the pins and needles. Jenny scanned the water, trying to find her bearings. A few feet in front of her, the riverbed curved upwards and met the ice. Had to be the shoreline. Even though her body screamed for air, she pushed forward and hoped Peanut was following behind.

She pushed to the ice-covered shoreline with every ounce of strength she had left. Her feet found solid ground and she pushed up through the heavy ice. The world screamed back to life in a blur of sound and pain.

CHAPTER THIRTY

Every pore in her body screamed in protest. Her bones ached. Her lungs stung with each breath. She trembled uncontrollably. Somehow, she still had the deer skin clutched in her hands. Everything else was at the bottom of the river.

"P-Peanut," she shivered. "Peanut!"

Nothing. Jenny dropped to her knees on the riverbank and felt all the energy rush out of her. How could she be so clumsy? It was her fault. Everything was gone. Her spear, her backpack, her Jordans, *Starfish*, the tea, and worst of all, Peanut—gone in an instant.

In front of her the river bubbled. Peanut burst through the surface in a flurry. He meandered out of the river, stopped on the shoreline, and shook himself dry. His tongue was hanging out of his mouth. He limped over toward Jenny, looking wet and cold. Jenny envied him. He let out a low grunt, and she gave him a grunt back.

Almost sensing what she was feeling, he rubbed his head against hers. She stared into his eyes. There was something more than animal instinct in those eyes. He had compassion. He cared for her.

Jenny closed her eyes feeling his body heat and wet fur against her cheek. The image of the backpack slipping out of her hand, down into the murky waters, played over and over in her mind. Everything she had worked so hard for at the bottom of the river.

The coyote fur around her shoulders was soaked through, along with everything else she was wearing. The only thing covering her feet now were wet socks.

"We will die out here from hypothermia," Jenny said. "And it's all my fault." All she wanted to do was sleep. She felt so tired.

She took a deep breath. Her eyes shot open. Peanut looked at her. Time to figure it out.

"We need to make fire."

She felt for her knife and flint. By some miracle, they were still in her pants pocket.

As she struggled to stand up, the numbness in her feet was starting to spread. She wobbled a bit as she stood up. Her feet ached from the cold and her entire body shivered.

The riverbank was littered with fallen trees. A few feet ahead, a thick tree line created a tall wooden wall that looked impenetrable. She managed to peel off a few strips of bark and find a few dry sticks. The ground was covered in snow. Finding dry leaves would be impossible. Her heart rate quickened and it became harder to think clearly. Panic rose in her chest.

She dropped the bark next to Peanut, who sat still on the ground. His eyes lazily scanned the area. Jenny worried he might be suffering from the extreme temperatures. She managed to snap off a few small twigs from the branches along the tree line. It was hard to grip them firmly with her shaking hands. With her meager supply of wood, she cleared a spot in the snow and piled it all together. The knife and flint managed to make sparks. Unfortunately, none of the sparks were catching onto the twigs and bark.

She grabbed one of the twigs and tried to snap it into smaller pieces, but her hands were shaking too much. She put the twig in her mouth and bit down hard. It tasted exactly how she thought it would. Bitter and woody. She bent the twig with her teeth until it snapped and then and stripped off a thin piece of bark.

After a few more bites, Jenny balled up all the wood strips in her hand and piled up the strips of wood. Once again, she tried to make a spark with her knife and flint, but it didn't catch the wood. She tried again and again, creating a flurry of embers. Then she blew on the embers until they glowed a hot orange and finally caught fire. Jenny piled together all the other twigs and bark, careful not to smother the flame.

The flame grew, enveloping the bark and twigs. The warmth from the fire increased and started to thaw her cold hands and feet.

"Peanut, come close to the fire. Don't be scared."

He slowly limped toward Jenny, taking a wide path around the fire, and slumped down next to her. He didn't look good.

"Let the fire warm you up." Jenny stood up and gathered more wood from the tree line. Soon she had a large enough pile to last them through the night.

Drying the clothes would be tricky. The problem was that removing them and letting them dry by the fire meant she would be naked, and possibly freeze to death. Had to find a balance and stay warm.

She poked a few spare twigs in the ground around the fire and draped the deer skin over it, then her coyote fur. They were both heavy with water.

She sat as close to the fire as she could without getting burned. Her toes stung as they started to warm up. Her clothes were damp against her skin. Her throat ached and her nose was thick with congestion. A serendipitous sneeze confirmed her fear. She was sick. Another sneeze followed and she let out a big sigh.

As her stomach growled angrily, she thought of the squirrel she'd impaled with her spear. Their dinner, gone. Now she had no way to hunt for food. Things were looking bad. They were too far out to head back, and she had no idea how much farther there was to go. It seemed that the only option was to move forward. But how could she even walk without shoes? Her feet would freeze and then she would get frostbite and lose her toes.

The thought terrified her.

Peanut let out a sigh next to her. She guessed he felt similar. Would his animal instincts kick in if it got bad enough? Despite being in rough shape, he was still stronger than her. Her head spun with anxiety and dread. Every scenario looked bad or worse.

Peanut eventually fell asleep, but Jenny was too wired to even think about sleep. At some point the sun had fallen beneath the horizon and a crescent moon rose to illuminate the forest around her. A steady breeze blew through the surrounding river land.

When the furs were dry enough, she swapped everything out, first wrapping herself in the deer skin, and then stripping out of everything except for her socks and underwear. She hung her jeans, shirt, and hoodie on the twigs circling the fire so they could dry out. Then she removed her socks and dried them out as well.

The deer skin blanket was warm, but not warm enough. She felt chilled to the bone, but the deer skin managed to block most of the wind. Between that and the fire, she was able to retain some body heat. She wrapped the coyote fur around her head and curled into a tight ball, staring into the fire.

It crackled, sparks shooting up into the sky. How could she escape this? There had to be a way. There was always a way. She just needed to focus on the problem and come up with a solution.

The first problem was her shoes. She couldn't trek through miles of snow in just socks. Her feet would get frostbitten. She mentally ran through her inventory of tools until an idea hit.

The coyote fur could be cut in half and wrapped around her feet. Then maybe she could slip her socks over them to create a weird sort of moccasin. It wouldn't be perfect, but it might give her feet enough padding to walk across the terrain and stay relatively warm.

She held the coyote fur in her hands and thought about the animal it had come from. How she had impaled the beast and let it die a slow death. He deserved to die, no question. For one, he killed Peanut's mom Virginia. Plus, he attacked them again at the cave.

But she had speared him into the ground, letting him suffer and die slowly. It was a cruel thing to do, and she had grown to regret it. A quick slice of the knife would have been the right thing to do. The dark eyes of the coyote suffering, pleading to be killed, haunted her.

Those eyes reminded her of Rebekah, whose look of fear burned into Jenny's memory. Jenny was the root of that fear and she hated herself because of it. She became the thing she hated most, and Rebekah saw it in her at that moment.

There had been many times that Jenny had thought she would die here. But right now it felt inevitable. The socks might work for a short while, but she still needed food and had nothing to hunt with.

Tears welled up in her eyes, and the cold air made them sting. Her vision blurred. She cried. It was a quiet cry, one of mourning. This was really the end. No escaping it. No amount of problem-solving could save them now.

Sleep never came, but she wasn't trying. Jenny looked up at the stars.

It was a wonder how insignificant they made a person feel. Giant balls of gas spewing out light, traveling vast distances, to fall to earth at this moment. Those stars were the same ones Neanderthals saw thousands of years ago.

How arrogant she was, thinking she knew better than the Neanderthals because she carved one spear. They would have outlasted her by now. They were the ones who invented spears, and fires, and wheels. What had she done?

Out of nowhere, Eric came to mind. Jenny searched her soul for hate. She desperately wanted to blame Eric for where she was now, but found nothing. Partly because it was Jenny's fault they had fallen into the river, but also because she was tired of thinking about Eric.

The hatred was exhausting to maintain. In truth, Rebekah had a point, Jenny did escalate the situation and that had caused Eric to go after her. There really wasn't any other way to see it. Sure, Eric's reaction was wrong, no question. But Jenny knew she had some level of fault as well, all over a pair of AirPods that seemed insignificant now.

She noticed she was feeling an emotion she couldn't put a name to. She had never experienced this one before. A sense of calmness had washed over her, and she stopped crying. She knew she was ready to die. There wasn't fear or panic in the feeling. Just simple acceptance.

This would be where it ended for her. She had few regrets: There were books she wished she would have read, affections she wished she would have pursued—she would die never experiencing a first kiss. She wished she could have seen her father one last time. Why didn't she take Rebekah up on that offer for help?

Stupid, she thought. So stupid.

Jenny scooted over beside Peanut. With her head propped against his back, she faced the river and watched the stars against the ice, quietly hoping that death would take her while she slept. That would be best. Fade out, turn down the volume, and drift away. The stars twinkled above, passive to the quiet event that was the end of her life. After a while her eyes grew heavy and she fell into a dreamless sleep.

CHAPTER THIRTY-ONE

Morning came slowly. The sky was cloudy and gray. The air was unseasonably warm, considering a blizzard had just rolled through. Perhaps the last and final burst of warm weather until the spring.

Jeff had arrived at his deer stand in the Balsam Lake Mountain Wild Forest preserve around four in the morning, well before the sun was up. His alarm had gone off at two this morning, and he was out the door in under a half hour. Hunting weekends always felt like Christmas to him. Preparing the night before, laying everything out, getting his truck ready, making sure he had all the tools. The buildup was torturous but exciting.

Driving out was quick, the roads were clear, and few other people were up this early, so it felt like his own little dystopian future. A lone man against the world, hunting for his dinner. Jeff loved imagining the end of the world was coming.

In fact, even though his wife didn't know, Jeff had been preparing for the end of the world. The way things were going these days, it never hurt to be ready. He had found a small online community of people who called themselves "preppers," and they all posted their survival kits. It usually ranged from go-bags, to closets, to full-on basements stocked with supplies. One of the major posters had built a bunker in his backyard. Truly ready for the end of the world.

The best part about hunting in these woods was the silence. Sitting in the deer stand felt like meditation. Just Jeff against the world, rifle in hand. If he held his breath, there wasn't a sound to be heard. He tried explaining this to his wife, but she didn't get it. Thought it was a weird hobby. She would never understand how calming it was, man sitting among nature, being one with it. Finally able to breathe and get away from the stress of life.

The deer stand was made of steel and built against a tall oak, about twenty feet off the ground. At the top was a narrow little platform, a small metal seat. A narrow ladder led down to the ground. Nothing high tech or remarkable.

After sitting for two hours, Jeff's butt had fallen asleep and he was feeling the need to stretch his legs. So far, he hadn't had any luck spotting game, so he decided it was a good time for a break to stretch his legs and empty his bladder.

He slung his .375 Ruger Rifle, with Leupold VX-6 scope, over his shoulder and made his way down the ladder. He unzipped and relived himself on the tree.

Something behind him made a noise. Jeff glanced over his shoulder and saw movement in the distance. He quickly finished and grabbed his rifle with both hands. He took a breath and tried to calm himself, but the adrenaline flowing through his system made it hard.

He saw another movement. It was either a deer or a bear, hard to tell. He had hunting tags for both, so it didn't matter either way. Jeff focused and looked down his scope. In the lens he could see a brown bear through a thick tree line, laying near a frozen river.

The bear was just waking up, probably getting ready to move. He would have to take his shot now. No time to climb up the stand for a better angle. He exhaled and held his breath, willing his heart to slow down. The scope swaying slowed, the crosshairs lazily swinging over the bear. Jeff focused on the rhythm of the sway. *Right, left, right, left.* Slowly, he wrapped his finger around the hairpin trigger. *Right, left, right . . .*

He pulled the trigger, his shoulder shaking violently, and the sound of the world went away. Nothing but a high-pitched ringing sound. In the distance, the bear slumped over and went still. Then something Jeff had never seen before happened. Someone wrapped in fur jumped up from behind the bear. The fur fell away, and a small half-naked human stood over the bear, screaming.

CHAPTER THIRTY-TWO

A roaring thunder ripped Jenny from her deep sleep. The world had exploded around her in a blaze of sound. Her eyes struggled to find focus in the dim light of the morning. Her side burned with intense pain. Something was wrong.

As she stood up, the deer skin fell away. She turned to see Peanut laying still on the ground, blood pouring out of his ribs. Jenny screamed as a white-hot pain flashed through her right side. She fell to her knees and stumbled toward Peanut.

Blood was everywhere. Near her bottom rib, there was a large gash in the side of her abdomen. She lowered her shaking hands toward the wound and touched it. A white-hot flare of pain shot through her side. The wound was deep and blood oozed out. How did this happen? Did Peanut bite her?

Ahead of her, Peanut made a groan. Jenny crawled toward him to see an even larger wound in the center of his ribs, blood pouring out onto the snow. His breathing was slow and labored.

Snow crunched behind her. Footsteps, running closer. She whirled around and saw a large man running toward them. He was dressed head to toe in thick camo clothing. A light orange vest was pulled tight over his jacket. He held a large rifle in his hands.

The large man pushed through the tree line and came to a stop on the shore, seeming out of breath. His face was bright red. He lifted his gun and aimed it at Jenny.

"You, little girl. M-move out of the way, th-there is a bear!" the large man said. The gun shook in his hands.

"Don't you dare shoot this bear again." Jenny spread her arms out as wide as she could, standing between the gun and Peanut. When she stretched out her arms, pain flared up her side again, and she flinched.

"Are you crazy? That's a wild animal!"

"No, he isn't. He is my bear. He is trained. He won't hurt you."

"I . . . Look. You're clearly hurt."

"Yes, I think you shot me."

"Let me take you to a hospital."

"No, you're going to take us to the closest vet."

"Excuse me?"

"We need to save this bear. He can't die here."

The large man stumbled over his words and lowered his gun toward the ground.

"Look, little girl, with all due respect—"

"I am not a little girl! I am Jenny Woods, and we are going to save this bear, or I will make sure you go to jail for a very long time."

"Now, this was all a misunderstanding. How was I supposed to know you were next to this bear?"

"Look, what's your name?"

"Jeff. Wait . . . wait a minute." His eyes went wide and he gasped, putting a hand over his mouth. "Are you Jenny? The Jenny? You're the… You're her."

"Yes. Look, Jeff, I need your help. This bear is very important to me. He saved me. You have to help us. If we can get him to a vet, he might live."

". . . I'm gonna regret this. Fine, okay. But you can't press charges on me for shooting you."

"Deal."

"If he so much as makes one aggressive move toward me, I'll shoot him."

"He won't. Come on."

Jeff slung his gun over his shoulder and started for the tree line. "My truck is nearby. If you can get him through that tree line, I can drive up to the other side. It's a big fine to drive on this land, so . . . just don't tell anyone, okay?"

"Okay."

Jeff ran off to get his truck, and Jenny grabbed her cold, but dry, clothes off the sticks. At that moment, it crossed her mind that she had been half naked in front of a complete stranger. Thankfully, Jeff didn't seem like a creep, but still. This was all kinds of weird. The gunshot wound ached and made it hard to dress quickly. Once her pants were on, she wrapped the coyote fur around her abdomen and used her belt to sinch it tight against the bullet wound. It wasn't a good tourniquet, and hurt like hell, but hopefully it might help stop the bleeding. All she could do was hope it wasn't life threatening. She threw on her shirt and hoodie and dashed back toward Peanut.

He looked bad. Really bad. There was a lot of blood on the snow. Jenny couldn't even begin to process her feelings, there simply wasn't time. For now, she had to get him through the thick tree line. She took his face into her hands and stared into his eyes. They came into focus and looked back at her.

"Hey. Hey, you. It's going to be okay. Okay? Don't you leave me." She pointed back to the tree line. "We just need to get through there, and we are home. Got it? Twenty more feet and we are home free, buddy."

Peanut looked at her face and let out a big sigh.

"No, don't you give up. Not now. We are too close. Come on, Peanut."

Jenny stood up and tried to lift him up by his good front paw.

"Come on, Peanut. Let's go." She tugged hard. He didn't move. She pulled even harder, worried she might be hurting him.

"Peanut! I said let's go." She pulled as hard as she could, muscles straining hard, heels digging into the cold ground. Her side burned with pain.

Peanut kicked with his back legs. He struggled to find his footing and stumbled. Jenny wrapped his arm around her shoulder and hiked him up onto her back. Her legs buckled under his weight and she fell to her knees. Even after losing weight he was still heavy, and now he couldn't support himself.

Jenny pushed up as hard as she could. Her legs shook as they strained to stand up. She let out a scream and pushed with everything she had, dragging them both forward a few inches. Everything hurt. Her entire body was in pain and it was hard to focus. Her side felt like it was on fire. Peanut kicked with his legs, trying to stay upright. Inch by inch they struggled together. Jenny's side was pulsing now as pain burned through her, and tears ran down her cheeks.

The distance to the tree line seemed as big as football field. It felt insurmountable to Jenny, like her body would collapse at any moment. With each step, she thought the next one was the last. Fall to the ground. Bleed out. But they kept moving. They didn't fall. The tree line grew closer.

They reached the thick bushes of the tree line together. Jenny fell through into the forest behind, but Peanut got stuck halfway. Jenny rolled and tried to stand up, but her arms nearly collapsed under the effort. Her strength was running out. The pain in her side grew worse.

Jenny crawled toward Peanut and grabbed him by his good paw. She spun her body around so her feet could dig into the snow and dirt. The muscles in her hands strained as she pulled Peanut's paw through her legs. Digging her feet into the snow, she could use her full body strength to pull him toward her. Peanut started kicking his legs to try and help. Together they made it through the tree line and Jenny rolled over, toes numb, hands sore, and completely exhausted. Peanut just lay on the ground next to Jenny, and they both lay there together, breathing heavily.

The sound of a car engine grew closer, and it hit her all at once: they were going home. The truck barreled into the clearing, snapping a few small trees in its wake, and came to a stop near them. Jenny sat up and watched as Jeff did a three-point turn, backing up as close as he could get to them both. Then he hopped out of the truck and came around to the back. He had left his rifle in the truck, but he had a handgun around his waist. The strap that locked the gun in place was open.

"You holding up all right, little lady? That gunshot wound nicked you too, ya know."

"Oh, I am well aware, Jeff. It's much more than a nick. I used a belt and coyote fur to make tourniquet."

"I think tourniquets only work on limbs."

"Not the time."

"Right. How are we going to do this, Jenny?"

Jenny raised up her hands toward him, and he grabbed them and carefully pulled her to her feet.

"We will have to lift him into the truck. I'll pull, you push. Sound good?"

Jeff nodded. Jenny pointed toward Peanut's good paw, and Jeff dashed around toward it. Jenny carefully took Peanut's broken paw under her arm.

"This might hurt a little, big guy. Just trust us, okay?" Jenny said. Peanut's eyes were unfocused.

"Something wrong?" Jeff asked.

"No. Let's do this."

Together they lifted Peanut onto their shoulders. They walked him toward the truck, his feet dragging on the ground behind them. They set him down into the bed of the truck.

"You push from behind and I'll pull," Jenny said.

Jeff nodded and she hopped up into the truck. She pulled Peanut by the good paw, and Jeff pushed from behind. Peanut kicked and huffed, trying to help. At least he still had some fight left in him.

Peanut flopped into the truck, and it sank lower under his full weight. Jeff pushed him into the truck bed, and closed the tailgate behind him.

"Don't worry, little lady. I have some great off-roading shocks installed. Ya know, just in case," Jeff said as he handed her his jacket.

"Uh . . . good to know. And thanks for the jacket."

"Yeah least I could do. You look a little cold."

Jeff ran around to the front of the truck and hopped in, slamming the door shut. From the inside he turned back and yelled:

"Hold on back there Jenny. I'm about to break a lot of laws."

CHAPTER THIRTY-THREE

It wasn't long before they were speeding down Highway Seventeen. In the bed of the truck Jenny held the deer skin against Peanut's wound. Looking around the highway, it was strange to see other cars. People with entire lives passing by as if it was just another day.

"I didn't realize how much I missed seeing humans," Jenny whispered to Peanut. His breathing was haggard, and it felt like every breath was a struggle. The truck was going at least ninety miles per hour, probably as fast as the old thing could go. The wind felt good against her face. Relaxing. Almost good enough to keep her from noticing the pain in her side.

Under her hoodie, the coyote fur and her shirt were stained red. Not only was Peanut in bad shape, but Jenny could tell she was losing blood too. Her side ached with pain, and it started to creep into her mind that this gunshot wound in her side could actually be serious. The loss of blood made her mind feel slow and dull, like that one time her father let her drink some wine. But she tried to push through it all. To hold on. For Peanut.

"How much longer?" Jenny yelled through a little window looking into the cab of the car.

Jeff turned back toward Jenny. His thin gray beard failed at hiding his thick round chin. Jenny guessed he was older than her dad. Around fifty. Maybe it was the blood loss, but she felt no anger toward him. All that mattered now was getting Peanut to a vet. The accident was upsetting but they were free. She had survived. A smile crept across her face and then a knot grew in her throat. Tears of joy streamed down her face. Layer by layer, her stress melted away. A heavy weight lifted from her shoulders. She felt as light as air. She had made it out alive.

They pulled up next to Animal Hospital of Sullivan County. Jenny could tell right away that this place was closed. The "open" sign was off and the inside looked dark.

"It's too early, Jeff. They aren't open yet."

"Well, shit. Okay, let me Google here . . ." Jeff typed in a search in Google Maps. Jenny stared at the bright screen. It looked familiar, but different.

"Did a new iPhone come out?"

"Oh yeah, this is the newest one."

Jenny didn't miss phones. Well, except for how convenient they made life. That she missed.

"Looks like there's one down the road a bit. Catskill Veterinary Clinic," Jeff said.

"Let's go. And can I borrow your phone? I need to make a call."

Jeff slid the phone through the small window and looked her in the eyes.

"Take all the time you need."

The truck peeled out of the parking lot, the tires screeching against the pavement. Jenny dialed the number she knew by heart.

Ring.

It was early. No way he would be awake yet.

Ring.

He might not pick up the unknown number.

Click.

"Hello?"

Jenny's heart melted. The rich sound of her father's voice filled her ear. Tears welled up in her eyes.

"Dad?"

"Jenny? Is that you?"

"Dad, it's me."

"This better not be a prank call." He sounded angry. She knew what to say.

"It really is me, Dad. I'm not dead. The Woods Stubbornness wouldn't allow it." She heard his voice catch. He was crying.

"Jenny, I missed you so much. I thought you were. . . that you . . ."

"I'm not. I didn't . . . I missed you too. Dad."

"Look, where are you? I'll come to you."

"I'm heading toward Catskill Veterinary Clinic, off Highway—"

"A veterinarian?"

"It's a long story. A man named Jeff is taking me and... a friend

163

there."

"Who's Jeff? What friend"

"It's so hard to explain right now dad. He's the man who accidently shot me and he's now driving me to the vet, with… a bear. I know, it doesn't make any sense. I promise it will."

Out of nowhere, blue and red lights flashed on down the road. A cop car was slowly speeding toward them.

"Wait. Shot you?"

"I think I'm ok. Just, can you get here?"

"Okay, I don't understand, but I'm in the car now. I will be there soon."

"I have to go, Dad. Cops are coming."

Jenny clicked off the phone. There just wasn't enough time to explain everything to him.

"Jeff. Cops are on our tail. What do we do? We can't slow down."

"Yeah, I see. This is going to be a long day. I don't know how I will explain this to the wife. Hold on back there."

Jenny felt the truck lurch forward. Inside it looked like the speedometer was pushing past one hundred. Jenny pressed the fur skin into Peanut. Still breathing.

The cop car was gaining on them.

"How much longer?" Jenny yelled into the cab.

"Hold on, almost there."

They took a sharp right, hard and fast. It almost felt like the truck went onto two wheels. Jeff drove over the snow-covered lawn and into the parking lot of Catskill Veterinary Clinic. The truck bounced along the uneven terrain. Jeff hit the brakes and turned the steering wheel hard, spinning the bed of the truck around to the front entrance. He threw the truck in park and hopped out of the cab, running back toward the road.

"Where are you going?" Jenny yelled.

"To deal with the cops. Go inside and get help!"

The cop car screeched around the corner. Wasting no time, she hopped out of the truck bed and ran toward the clinic. She threw open the wooden door and ran inside.

A small older woman with short brown hair and bright pink scrubs behind the front desk let out a small gasp. The woman had a look of horror on her face, her mouth struggling to spit out words. Jenny had suspected she looked like a hot mess, but the lady's terrified look confirmed it.

"I need a doctor. It's an emergency," Jenny said.

"Please go or I'll call the cops." The old woman's boney hand picked up the phone and started to dial. A young man with short wavy hair and thick black glasses walked through a nearby office door. He wore a long white coat with the name "Eli D. Vince" stitched into the jacket, with the letters "DVM" after them. Doctor of Veterinary Medicine.

"Eli, my name is Jenny Woods. I'm the person who everyone thinks is dead but I'm not." This was a terrible way to start. He was going to think she was crazy. "I have a bear outside that needs your help. He was shot by a hunter and he is dying."

Eli stared at Jenny, studying her. Then he turned and slowly walked to the window. With one finger he pulled up the blinds and looked outside. In the distance Jeff was pinned to the ground by a cop, who was in the process of handcuffing him. Another cop was walking toward the truck.

"It would seem that time is of the essence," Eli said. "Linda, no need to call the cops. They appear to be here already. Please go get the large mobile stretcher and meet me outside. Ms. Woods, would you lead me to the bear?"

Eli grabbed two latex gloves out of a box on the tall counter. They walked outside just as the cop was approaching the back of the truck. Jenny watched him peer over into the bed, jump backward at the sight of Peanut. His hands fumbled for the gun at his side.

Jenny ran out and stood between the truck and the cop. "Please don't shoot. He won't hurt anyone."

The cop pulled his gun up and pointed it at Jenny. Her blood went cold. All she did was ask him not to shoot. Cops didn't hesitate to shoot people like her. Everything was happening too quickly.

Eli walked toward the cop with his hands out. "Please, officer, lower your weapon. The bear is a patient and the woman is a client. I believe you can make an exception for an emergency, yes?"

The cop looked at Eli and then back at Jenny. He stared at her and she watched the recognition click. He lowered his gun.

"You're the... from all the posters. Woods. Jenny Woods, that's you."

"Yes, that's me."

The cop turned and yelled over his shoulder. "Hey, Doug. I found Jenny Woods."

"Technically, Jeff found me." Jenny said, pointing to Jeff who was currently handcuffed and lying on the ground.

"The missing girl from the television?" Doug yelled back.

"Yeah, from the television."

"We all good, officer?" Jenny said.

Linda burst through the doors of the clinic with a large silver cart on wheels. Eli went to the tailgate and Jenny followed. They opened it and Eli hopped into the truck. He pulled the deer skin back, revealing the bloody wound in Peanut's side. Jenny watched his furry chest slowly rise and fall. Still alive.

"It's bad. Really bad. If we get him inside, I can stabilize him, but he needs surgery," Eli said.

"Okay, then we do the surgery," Jenny said.

"My facilities aren't big enough. But if we can get him an airlift to the Schwarzman Animal Medical Center in New York City, they can do it there."

"How can we get an airlift?" Jenny asked.

The cop who had pulled the gun on them cleared his throat. Jenny turned to see a walkie-talkie in his hand.

"I think I can get us an airlift."

CHAPTER THIRTY-FOUR

"**D**ad, turn back around and head to the city, we are flying to the Schwarzman Animal Medical Center," Jenny said into Linda's desk phone.

"Schwarzman Animal Medical Center?"

"Yeah, the big one, in Manhattan, near um . . ."

"East 62nd and York," Linda interjected.

"East 62nd and York."

"I'm confused. Why am I going there?"

"I'll explain everything when we get there. Ow!" Jenny shot a glance at Linda, who was stitching the bullet wound in Jenny's side. "Have to go now, sorry!"

After Eli and the cop wheeled Peanut into the operating room, Jenny collapsed into the chairs by the waiting area. When she finally peeled off her hoodie, Linda saw the bloody shirt and instantly went into nurse mode.

Since Peanut was occupying their only operating table, Linda improvised and threw some towels onto the front desk. Before Jenny could get two words in edgewise, Linda removed Jenny's shirt and peeled away the coyote fur that had acted as a tourniquet. When Linda saw Jenny's thin figure, she gasped.

Looking into the window, Jenny saw her reflection for the first time. Her hair was an uneven smattering of chunks. Her cheeks had a slight sunken in look and her pants were barely hugging her hips. Her skin was covered in dirt and blood.

Linda insisted on stitching the wound. The bullet only grazed her, which was the best outcome when getting shot, according to Linda. She also said Jenny lost a serious amount of blood and she needed to go to a hospital. Jenny wanted no part in that until Peanut was stabilized, so as a compromise, she let Linda stitch her wounds.

"How much longer?"

"You or the bear?" Linda said.

"Both."

"The bear will take a while. You, almost done." Linda dabbed a cotton ball over the stitching. The peroxide burned her skin.

"Got a shirt I could borrow?" Jenny asked, sucking in a breath from the pain.

"I think I have a set of scrubs in the back. Let's get you in some clean clothes."

While they waited for Eli to finish with Peanut, Linda cleaned Jenny up. She helped wash all the dirt and blood off her skin. Then she let Jenny change into a clean set of blue scrubs. She had an extra pair of shoes at her desk and let Jenny wear them. They were a little small, but better than anything she'd worn in a while, so she didn't complain.

Then Linda took a pair of scissors and sat Jenny down in a chair in the waiting room. She threw a towel around Jenny's shoulders and started to cut.

"Gotta have you looking nice, now."

"Why?"

"The cameras, dear. The media will catch wind that you're alive, if they haven't already. You're going to be on TV soon." Outside, there were at least a dozen cop cars blocking the road. A small crowd of people gathered near the parking lot.

"I don't really care what I look like. I didn't do anything special."

Linda's scissors stopped cutting as she looked Jenny in the eye. "Honey, everyone wants to see the girl who survived."

The last thing Jenny wanted was to be on TV. She wanted to see her dad and hug him until it hurt. And then she wanted to see Peanut.

When Linda was finished, she gave Jenny a compact mirror from her purse so she could look. Her hair was incredibly short, but it looked much better. Jenny could see in her gaunt face how much weight she'd lost.

Through the window Jenny could see snow starting to kick up violently, and the crowd held up their arms to protect from the wind. An orange-and-white airlift helicopter set down in the parking lot. Two EMTs dressed in dark blue ran into the clinic. They stopped and looked at Linda.

"Where is the bear?" one of the EMTs asked.

"Behind that door." Linda pointed. The EMTs ran past, but Jenny noticed their stares lingered on her. One patted the other on the shoulder.

"Let's go!"

Jenny looked at the floor but felt their eyes looking at her as they walked past. This must be what it felt like to be a celebrity.

Jenny grabbed a winter jacket from the lost and found and followed the EMT's as they brought Peanut to the helicopter. Jenny stepped into the helicopter and no one stopped her. Within ten minutes, Peanut was loaded and ready to be airlifted. The EMTs said they gave him a sedative so he wouldn't move. There was a white band of gauze wrapped around his midsection. Jenny stared at his chest, and watched it expand and contract. Then the EMT's helped Jenny get fastened into one of the seats and gave her a headset.

Outside the helicopter Eli and Linda stood with a small crowd of cops, and Jeff, who was still handcuffed but allowed to stand and watch. Jenny stared and tried to memorize all of their faces.

Then the helicopter lifted and rose high above the ground. Jenny felt her stomach sink to the floor like she was riding a rollercoaster. The helicopter shot forward and the ground below zoomed past. The sun had just started breaking through the horizon. It painted the clear sky in brilliant yellow orange. Below, the cars and houses looked tiny, like models. Each one held a human with a story. When they came upon that familiar New York City skyline, Jenny nearly cried at the sight of it.

They touched down on the roof of the Schwarzman Animal Medical Center with a soft bump. The two EMTs dashed out of the helicopter and immediately started unloading Peanut. Jenny wasn't sure what to do, so she hopped out and helped pull the gurney from the back of the helicopter. She wasn't going to let Peanut out of her sight.

The gurney bounced out of the back of the helicopter and onto the roof. Jenny kept a firm grip on its metal railing. Three people rushed toward the gurney, all wearing scrubs. A woman stepped forward from the trio and talked to one of the EMTs. Jenny couldn't make out what they were saying over the roar of the helicopter.

The trio grabbed the gurney and wheeled it toward the roof door leaving the EMT's with the helicopter. Jenny ran with them and couldn't help but catch the glances back at her.

Inside the waiting area were a few people with small animals, along with a nurse. The trio and Jenny dashed past in a hurry. All the folks in the waiting room stopped and watched as the group ran by.

They ran down a long hall and took a left through a set of big metal doors. They stopped the gurney outside of a large room with a glass window. Inside Jenny could see a giant light pointing toward a metal table. Two nurses in scrubs were setting out tools for surgery.

The woman who spoke to the EMTs earlier turned toward Jenny. The other two took Peanut into the room.

"Afraid you can't go any further Jenny," the woman said.

"I can't leave him. I have to be with him." Jenny felt ready to fight this lady. She wasn't going to give in.

"Hey, it's okay." The woman leaned forward and gave Jenny a hug. "He is going to be okay. The bleeding was stopped by the doc you just came from. All we have to do is a small surgery and stitch up his wounds, and then he will be good as new."

That hug, such a small act of kindness, and yet one that Jenny had so desperately missed. Layers of fear and anxiety melted away. Maybe it was the exhaustion, or starvation, or bullet wound in her side, but Jenny couldn't let Peanut go. It was just too much.

"I just, I really can't leave him. I need him." How could she leave her best friend's side?

"What is his name, Jenny?"

"Peanut."

"Let me take care of Peanut, just for a little bit, and then I will give him back to you."

"Okay. Also, his right front paw, I think it's broken. Can you take a look at that too?" Jenny said.

"Yeah, we can take a look at that. He is in good hands here. Trust me. You need anything, just ask, okay?" The doctor stood up and moved to exit through the surgery door.

"Wait, what's your name?" Jenny asked.

The doctor turned. "Virginia."

Jenny smiled. "That's one hell of a coincidence."

"Why is that?"

"That was his mom's name."

CHAPTER THIRTY-FIVE

The nurses at the Schwarzman Animal Medical Center were unbelievably nice to Jenny. They let her sit in one of the small examination rooms, away from the waiting area, for privacy. She tried to remember everyone's names, but it was getting hard to remember all the people she'd encountered. Exhaustion had caught up with her.

One of the nurses, a middle-aged woman with red hair who went by Deb, brought Jenny a cup of homemade soup and some fruit from the employee break room fridge. They said Jenny couldn't handle any complex foods right now because her body was in starvation mode. Had to be careful, or else her stomach wouldn't react well. Deb wouldn't say who gave up their lunch, and Jenny was touched by yet another act of kindness. When the door to the break room opened, she started to say the line she had been rehearsing in her head.

"Deb, I just want to know who gave me their lunch—" Jenny stopped mid-sentence. Her father stood in the doorway.

"Hey, Jenny," he said, but she was already running toward him. Their bodies collided with a thud and she hugged him hard. He hugged her back and they stood there, both crying, for a long time. There was so much to say. Jenny could barely keep one thought in her head long enough before three more popped up in its place. She had to tell him everything all at once.

They sat in that small room for what felt like hours, laughing and crying. Jenny told him everything she could remember from the first day up until now, and he just listened. He was always such a great listener. His soft brown eyes watched her, absorbing every word.

As she looked at his face, it almost felt like a dream. There was a strange distance between them, as if the Jenny who she'd been was gone, and replaced with a woman who looked and acted the same but was different beneath the skin. Being away had changed her, and had changed him as well. She could feel it. He had a few wrinkles near the corners of his eyes that weren't there before. Above his ears were a few more wisps of gray hair.

"One thing I don't understand. The one woman you met. What was her name?"

"Rebekah."

"Right. I don't understand. Why didn't you ask her for help?"

"I don't really have the words to explain it. I wasn't myself in that moment and it scared me."

"Okay, I'm sure there are things that will take me a long time to understand."

"Me too," Jenny said, and they both laughed.

"I'll be honest, you look like crap."

"Yeah? Well, you look like you aged five years old man." She missed their banter.

"Touché. Guess stress does that to a person."

"I hate that you thought I killed myself."

"I didn't know what or who to believe. None of it made sense."

"It's the Woods Stubbornness that got me through. That and the lucky pocketknife." She pulled it out of her pocket and held it out to him. He took it in his hands and flipped it open.

"Wow. Grandpa would be proud. It really is a lucky knife."

There was a knock at the door, and a man in brown pants and a gray suit jacket opened the door.

"Hello, sorry to interrupt. My name is Detective Rodriguez."

Jenny's dad stood up and faced the detective.

"How can we help you, officer?" he asked.

"I need to speak with Jenny about some serious business."

"Well, she is still a minor, so you can speak to me."

"It's okay, Dad. I can handle it," Jenny said. Her father crossed his arms.

"Jenny, as you know, attempted murder is very serious," the detective said.

Her dad couldn't help but interrupt. "Now wait a minute. What's this about attempted murder?."

"Dad, please. Let them explain—" Jenny started, but her father spoke over her.

"And what about a lawyer? Don't we have rights here?" Her dad's face grew red. The detective held his hands up.

"Wait a minute, why would you need a lawyer?" the detective said.

Jenny and her dad looked at each other.

"I'm here because a classmate of yours has come forward. They said that . . ." the detective flipped open his notepad. "Eric Wilson lied about your attempted suicide. This classmate alleges that Eric pushed you into the ravine during the class field trip. Is this true?"

Jenny's mouth dropped open. Never in a million years did she think people would speak out against Eric.

"Um . . . yeah. Yes, that is true. He pushed me." They sat in silence while the detective scribbled in his notepad. Then he stopped and flipped it shut and looked at them both.

"Thank you, Jenny. Attempted murder is a serious charge. Not only did Mr. Wilson attempt this, but he then tried to hide the fact afterward, claiming you had committed suicide. The state takes this very seriously, Jenny. Would you be prepared to testify in front of a grand jury?"

Jenny looked at her father, whose expression was just as surprised as hers. Everything was happening so fast it was getting hard to keep up.

"I don't know."

"Ok. Think about it." The detective handed her his business card. "I will be in touch in a few days. We have more questions, but for now, rest. It's good to have you back, Jenny." He nodded to her father and left the room.

Jenny felt a wave of exhaustion wash over her. The events of the day had been overwhelming and she needed sleep. There was another knock at the door. Virginia popped her head in. She was in a different set of scrubs and she looked tired, like she'd just run a race.

"Hi, Woods family."

"How is he? Is he going to be okay?" Suddenly nothing else in the world mattered to Jenny.

"Well, the good news is that we were able to repair the damage. Thankfully, no vital organs were damaged, though he does have some injury to his ribs that will take time to heal."

Jenny felt a wave of relief wash over her. He was going to be okay. "That's amazing."

"That said, there is some bad news. His paw, the one you mentioned earlier, Jenny. We did an Xray and it turns out you were right. It was broken. It looks like it had been broken for a while. When we took a closer look, we found that it was infected and starting to spread. Had you not come sooner, Jenny, Peanut would be dead."

"Oh, wow."

"We had to amputate. I'm sorry." Her words hung in the air like icicles.

"What does that mean? Can he survive without it?"

"Yes. His life will never be as it was, but maybe he can discover a new one."

"What will happen with him? Can he be released back into the wild?" The thought of saying goodbye to him was too much to think about. He would need to go home eventually.

"My nurses have been on the phone with all the local zoos all morning. The Bronx Zoo has agreed to house him, at least temporarily, until he gets strong enough to go back out into the wild."

"How much will that cost us?" Jenny's father asked. The doctor laughed in response.

"Mr. Woods, are you kidding? This bear is an overnight celebrity. The news of Jenny's story is already breaking on all the news. Once my nurses explained who the bear was, the zoo practically begged to take him. People are going to travel from all over the world to see this famous bear."

"Oh. Well. That's good." Jenny's dad was too stunned to say more.

"Wait, Peanut and I are already on the news?" Jenny said.

"Jenny, there are dozens of news trucks parked outside right now, all waiting to meet you. They want to hear your story. They want to know how you survived. They've already given you a nickname."

"What is it?"

"Jenny of the Woods."

CHAPTER THIRTY-SIX

In the days after she arrived back to civilization, her story spread like wildfire across the nation. Everyone wanted to interview her and hear her story. One news outlet called it *"The Harrowing Story of Jenny of the Woods."* The only thing worse than going viral was going viral with a bad haircut. A photo of Jenny with her short hair was plastered all over the front page of the New York Times. Thank goodness for Linda, at least she had cleaned it up. When Jenny walked into the salon she had been going to for years, her stylist, Amanda, gasped and nearly cried. After they had hugged for a long time, Amanda managed to salvage what was left of Jenny's hair by balancing out the unequal patches into short uniform cut that didn't look half bad.

The hardest conversation she had was with her doctor, who said that the road back to normal would be a long one. The damage living in the wilderness did to her body had been detrimental. Near constant starvation had whittled forty pounds of weight away from her, which had adverse effects on her kidneys and liver. Malnutrition from only eating meat had done damage as well, and the doctor required her to be on a very strict diet for at least a year, with monthly check-ups after that. Jenny had no appetite for meat, and he was willing to work with her new pledge to be vegan.

She had a minor UTI from the lack of proper care. There were about a dozen ticks to remove from her body, along with a nasty flatworm in her stomach that she had to take pills for. All of this would have been manageable, but the part that nearly sent her over the edge was that she had frostbite on three of her toes. Meaning, they had to be amputated. After the surgery, when she saw her nearly toeless foot, she couldn't help but laugh. It seemed that Peanut wasn't the only one losing body parts. After all it could have been worse. There was also a nasty scar from the bullet wound under her rib cage. The doctor did note that Linda had done an amazing job of stitching Jenny up.

Her muscle mass had also decreased significantly due to the starvation. She had to meet with a physical trainer named Buddy once a week who helped her rebuild muscle, and re-learn how to walk, which was surprisingly hard with only seven toes. Buddy was so upbeat it was annoying but also endearing. He pushed Jenny until it felt like her muscles would break. They never did, but if they did, she was convinced Buddy would find a way to smile about it.

Jenny reluctantly traveled down to Manhattan and did TV appearances on *Good Morning America*, the *Today Show*, and *Jimmy Fallon*. She also did interviews with newspapers and podcasters. The questions were the same, no matter where she went: What was it like? How did you feel? Were you scared?

On one appearance, Jenny made a point to talk about her old beat-up black-and-red Jordans; how they weren't the best shoes for living outdoors but they were her favorite. She also talked about how she fashioned snowshoes out of them but ended up losing them in the river. A few weeks later, Nike sent her a brand-new pair of black-and-red Jordans and asked her to post on social media about them. Part of Jenny really wanted the new shoes, but Rebekah's voice popped into Jenny's head calling her materialistic. As she was thinking about it more, she realized that essentially, she was trying to profit off her own misery and suffering. There were people all over the world suffering, and they didn't get free Jordans for it. Jenny felt guilty for taking the shoes, so she sent them back. That was the last time she mentioned a product on air.

No one asked her the hard stuff like: How was confronting death on a daily basis? What did starvation feel like? How did it impact your mental health? Were you depressed at all? It was all fun fluff questions, she quickly realized. Fluff, that's all her suffering was to people. Something to talk about until the next big story. There was only one reason that Jenny kept doing all of these shallow interviews and appearances: Peanut. As long as people talked about her story, he would continue to get free room and board at the Bronx Zoo. So, before every interview she took a moment to remind herself just who she was doing all of this for.

A half-dozen clothing lines asked her to be their next sponsor. The sponsorships were mostly for hunting and survival clothes, but there was one persistent clothing line that wouldn't take no for an answer. A high-end fashion boutique called DuBois that sold dresses to fancy people in

Harlem. Curiosity got the best of her, so she sent an email to the head designer, explaining that she wasn't really a fancy-dress kind of person. The designer, Francine, wrote her back and said that it didn't matter. She was moved by Jenny's story and simply wanted to design clothes for just her. She started sending Jenny beautiful clothes. Pants, cardigans, shirts, and blouses, all claimed to be hand-sewn by Francine herself. A dress never showed up, which made Jenny respect Francine even more. Jenny admitted to herself that she did need to upgrade her wardrobe for college, so she worked out a deal where she would work part-time with Francine at DuBois to earn the clothes.

As much as Jenny wanted to put all of this behind her, her father felt otherwise. For the longest time, Jenny refused to even talk the Grand Jury. Her father kept trying to bring it up, and Jenny kept avoiding it. It seems like he really wanted to get even with Eric. Jenny didn't want to hear anything about it. She just wanted to move on and get ready for college. One evening during dinner, things reached a boiling point. They were eating quietly when her father came right out and spoke his mind.

"I'm sorry, but I have to say something. You're not going to like it," he said.

"Dad, don't do this now."

"Just think of the money, Jenny. Just . . . would you think of that for a moment?"

"Money? That's what this is about to you?"

"Jenny, you know his parents. We could get so much from them. It would help us out so much . . . Could pay your tuition, and leave you more for the future."

"Dad, please don't do this to me."

"What am I doing to you?"

"Can't you hear yourself? Don't you see what you're trying to do?"

"Explain it to me, Jenny. Please, tell me. What am I doing?"

"You're trying to get rich off my suffering."

"No, baby, no it's not that . . . I mean, I guess it could look like that when you frame it that way. It's also about getting justice."

"If it was about getting justice, you would have led with getting justice. It's about money to you. That's the truth."

"The suffering happened. It's in the past. This will help us move forward."

"Maybe it's in the past for you, but not for me. I relive it every day."

"Just . . ."

"We don't even need the money, dad. I don't care about justice, or revenge. I don't care about any of it. I'm done. I'm trying to move on. I

177

don't want to keep going back to it. I want to be done."

"Just please think about it. For me. Would you do it for me?"

"What about me, Dad?"

"Jenny, he tried to kill you. I couldn't protect you. What am I supposed to do now? Let him get away with it? I want to kill him."

"You don't even know that that feels like."

"You do?"

"I want to focus on college, Dad. I'm done with high school. So, done. I'm not even going back to finish my classes. I'm just going to take the GED test and be done with it all."

"Wait, you don't want to finish out the year?"

"Not in the least."

"But don't . . ."

"*Stop!*" Jenny slammed the table with her fists. Her father's face had a fear in it that she had never seen before. "You. Don't. Control. Me. I'm not the Jenny I was before; do you get that? You don't understand the things that are important to me now. Worse, you aren't listening to me. I'm trying to tell you, right now, but you won't even listen. I don't want money. I don't want things. I don't want interviews, or movie deals, or book deals. I don't want justice. All that I want is to move on. Got that?"

CHAPTER THIRTY-SEVEN

Jenny arrived at Webster Diner early, situating herself in the usual booth. Back corner, full view of the diner. She stared out of the window, watching the bustling street. Cars crowded the intersection outside, blocking a bus from crossing the street. Morning commuters started their long trudge to the D train up the snow-covered Bedford Avenue hill. A part of her yearned for the quiet solace of the forest.

When her tea arrived, she gripped the mug. The warmth radiated through her hands. She looked down and saw they were trembling. Jenny wasn't sure why. Was she nervous for the conversation that was about to happen? Her therapist would probably say there some kind of post-traumatic stress trigger in the environment. Jenny knew this wasn't trauma from her survival story... this kind of trauma had been established well before that.

As she was stirring her tea, the front door of the diner chimed. Jenny didn't look up, but felt butterflies in her stomach all the same. She knew without seeing that her mother had arrived. She didn't want to see another face full of sorrow, they were all too common these days.

Jenny looked up at the same moment her mother turned towards her. They made eye contact and, to Jenny's surprise, her mother was nothing but smiles. For some reason that made it worse, and Jenny felt an abundance of emotion well up in her chest. Her mother must have known, because she swooped in for a hug before a tear could form. The hug was strong, and Jenny couldn't help but let out some tears. Even after it felt like they had hugged for much longer than would be socially acceptable in public, her mom held on a little longer.

Jenny pulled back, and her mother finally let go. They took their seats

179

in the booth and Juan the waiter saw his opening. Her mother ordered coffee, with cream and two sugars. After he left, silence hung in the air.

"Jenny... I don't even know where to start."

"Me either. Life is weird, isn't it?" Her mom laughed.

"Yes, life is weird. So, Jenny of the Woods huh?"

"Yeah."

"A little too obvious if you ask me. You made the journalist job too easy with that last name." This time Jenny laughed.

"Yeah, not sure who came up with it first... But I'm stuck with it now I guess."

"I want to hear as much as you want to share. Doesn't have to be now, doesn't have to be all at once..."

Jenny let out a shaky sigh of relief.

"I had a lot of time to think about this conversation, and I've decided I want to tell you everything. Do you have some time? It might take a while."

"Jenny, there is no where I'd rather be than here with you."

Jenny told her everything. Every detail from the start of the bus ride through the fight she had just had with her father. Jenny talked for what felt like forever. Her mother asked clarifying questions here and there, but mostly she just listened.

Once Jenny finished, her mother sat back, and breathed a heavy sigh. It was as if Jenny had just transferred the full emotional weight of her journey to her mother. Jenny studied her face, watching as emotions washed over her.

"Jenny of the Woods? More like Jenny of the Bronx. That's where you come from, that's where you were born. Your spirit is unbreakable and the forest had nothing to do with that. That's us Bronx women. We are tougher than most. That's what you are now Jenny. You're not a girl anymore, you're a woman. I can see it looking at you now.

"Thanks."

"That bear though, I actually thought that you were going to say it wasn't real or something."

"Wait what?"

"Yeah, like, I thought maybe you had dreamed it all up to help you cope or something. I think I saw something like that in a movie once." Jenny laughed again.

"No, he's very real. Or else everyone is lying to me. We can go see him at the zoo if you want. I can introduce you to him."

"I'm going to take a rain check on that. Not about to have my hand bit off."

"Don't worry, just give him peanut butter and he's your best friend."

"That's going to be a hard no from me."

"I thought Bronx women were tough?"

Her mom smiled. "I know my limits."

There was a moment of silence. Her mother looked out of the window. Jenny could tell she was working up to say something.

"Jenny I just have to say…"

"Mom"

"What?"

"Are you going to talk about my childhood?"

"There is something I have to tell you."

"I don't want you to think I asked you here to rehash all of that. I promise that's not it."

Her mother sighed. She was clearly trying to communicate something but was struggling to find the words.

"Has your father said talked about anything new in his life since you've been back?"

"New? No, not really… it's weird, I missed him so much while I was gone. Since I've been back everything has been moving so fast and we haven't really had the chance to just stop and talk to each other."

"That's your father, always moving, never slowing down. Sounds like there is a bit of that in you too."

"Not sure if that's an insult or…"

"Not an insult. Not at all. Since he didn't share, I guess I'm breaking the news… Once you disappeared, he and I started talking again."

"Wait, talking? Or, like, talking talking?"

"It's complicated."

"I don't think it's all that complicated. What's going on?"

"He was struggling with it and I was too. So, we started talking to each other more. Then, when they told us they thought you were dead, we started grieving together."

"He didn't tell me any of this."

"Your father had a very hard time, Jenny. I'll let him tell you the full extent but he's probably thinking right now by not telling you he is protecting you. I'll just say that he went to a very dark place. When we held your funeral…"

"Holy crap, I didn't even think about that. Y'all really held a funeral for me?"

"Of course. We were told you died. So, we did what people do in that situation. Even so, your father never really believed you were dead. He said until there is a body, he wouldn't give up. That's the Woods stubbornness."

"Trust me I know all about that stubbornness. Is it weird that I wish I could have been at my funeral, like Tom Sawyer?

"Maybe a little, but I like weird."

"Well, I want to hear all about how that went, but it seems like there's more to your story."

"There is. After the funeral we kept talking. He didn't have anyone. He started drinking a lot. Nearly lost his job after he got into a physical fight with a co-worker. Rather than fire him on the spot, they took pity and told him to take some time off. So, he did, and we spent more time together.

"So, y'all talking talking?"

"We are, kind of, talking talking. But it's very complicated, as I'm sure you can imagine."

"Why hasn't he shared any of this with me? And why haven't you come around if you're like kind of together? Which is weird for me to even be saying."

"Having survived everything you went through was the answer to our hopes and prayers, but you didn't know what you were coming back to. Your father and I are broken, damaged, people Jenny. He's fighting to be there for you right now. And he's trying to put on a strong face, but he hasn't healed. This whole thing messed him up pretty bad. He's different from the person you knew. We didn't want to spring everything on you all at once after we found out you were alive. We decided it would be best to ease all this in slowly as you readjusted."

"I guess that makes sense, but it's still a lot to process right now…"

"I completely understand."

"He seems angrier. We are currently having a pretty hard fight about this stupid trial. He got really upset. I don't remember him ever being that angry."

"Yes. The trial… tell me what you're thinking about that Jenny."

"I don't want money and I don't believe anything I say will result in actual justice. So why bother? Rebekah said I should forgive him, but I'm struggling with that too."

"Can I be honest with you?"

"Please, that's why I wanted to meet."

"Rebekah sounds like a white woman." Jenny laughed.

"Well, you got that right."

"It's something I've heard many times before. Forgive, so that you can move on and heal. So that everyone can move past this. Franky, I think that's all a bunch of bull crap."

"You have no idea how refreshing it is to hear that."

"Jenny if you don't want to forgive him, then don't. He's an evil child, and I think it's ok to stay angry at evil. Rebekah sounds like an older woman, like me. Women of our age have been told all our lives to sit down, be quiet, move on, be gentle, and smile more. When we are told that over and over and over, sometimes, despite our best resistance it can become an internalized belief. I want you to hear me: you don't have to be any of that. You can be whoever you want to be Jenny."

"So do you think I should testify?"

"I appreciate you asking me for advice, but I'm not going to tell you what to do. You've got too much of that going on right now. The only thing I will do is promise to support your decision no matter what. You want to ignore it all? Let's ignore it baby. You want to forgive Eric? I'm there with you. You want to testify? I'll be in that court room. In the end you have to decide for yourself what you want to do. You can't let anyone else tell you what to do or else you'll end up like me."

"What do you mean by that?"

Her mother paused and stared out of the window.

"I made a big mistake. Something that has haunted me all of my life."

"I didn't ask you here to force you to apologize for anything. I just wanted to see you, talk with you."

"And I appreciate that. But I think it's time you heard my side of the story. Have we ever talked about it, woman to woman?

Jenny thought back. The few times she hung out with her mom, they always talked around it.

"I guess not, no. But I'm not mad about it anymore, you did what did. You don't have to apologize."

"Jenny, I did the one thing a mother should never have to do. I left you."

Jenny let the words hang in the air. It was a stunning thing to hear out loud for the first time.

"I let my family come between us, I let them control me, and now I have no one." Her mother started crying. Jenny couldn't help but feel emotional.

"What do you mean you have no one?"

"Back then, my family never approved of your father. After you were born, they were openly hostile. They refused to see you. All they talked about what how I made a mistake, and how you were a mistake. They begged me to leave you both. They offered money, a car, a new home…. Anything to get me to leave."

"Wow."

"Then they started being more hostile. They called your fathers office and made false complaints against him. They reported us to ACS repeatedly, with false claims of abuse. Something inside of me broke. I wish I could say something even slightly noble to defend myself, like I left you to protect you from them. But that's not true… the truth is after years of this, I started to think it was true. That marrying your father and starting a family was a mistake."

Her mother paused, and Jose sensed his opening again, and quickly refilled her coffee. Jenny decided he had earned a great tip today.

"So, I left you and your father and went back to them. It was fine for a while. All those promises they made never happened. The car and the house never materialized. However, things seemed peaceful again, so I convinced myself that I made the right choice. You remember the time we saw the movie together in Harlem?"

"Yes, when I got my period."

"Yes, so, they didn't know I was seeing you that night. Somebody saw us and snitched to my family. All of that "peace" was gone and they went right back to their old ways, telling me that you were a mistake, that I should never see you. That movie night was the first time I got to be a mother. It awakened something in me."

"So, what happened?"

"Soon after we got into a big fight, and I found out they had never stopped making false complaints to ACS. For years they were trying to get you taken away from your father. That was the final straw. I told them off, to put it lightly. I told them I would never speak to them again, and that if they ever made another complaint, I would burn their house to the ground.

"Woah."

"They believed me because I meant it. So, there I was, alone in the world with no one… but at least I was free from my family."

"I don't even know what to say. Are they, like, still alive? Is there just a random family in the Bronx that loathes me?"

"I honestly don't know. I've not talked to them, and they haven't tried to talk to me. Frankly, I don't care. But I know from a friend that they haven't made a single call to ACS."

"This is a lot to process."

"I know. Take all the time you need. My point to all this is I let people get in my head. I let them have control over me and my life. People think they are helping you, but they are just telling you what they want you to do. You have to decide what you want to do because you're the one that has to live with it. Sure, you will get it wrong from time to time, but at least you get to own that. So, whatever you want to do with that trial, make sure it is you making the choice. Not your dad, not Rebekah, not me, not the public opinion or the tweets. You, and only you, can decide."

"Thank you for saying that...I feel like I'm just meeting you for the first time. There so much I don't know about you..."

"Well... Did your father tell you I went to school for botany?"

"What? No! That's so cool."

"Thanks. I guess we have a lot of catching up to do."

"I have a botany related question for you... this is something that bothered me the whole time I was stuck in the forest... what the heck does poison ivy look like?"

CHAPTER THIRTY-EIGHT

After a short and thorough search, a small law firm in her neighborhood agreed to help prep Jenny for testimony for the state's trial against Eric. They also drafted a few rejection notices for television and movie deals.

On the day of the testimony against Eric, Jenny wore a white blouse and green cardigan by Francine, and a new pair of Jordans she bought herself. Her feelings toward the trial had been evolving over the past few days. Her father had been avoiding discussing the topic for her after the fight, but she knew what he wanted out of this: to see Eric reprimanded for once in his spoiled life, as he put it bluntly in their first meeting with their lawyer, Maria.

Maria was a small, frank woman with long flowing black hair. After their first meeting, Jenny knew she was the one to represent her. Maria completely understood how much Jenny didn't want to be in the limelight. She made no attempt to push Jenny to make money off her story, unlike the other law firms she had visited. Maria only seemed interested in representing Jenny, and not the money Jenny could make. Plus, her favorite book was *To Kill a Mockingbird*, so Jenny knew she had good taste.

Maria sat with Jenny in a small room in the courthouse, calmly helping Jenny prepare for the testimony. Jenny latched onto Maria's calm energy. The butterflies in her stomach made it hard to sit still. Jenny paced around the room

"You remember everything we discussed?" Maria asked.

"Yes. Don't elaborate my answers. Be straight to the point. Only discuss facts and try not to get too emotional."

"Good. First up will be the prosecution. You've prepped with the

186

state lawyer multiple times. You feel okay there?"

"Yes, I'm okay. Glad we prepped with him."

"After is the cross-examination. The defense lawyer will ask you harder questions."

"Right." Jenny knew she could do this.

"They will likely push hard on the suicide angle. That's okay though because it's all false. There is no truth to those words, so don't let that unsettle you."

"I will answer his questions truthfully."

"Unless the state attorney objects."

"Unless he objects. Then we wait to see what the judge says."

A tall uniformed man entered the small room. He moved quietly for a such a large figure.

"Ready, Ms. Woods?" the bailiff asked in soft voice.

Jenny looked at Maria, who gave a small businesslike smile.

"You will be great. Feel nervous?"

"No. Yes. I feel good. Calm," Jenny said.

"Good."

Jenny flashed a smile and followed the bailiff. They entered another small room, and the bailiff stopped and waited. Jenny could hear muffled voices on the other side of the door. Then there was silence.

"All right, kiddo. Let's go," the bailiff said. They stepped out into the courtroom.

The room was packed. The jury was a menagerie of stone-faced people. Not a single open seat in the audience. Her dad and mom sat together in the back next to Maria. It was weird seeing them together in public. That was going to take some getting used to. As she stared out over the crowd, lost in thought, her father flashed Jenny a smile, and she smiled back at him as if they were the only two people in the room.

Jenny looked over to where the Defense was seated. Eric was sitting with his head down, staring at the table. This was her first time seeing him since that day. In her imagination, he was bigger, but sitting in front of him now he just seemed small and weak. Somehow that made it easier to see his face again. He didn't have power over her anymore.

The bailiff directed her to the witness box. It was a tall wooden stand with a chair and microphone on the inside.

"Please raise your right hand," the bailiff said and Jenny complied.

"Do you solemnly swear that you will tell the truth, the whole truth, and nothing but the truth, under pain and penalties of perjury?" The bailiff asked.

"I do," she said. The judge looked at her and motioned to the chair in the box. He was old, and a crown of white hair circled his otherwise hairless head. The black robes made him seem daunting, but the smile on his face seemed no more threatening than some old grandpa.

"You may be seated, Ms. Woods. Prosecution, you may examine your witness," the judge said. In all their practice sessions, the state attorney wore a black suit and white shirt. The only thing that changed from sessions to sessions were his ties. Jenny had been working to figure out if he just owned one suit or multiple black suits. But his ties were always great. Today he sported a blue one with gold-embroidered roses.

"Ms. Woods. I think by now many of us are familiar with the harrowing story of your survival. What we are focusing on today is the circumstances surrounding the start of your journey. When did you and your class arrive at the Balsam Lake Mountain Wild Forest preserve?"

"September twenty-fourth earlier this year. Sometime around noon," Jenny answered.

"Who was the teacher who supervised this class trip?"

"Mr. Blumfit. Uh. Henry Blumfit. Our history teacher."

"And how would you characterize Mr. Blumfit's control over his students?"

"I would say it was very relaxed. Students could get away with a lot in his class."

"Would you say that the students knew this?"

"Yes. Everyone knew he was a pushover."

"Thank you. How would you describe the environment on the bus, that morning of the twenty-fourth?"

"Chaotic."

"Can you walk us through your personal experience that morning?"

"I had put on my AirPods to ignore people so I could read. Then Eric Wilson removed them from my ears. When I asked for them back, he pretended he didn't have them, and when I asked again, he threw them out the window."

"Did anyone try to stop Eric?"

"No. People just laughed."

"What happened next?"

"Eric pushed me down. I said something and then he started to hit me."

"Did Mr. Blumfit do anything?"

"When he heard the commotion he came back, separated us, and told me to sit down or else he would give me a detention."

"Did you try to explain what had happened?"

"Yes. But he didn't want to hear it and told me to sit down."

"Thank you. So to summarize, you and Eric were not friends?"

"Correct."

"Moving forward, when the bus arrived and everyone disembarked, you were paired off with Logan Camillo, is that correct?"

"Yes."

"Then what happened?"

"We hiked along the trail. Logan and I talked. At some point there was a commotion at the front of the line. Someone had fallen down, so we all stopped. Logan had said that Eric was going to pull a prank."

"How did Logan know this?"

"He said Eric told him."

"Objection. Hearsay," the Defense said.

"Sustained. Prosecution?" The judge said in response.

"Moving on. Then what happened, Jenny?"

"While Mr. Blumfit was helping the person who fell, Eric approached us."

"What did he say?"

"That the person falling was a distraction."

"A distraction for what reason?"

"The next thing I know he pushed me off the trail."

"I would like to enter into the record a report regarding the trail that Jenny just mentioned. We engaged with the Parks Department to survey the area. Accordingly, they found that Jenny fell fifty feet down through rocky terrain and trees. The Parks Department is quoted in the report having said that Jenny is 'one lucky woman' for not having broken her neck, or worse. In the report you will see photos looking down the cliff that Jenny was pushed down. Please note because of the sheer distance, the bottom of the ravine is not visible from the perspective at the top."

All this information was news to Jenny. She knew she was lucky to survive the fall but didn't know the full extent of her good fortune, if it could be called that. She told herself to ask Maria to see about getting her a copy of that report. She looked over at the jury and one woman was staring at the photos and had her hand over her mouth. Eric was staring a hole into the ground.

"No further questions, Your Honor."

The judge nodded and turned toward the other lawyer. Maria had run Jenny though a lot of questions he might ask. They had spent hours prepping and talked at length about how they might push the suicide angle.

"Defense, do wish to examine the witness?"

"Yes, your honor." A tall man with a red tie, slicked-back gray hair, and broad shoulders stood up from Eric's table. He looked expensive. Paid for by Eric's parents, Jenny figured. He looked Jenny in the eyes and she met his gaze. They stared off and he broke first.

"Please proceed," the judge said.

"Thank you. Ms. Woods, my client has admitted to taking your headphones and does regret this action. Once Mr. Blumfit calmed the situation down, how did you feel?"

"Frustrated," Jenny responded.

"Because you didn't agree with your teacher's decision?"

"Yes."

"Then what did you do?"

"I said something dumb to Eric to make him mad."

"You took matters into your own hands, defying the instructions of your teacher. What did you say to my client?"

Jenny couldn't help but smirk. It was so obvious to her that he was trying to trick and discredit her. Hopefully the jury saw through it all. "That I had filmed a video that made him look bad."

"Why did you say that?"

"Because I was upset that Eric had destroyed my AirPods."

"Did you actually shoot the video, though. The one that you claim made him look bad?"

"No."

"So, you lied to Eric just to try to make him angry. Is that correct?"

"Yes."

"Are you aware that the altercation caused a hairline fracture to my client's orbital socket, and a minor concussion?"

"No, I wasn't around after the field trip." Her quip managed to get a few chuckles in the audience.

"Your school has a zero-tolerance policy. Are you aware of this?"

"Yes."

"So, according to that policy, upon arrival back at the school, action would have been taken against both you and Eric for the altercation."

"Okay."

"And that Eric would have been properly punished for the destruction of your headphones."

Jenny sat, waiting for a question.

"Yet, you took matters into your own hands and my client suffered injuries because of your actions."

"I'm sorry he hurt himself punching me."

The tall lawyer stared at her and Jenny stared back at him, unblinking. Maria had said he might try to find a way to get an outburst from her.

Jenny felt calm. This was nothing compared to fighting a wild coyote. She knew she could do this.

"Let's fast-forward to the alleged incident. You stated that my client had created a diversion at the front of the line and was also at the back of the line at the same time. How is possible?"

"He had someone fake an injury."

"So, you are alleging that my client planned out an elaborate situation, all while under the effects of a fracture and minor concussion, to get revenge on you?"

"Yes."

"Is it true that your mother left you and your father at a young age?"

Jenny felt a blossom of anger in her chest. Maria said the Defense might try to bring this up. Jenny didn't want her personal life thrown out in front of all these people. To bring up her mom was low. The state lawyer stood up.

"Objection, Your Honor," the state lawyer said.

"Defense?" the judge said.

"Your honor, my client alleges that he did not push Ms. Woods. Rather, that she had made an attempt at suicide. I'm simply hoping to illustrate why this was likely."

"Overruled. Ms. Woods, please answer the question."

"Yes."

"Thank you. And Ms. Woods, isn't it also true that your father struggled to support you?"

"Objection!" the state lawyer was looking red in the face.

"Sustained. Defense, get to the point."

"Ms. Woods, how many friends do you have?"

"One." Which was kind of a lie. Peanut wasn't a human but he was her friend.

"So, you were not a popular girl at school?"

"No."

"So then, Ms. Wood, why would my client, a smart young man with a bright future ahead of him, attempt to murder an unpopular girl that he hardly knew?"

"That's a great question," Jenny said with a calm smile. The Defense looked irked.

"You tried to commit suicide and now you are trying to avoid the consequences by blaming my client!"

The state lawyer was about to object. Jenny could see it coming but she broke Maria's rule.

"You're wrong," Jenny said. The Defense looked surprised. The state lawyer paused.

"Excuse me?" the Defense said.

"If I wanted commit suicide, why did I fight so hard to survive?"

"Well, I mean . . . there are—"

"If I wanted to be dead, I would be dead."

Jenny stared down the defense lawyer. She looked at Eric and saw fear in his eyes. She recognized the fear, the coyote had the same look when she thrust her spear into its chest. Eric was afraid for his life. It was telling to see that the possibility of being in jail evoked that kind of response in him. However, she wasn't ignorant to the history of justice in America when it came to young white men, so she held little hope he might actually face consequences.

"N-no further questions, Your Honor." The Defense looked shaken.

A murmur spread throughout the courtroom. The judge banged his gavel.

"Quiet, please. Prosecution, do you wish to reexamine?"

The state attorney stood up and straightened his tie.

"No."

The judge cleared his throat to speak and turned toward Jenny.

"Thank you Ms. Woods. That will be all." He turned to the defense lawyer.

Jenny tuned out whatever they were saying and left the witness box. She was done. She did her part. She made her way to the back of the courtroom and sat next to her parents and Maria. Maria leaned over and gave her shoulder a squeeze and nodded in approval.

Her mother gave a head nod of approval, and father leaned in and said, "Good job," but she could hear in his voice that he was struggling to hold back his anger. She couldn't imagine what it was like for them both, to have your marriage history aired in front of all these people. Jenny looked around at all the other faces in the court room, wondering why they were all here. The defense attorney stood from his chair.

"The Defense calls Logan Camillo."

CHAPTER THIRTY-NINE

Jenny watched as the bailiff led Logan to the stand. He looked tired and his skin was pale. The lighting made him look sickly. Much worse than when Jenny last saw him last. After he was sworn in, the defense attorney rose and walked toward the witness stand.

"Mr. Camillo, based on your personal knowledge and observations, was Ms. Woods popular at school?

"No, she didn't have many friends."

"How many friends would you say she had?"

"I don't know. We didn't talk much."

"Let's get right to the incident at hand. You were assigned to be Ms. Woods's walking partner, correct?"

"Yes," he said. His voice sounded small.

"Can you walk us through what happened from your point of view, after the commotion at the front of the hiking line brought things to a stop?"

"Eric came to the back of the line and asked me for some painkillers."

Jenny's mouth hung open. She couldn't believe what she was hearing.

"Did he say anything about planning a prank?"

"No."

"Did Mr. Wilson push Jenny off the hill?"

"I don't think he did, no."

The whispers grew louder. Someone in the back stood up and shouted, "You're a liar!" Jenny was shocked but happy to hear it said out loud. The judge banged his gavel. Logan burst into tears.

"Order! The people will remain quiet or I will clear out the courtroom."

The buzz died down, but the room was electric with energy. There was a tension in the air. The only thing Jenny could focus on was Logan. He looked sad and distraught on the stand. Jenny pitied him. Clearly Eric had somehow convinced him to lie under oath and he looked completely defeated.

"Did Jenny throw herself off the cliff?

"No . . . no, she didn't."

The defense lawyer paused. His face contorted into a look of confusion. People quietly whispered around her. Something was happening.

"Mr. Camillo, in previous statements you had said that Ms. Woods did, in fact, throw herself off the cliff.

"Well . . . the more I thought about it, the more I remembered she didn't."

"Might I remind you that you are under oath."

"Okay."

"The Defense rests, Your Honor."

The lawyer looked confused. Something had gone wrong. Jenny tried not to get her hopes up, but maybe there was a sliver of a chance.

"Prosecution, the witness is yours."

"Mr. Camillo, in your sworn statements you say that Ms. Woods was, and a I quote, 'crazy' and that 'she threw herself off the cliff.' But now you are saying she didn't. I will remind you that lying under oath is a serious crime. Can you please state again what actually happened?"

Logan locked eyes with Jenny. There was anger painted all over his face. He balled his fists and stood up. His hands were shaking.

"I . . . um . . . I'm sorry, Jenny. She was pushed. Eric pushed her and tried to make me lie about it all!"

The court room erupted. It was as if everyone leaped to their feet all at once and started yelling. The defense lawyer was red in the face, shouting at the judge and waving his hands. The prosecution lawyer turned away from Logan, speechless. The judge banged his gavel over and over so hard that Jenny thought it would break.

Logan looked up and met Jenny's eyes. Jenny mouthed the words 'thank you.' Logan looked back at the floor and wept. Eric's jaw hung open in pure shock.

The judge said something to the bailiff and the room was cleared out. Everyone in the audience was ushered out of the courtroom and into the hallway. Maria led Jenny and her parents away from the crowd and into a small hallway off to the side. Her father said what everyone was thinking.

"What happens next?"

"It depends on how the judge wants to handle it, but they may declare a mistrial or   strike the witness's testimony from the record. Or his statements may stand."

"But what will happen to Eric?" her father asked. "We should stay and see what the verdict is. They will send him to prison, right? They can't let him get away with this."

He looked upset. Jenny smiled at his protectiveness.

"Dad, it's okay. I don't care what happens to Eric. I have somewhere better to be."

CHAPTER FORTY

Jenny had worked to get to know the staff at the Bronx Zoo as soon as Peanut took up residence. She had been there every day since he was released from the hospital. No one really said anything officially but they never charged her admission. They gave her a lot of leniency and a ton of freedom for a guest of the zoo. Peanut had more than doubled the ticket sales for the zoo, so that made up for it.

They had built Peanut his own small enclosure near the Rhino enclosure, at the center of the Zoo. He was a special case here, so they had to do a bit of modification to house him.

The staff had given Jenny a key to Peanut's enclosure. The animal caretakers had agreed it was important to let Jenny come so Peanut would acclimate to his new environment. Evidently there was some pushback from the higher-ups about this decision. Something to do with expensive insurance premiums. The caretakers had told Jenny not to worry about it, so she didn't.

Jenny closed the metal door behind her and walked into the enclosure. There were a few tall trees near the back, and a sloped rock outcropping that led down toward the fence people stood behind to watch. It was a cold December day, but there wasn't much snow on the ground yet. Peanut was near a tree in the back, digging away at something. The caretakers had tried to ease him into hibernation, but said that due to the events of the past month it will take some time. He hadn't noticed her yet. She had a small black bag at her side, which she set down near her feet.

"Hey, Peanut, yip-yip!" Jenny said.

Peanut immediately turned his head and stared at her for a moment.

Then he came barreling toward her. The doctors had built him a custom prosthetic leg made of steel and thick rubber. It wrapped around his amputated paw. It took him some time to get comfortable but after a few days on it he was running around like usual.

He stopped in front of her and let out a big puff of air. Jenny let out a low grunt and made herself big, throwing her arms out wide. This was their greeting now. Thanks to the regular feeding schedules he was starting to fill out.

"Hey, big boy. You're starting to get some weight on you I see. Are you getting taller too?"

He plopped down and clicked his teeth at Jenny.

"I miss you every single day, Peanut. I brought you a treat."

She reached into the black bag and pulled out a Ziplock bag full of Strawberries: a newly discovered favorite snack of his. Peanut tried to snatch one out of her hand.

"Hey! Wait a sec, be patient."

He let out a huff. She huffed back at him.

"There, how hard was that?"

She tossed him a strawberry and he caught it in his mouth, practically swallowing it in one bite. Outside the fence, a small crowd gathered. Her parents stood in the crowd, smiling. Jenny had begged her father to come meet Peanut, not from the other side of the fence but in person. Eventually she wore him down and he practically peed his pants when they met. The entire time he couldn't stop shaking. He'd said it wasn't the bear he was afraid of, but rather being mauled by it. Jenny couldn't blame him. That had scared her too. He appreciated their friendship from afar and behind a strong fence.

After an hour or so, Jenny felt the events of the day catching up with her. She gave Peanut one last hug, grabbed her bag, and turned to leave. After a few steps she stopped and looked back. Peanut sat on his back legs and stared at her with his big brown eyes.

"I'll be back tomorrow. I promise," she said. He didn't move. He looked like he was about to start pouting. "Fine, fine. You know I have it with me."

Jenny reached into her back and pulled out a peanut butter and jelly sandwich. She unwrapped it and tossed it to him. He caught it in midair and ate it in two bites.

EPILOGUE

It was dark out. Her father had long since gone to bed. Ever since she returned, falling asleep in her bed had been a struggle. One of the many things she had fantasized about in that cave was a warm comfy bed. Now that she was back in civilization, she missed cave. The smell of the forest, the feel of the soft earth. Hopefully some animal had taken up residence and put it to use.

Since she couldn't sleep, she went to the kitchen and put a pot of water on the stove. So easy. Just a flick of the knob and fire. As the water was heating up, Jenny pulled a small stone out of her pocket, one she found in her backyard and cleaned. She plopped it into the pot. There was something about the stone and water that gave it a flavor she liked. Made her feel weirdly nostalgic. Almost better than tea. Almost.

When the water was ready, she poured it and the rock into her ceramic mug. She stepped out onto the balcony and sat on the deck chair. The night was chilly but it didn't feel cold. As she sipped her hot-rock water, she pulled her legs up beneath her and let the sounds of the Bronx waft over her. She could make out a few stars in the sky, but city light obscured most of them.

A while later she went back inside into her room. She picked up the coyote fur from her bed and held it, letting the memory and emotion wash over her. A little while later she crawled under her warm comforter, wrapping it around her shoulders. The mug was almost empty, so she drank the last of the hot-rock water and set it aside. She grabbed *The Guns of August* off the nightstand and read until her eyes grew heavy.

ACKNOWLEDGMENTS

This book would not have been possible without the help of many devoted readers who gave their time and feedback. Thank you to the book club of Waterloo, Iowa: Diane, Jen, Rochelle, Tina, Mary, Fayeth, Karen, Lisa, and Linda. Thank you to the book club of friends: Mic, Jace, Kristin, Michaela, Maureen, Amanda, Caitlyn, and Gianna. Thank you to the independent readers: Judy, Florence, and David. A special thank you to Andrea Vande Vorde for her incredible editing skills at vandevordedits.com. I'm blessed to have you all in my life!

ABOUT THE AUTHOR

Joseph lives in The Bronx with his wife Anais, son August, and dog Parker. Growing up in Iowa and Idaho, much of the research for this book was absorbed firsthand from survivalists, farmers, and mountain men. Learning how to purify water, start fires, hunt wild game, and live off the land came hand in hand with growing up in these places amongst wilderness. This is his first book and it is dedicated in loving memory to his cousin Ted. Connect at Josephstamp.com.

Made in the USA
Las Vegas, NV
09 August 2024

91b2084b-4dbc-4095-b09c-8becf0f892b0R01